CHRONICLES

OF AVE

VOLUME 1

CHRONICLES
OF AVE
VOLUME 1

STEPHEN ZIMMER

SEVENTH STAR PRESS

Cover art: Matthew Perry
Cover art in this book copyright © 2013 Matthew Perry & Seventh Star
Press, LLC.

Editors:
Rodney Carlstrom on *Moonlight's Grace, A Touch of Serenity,*
and *Winter's Embrace*
Mary Bickett on *Into Glory Ride, Land of Shadows,* and *Lion Heart*

Published by Seventh Star Press, LLC.

ISBN Number: 978-1-937929-30-5

Seventh Star Press
www.seventhstarpress.com
info@seventhstarpress.com

Publisher's Note:
Chronicles of Ave, Volume 1 is a work of fiction. All names, characters,
and places are the product of the author's imagination, used in fictitious
manner. Any resemblances to actual persons, places, locales, events, etc. are
purely coincidental.

Printed in the United States of America

First Edition

Acknowledgements

To my mother, who I love more than I can ever put into words. My heart is broken with this first book to be released since she left, but in carrying onward I honor the love, support, and encouragement she gave me all throughout our time together in this world. The world turned grey when my dad left, and now all appears in darker shadow, but I must continue to fight, move forward, and become the person that mom saw in me. The road seems impossibly long, but with this book release may my mother, wherever she might be, see that I am doing my best to keep moving.

To Rodney Carlstrom, who I extend my heartfelt gratitude and appreciation for helping me bring more of Ave to the readers by being such a dedicated editor with the three latest tales in this project. I am the better for the experience, and am thankful he pushed me to grow as a writer. I worked hard not to disappoint, and it is my sincere desire that Rodney saw that reflected in this release.

To Matthew Perry, whose artwork is such a blessing to have on the covers of my books. He is, without question, one of the most dedicated and hard-working people I know. It is definitely wonderful to see the magic I feel in the stories evoked in the imagery created by Matt.

To my readers, all around. I thank my readers, all of whom are friends in the sense that friends support you in pursuing your dreams, for being patient during this past summer, the darkest time of my life without question. Bringing my readers new adventures gave me something to hold onto as I picked myself up again and endeavored to move forward. May this book show them that I am moving forward, and I hope they find light and inspiration woven into the tales, of a kind that can see all of us through the darkest of experiences.

Dedication:

To the One who calls all of us to be the
best versions of ourselves

To my mother, a light forever shining.

The Tales:

Introduction to Volume 1

I am really excited to present this collection of short stories to readers as they give me a chance to reveal a world that I've been exploring and enjoying for a fairly long time now.

I want to state, first of all, that all of the tales here are stand-alone stories. You do not need to have read any of the Fires in Eden books to enjoy these, or have prior knowledge of the world of Ave. That being said, if you have read the Fires in Eden series, the short stories will broaden and deepen your experience of Ave, and bring more light to many things referenced along the course of the series.

Ave is a world filled with a diverse array of cultures, creatures, and settings, and I am confident that this collection will convey that reality. In Volume 1, you get to venture to Trogen lands, Gael, the Empire of Heaven, the great forests near to Ehrengard, the Shadowlands, and the lands of the Amazu people!

The Trogens and some things you will encounter in the Shadowlands are not directly inspired by a particular history or culture of our world, but with the others you will find cultures inspired by medieval Ireland, Germanay, China, the Normans, and the Zulu people.

I invite you to come explore Ave with me! Adventure awaits! I hope you enjoy the twists and turns and find all the things you encounter to your liking. I also hope you glean a little inspiration from the actions and mindsets of some of these characters, many of whom represent a light in the darkness.

So, without further delay,, saddle up on your sky steed and into glory ride!

-Stephen Zimmer
September 3, 2013

Into Glory Ride

Into Glory Ride

"There are far, far better things ahead than any we leave behind."
-C.S. Lewis

The Amnoros crept along the face of the cliff. The four-legged creature navigated a precarious footpath that would have been all but invisible to a Trogen, even the most veteran dwellers of the Iron Mountains. A plunge of well over a thousand feet was a mere handspan to the left, where the waves of the Northern Sea crashed like thunder into the rocky shorefront.

The Amnoros moved along with keen precision and astounding equilibrium, displaying an adept level of grace that belied the creature's stout appearance. Marragesh's thighs felt the movements of the Amnoros, as he remained careful to keep his own posture in alignment with the white-furred creature. Trogen riders had toppled with their Amnoros steeds to their deaths before, though such tragedies were rare.

Marragesh remembered his first forays with Banca out onto the cliff facings. His heart had thumped rapidly against his chest, and he had broken out in a cold sweat, feeling they would fall at any moment. He had always returned from such excursions with sorely rattled nerves, but in time he had grown confidence in the extraordinary climbing abilities and balance of his Amnoros steed.

The bodies of the Amnorosen were well-suited for the task. Their cloven hooves had small dew claws at the tips, in addition to inner pads. Both characteristics strongly enhanced the creature's traction even on rain-slicked surfaces.

While the Trogen's body remained still, his eyes were constantly roving, carefully scanning the aqua skies for any signs of the great eagles that plied the seacoast for their quarry. The huge birds occasionally sought to dislodge Amnorosen from the cliff faces running along the northern edge of Trogen lands. The great birds would dive in and knock an Amnoros off balance, following the doomed creature on its plummet to the rocks below, where a bloody feast would quickly commence.

There were other dangers to be wary of in the area, even worse than a great eagle on the hunt. The skies were devoid of the threat Marragesh was most concerned about much to his relief.

The lands of the Sea Wolf clan were situated very close to the territory occupied and warded vigilantly by the Elves. Flying on their leonine sky steeds in great clusters, the Elves vigorously guarded the lands they had seized so many years ago from the Trogens.

Containing rich mineral deposits and shallower waters filled with shoals of fish, the loss of the area had been a terrible misfortune in itself. Yet it was the fate of the large population of Trogens who had been surrounded and enslaved, forced to live in squalor and serve Elven masters, that burned the fiercest in the hearts of all Trogens.

There was little that could be done, as the Elves had already existed for ages when the first Trogen clans began to form. Highly advanced in the crafting of weapons and armor, with dominance of the skies and seas, the Elves maintained their advantage with a relentless fervor.

When the Trogens did manage to gain skills or abilities that could strengthen their ability to defend their lands, the Elves reacted with overwhelming strength. It was a large-scale, extended Elven campaign that had ridded the mountainous forests of the creatures the Thunder Wolf clan was named after. The massive wolves had just begun to be used as warriors' mounts at the time of their eradication, and were evidently formidable enough to be deemed a threat by the Elves.

From time to time, Marragesh espied the sleek war galleys of the Elves on the horizon. The vessels patrolled the coasts regularly, ensuring that the Trogens could never establish a sea force of their own. The Trogens could not hope to get a vessel of any significant size into the water, much less learn the art of harnessing the wind using sails.

It was all part of the constant pressure applied by the Elves, interrupted by punishing raids that were launched randomly, without any hint or forewarning. There were moments when Marragesh wondered why the Sea Wolf clan did not pull the edges of its territory back a little, to gain a buffer against the Elves, but he quickly admonished himself for such weak thinking. To do so would be an act of submission to the race that had tormented them for long ages. Even if it cost them their lives, Trogens were steadfast in the desire to defy their hated oppressors.

Marragesh looked forward, and saw that only a short distance remained to the lookout point commanding a spectacular view of the sea. It was little more than a narrow ledge, with some tufts of grass poking through the rocky surface, but it was a spot Marragesh preferred.

Making its way through the last few paces, with perfect poise, the Amnoros stepped from the pathway and onto the ledge. Marragesh guided the creature towards the back of the space.

Once he drew Banca to a halt, he swung his right leg behind him, and got down from the low-profile leather saddle. He patted the flank of the Amnoros firmly, feeling a deep sense of appreciation.

"You walk paths that not even a Trogen can see, Banca," Marragesh said to the Amnoros, still in bewilderment at the creature's ability to handle such hazardous footing so aptly. "Now go, rest and graze while you can. I need to keep a watch from here for awhile."

Banca could not understand his words, but the creature seemed to understand Marragesh's meaning. Needing little encouragement, the Amnoros trundled over towards a nearby clump of grasses. Marragesh watched his steed for a few moments, as the wind ruffled its outer coat of coarse, white fur, before turning his attention to the panoramic vista before him.

Sea and sky stretched on endlessly, drawing on Marragesh's sense of wonder with every moment that he gazed upon the view. As dazzling as the scene was, the Trogen warrior had a definite purpose. He stared out over the glimmering sea, alert for anything representing the approach of an Elven fleet.

A warrior of the Sea Wolf Clan, it had not been long since Marragesh had gone through his final rite of passage. As all Trogen warriors of his clan had done, throughout the generations, he had mastered his fears and ascended to full warrior status by swimming in the ocean with a pack of the lupine creatures that served as the symbol and inspiration for his clan.

Out of his element, he was at the mercy of the sleek, lengthy sea creatures, as they streaked through the salty waters all around him. Curiosity brought several of the Sea Wolves close to him, near enough that he could see the golden eyes within their long-muzzled visages.

Each time they swam away, disappearing into the murky waters. Marragesh completed the swim unscathed, and had emerged from the cold ocean waters as a full-fledged Trogen warrior, the proudest moment of his entire life.

Given scouting duties, he spent much of his time along the dangerous coastal region, though he had yet to match his longblade against the well-crafted weapons of the Elves. The desire to fight them ached within, a feeling that had grown considerably since he had started ranging the coastline. Like all Trogens, he had deep-rooted reasons for his simmering hatred of the Elves.

Long had the Elves plagued the Trogen race with their far-reaching, inland raids. Swift of foot, and using their sky steeds, sizeable forces of Elves participated in the periodic incursions, enough to overwhelm Trogen war bands of considerable size and experience.

Making the raids even more intolerable, they were punitive in nature, rather than conducted for any material gain. With the lone exception of the land they had taken from the Trogens, the Elves took nothing.

The tall, pale-skinned warriors killed and destroyed unceasingly. Trogen infants and frail elders alike were put to steel or flame, right alongside the warriors so often overwhelmed within a raid-stricken village. It had become abundantly clear over the years that the Elves desired to keep the Trogens in a constant state of upheaval, unable to get their bearings and develop their material culture.

With the animosity their violence engendered, and the enslavement of so many Trogens in the seizing of the lands to the north and west, there was no way the Elves could allow the Trogens to build in the way that the humans in the south did. The Elves saw to it that no fortification could be erected, and no crops could be grown to any significant degree, of the kind needed to sustain a great population of Trogens. Even a nascent attempt to do either was swiftly put to thorough destruction by the Elves.

Being situated so close to the Elves in a coastal area, the territory of the Sea Wolf clan bore the brunt of the deadly incursions. Yet the clan refused to abandon their territory, and took pride in their ages-old resistance. Many in the clan believed their steadfast defiance to be the primary reason the Elves had not pushed to conquer even more Trogen land.

As Marragash gazed across the ocean waters, and pondered the bitter legacy of the Elven raids, he thought of how it had been a considerable amount time since the last major Elven onslaught.

The next one was long overdue, and the realization raised the hackles on the back of Marragesh's broad neck.

***

As twilight settled across land, sea, and sky, Marragesh espied a conspicuous anomaly on the far horizon. He sat rigidly upright, his blood speeding in his veins as he carefully eyed a host of dark shapes in the distance.

There was no mistaking their forms, outlined against the sky in the last remnants of the sun's light. They were Elven galleys, sleek two-masted vessels designed with a low draft enabling them to beach most anywhere, whether along the banks of rivers, or on the shores of the oceanfront. Marragesh had seen the vessels many times before, but the numbers he now witnessed on the horizon indicated that something dreadful was afoot.

Sky warriors would undoubtedly be traveling along with them, steeds and riders resting upon the galleys for the moment they were unleashed on the Trogen lands. Marragesh estimated the vessels would reach the shorefront before the larger moon was at its apex.

A night raid loomed, one that would be conducted on a very large scale. The light of the rising moons had just begun to shower upon the cliff face, as Marragesh considered the options lying before him.

Trying to cross the cliff face at night would be a perilous undertaking, but he knew he could not wait until the dawn. The Elves would be among his people by then, spreading terror and death everywhere they roved.

The thoughts sparked the fires of anger inside him, and without thinking about it, his hand slid down to grasp the hilt of his longblade. Pushing his surging emotions back, he turned and strode over to the Amnoros. Gripping the leather of the saddle firmly, he hoisted himself up.

"I would not ask this of you, if danger was not approaching, Banca. Carry me safely," Marragesh remarked, in a low voice, patting the creature with his right hand.

The Amnoros did not protest, and dutifully started forward. Crossing the ledge, it took its first steps onto the natural pathway along the cliff face, where it resumed on the other side of the lookout spot. Chilly breezes brushed against them, ruffling the Amnoros' outer layer of fur, but the air did not contain the potency to threaten the steed's balance. Slowly, and methodically, Banca progressed upward along the cliff face.

Marragesh carried a signaling horn at his side, but did not make use of it. It was likely that the Elves had some forward scouts. He did not want to alert them to his presence, until he had a chance to disseminate the warning regarding their approaching flotilla.

If the past incursions were any indication, the Elves would speed up their advance if an open warning were to be sounded. It was far better to have time to prepare, and retreat to more defensible positions.

The trail broadened where it ascended on a sharper incline towards the top of the cliff. Banca was able to move a little more quickly with the surer footing. At the end of the pathway, at the top of the cliff, a narrow trail led back from the edge, heading inland. Once they had turned onto the new path, Marragesh spurred his steed to a faster pace.

A tight pass running between two great peaks stretched on ahead of him. Urging Banca to haste, he made swiftly for the entrance to the pass, trying not to think overly much about the deadly Elven force coming ever closer to their shores.

Listening to the rhythmic thumps of Banca's cloven hooves on the hard ground, Marragesh began to ponder an idea that was just beginning to set its roots within his mind. He glanced upwards, at the star-filled skies, knowing that something bold and unexpected had to be done to disrupt the Elven raid.

***

Still below the height where trees refused to grow, Marragesh made his way towards a cave familiar to all Trogen scouts. The place was used for sheltering small groups of Trogen lookouts, and to store some additional supplies and food. He called ahead, his voice cleaving the stillness, to prevent the warriors on watch from mistakenly attacking him in the darkness.

At the farthest edge of Trogen lands, there was no room for error. Hesitation meant death in a world where an Elven raid could fall upon a village at any time.

Shadowy forms emerged from the darkness, longblades in hand. The metal glinted in the moonlight, reflecting in the eyes of the warriors around him.

The Trogen sentries acknowledged Marragesh, and allowed

him to pass onward without incident. He paused long enough to warn them about what he had seen approaching the coast, and knew they would dispatch a couple of their number to send word to other villages in the area. He could hear their running footsteps behind him, as he continued down the rocky pathway. Though their faces remained somber as he rendered the grave tidings to them, their haste as he left betrayed their anxieties.

Returning to his thoughts, he was more determined than ever to see the idea through that was taking shape within his head. Risky, and all but certain to lead to one, dour outcome, it was an idea he could not act on alone.

***

After a little while had passed, he reached the Trogen outpost sheltered within the crook of a mountain rise. It was a place where he had been spending much of his time in recent months, as he was one of a group of young Trogen warriors who had heeded the call of a bold, clever veteran named Uzod. Seeking to advance Trogen capabilities in the face of the relentless Elven persecution, the older warrior founded the place now spread before Marragesh's eyes in the moonlight.

The winged shapes scattered about a large pen, in front of a lengthy, thatch-roofed byre, drew his eyes immediately. The four-legged creatures represented the first group of Harraks to be domesticated, and trained to fly with saddles, harnessing, and riders.

The creatures dwelled natively in the depths of the Iron

Mountains, needing little cajoling to fight Lavions, who were their natural enemies. Trogens had observed many Harraks in the wilderness, stirred from their dens during an Elven incursion. They had hurled themselves at Lavions despite being sorely outnumbered.

While smaller of body than the Lavions, the Harraks had their own strengths, most especially their powerful, bone-crushing jaws. One against one, they were at a significant disadvantage against the much larger Lavions, but in numbers they could contend with their airborne adversaries.

Banca showed increasing signs of skittishness as they approached the outpost. The breezes coursing over them undoubtedly carried the musky scents of the Harraks quartered there.

"Easy, Banca, easy," Marragesh said in a low voice to the Amnoros. "They are trained, and well-fed. These are not the ones that hunt in the mountains."

He did not want to stress the loyal creature unnecessarily, and decided to pull up on the reins a little earlier than he intended. Marragesh was sympathetic to the Amnoros, whose kind was normally harbored at another outpost utilized by Trogen scouts.

Swinging down out of the saddle, he patted Banca for a moment, before leading the big male over to a tree and tethering him. Silhouetted in the moonlight filtering through a space between a stretch of lofty pines, the downward tuft of fur on the creature's lower chin gave the steed a bearded appearance.

"You will be just fine here, Banca," Marragesh said, seeing the fear glistening in the widened eyes of the Amnoros. "Do not be afraid."

Another tendril of night air carried the scents of the Harraks to the distended nostrils of the Amnoros. Its extended pair of sharp black horns bucked dangerously, as the creature shuffled nervously.

"Easy Banca ... easy," Marragesh said.

He stayed a few more moments with the Amnoros, working to calm the beast's agitation. To the Trogen's relief, his steed began to settle down. Checking the tether to make sure it was secure, he gave a pat to Banca's flank.

"It will be alright, Banca," Marragesh said gently. "Understand that you are in no danger."

Marragesh turned back towards the outpost, and started forward. Before he had gotten very far, a figure bearing a great lance loomed out of the shadows.

"Marragesh!" called the familiar Trogen, who had reached full warrior status in the same group as Marragesh. Stepping into the open from behind a tree, his broad-shouldered form was delineated in the moonlight. "I did not expect you back so soon."

"Jarun," Marragash replied, gladdened to see the warrior he had grown up with, both of them having shared the same small village.

From the earliest days, when they had pestered the old village shaman without respite, to the day they dived into the icy waters of the ocean for the ritualistic swim with the Sea Wolves, the two had endured much together. When the call had come from Uzod for Trogen warriors to volunteer for an unprecedented initiative, one that many Trogen leaders saw as an impossible task,

Marragesh and Jarun had been among the first to participate.

"What brings you here, in the heart of night?" Jarun asked, his tone more pensive than curious.

It was not like a scout to return so quickly after setting out on a ranging. Furthermore, Marragesh was not prone to skittishness. Both truths readily explained the trepidation in his comrade's demeanor.

"The Elves approach our shores once again," Marragesh announced somberly, leaving no room for Jarun to assume it was some kind of jest.

"The Elves are coming?" Jarun's eyes widened. "In what strength?"

"A great many vessels. A very strong force," Marragesh replied evenly.

Jarun went speechless for a moment. His eyes narrowed, his voice lowering as he stated, "You know I lost two brothers on the last raid."

"We have both lost far too much. We must stop them, this night," Marragesh said, with iron determination.

The sharp edge of grief scraped at the boundaries of his mind, but he held the sorrowful feelings at bay. He knew Jarun still mourned the loss of his brothers, a pair of brave Trogens who had fallen defending against the last Elven incursion.

The loss of family was something Marragesh knew intimately. His village had been razed to the ground several years before, while he was on a long-ranging hunting foray with other young Trogens.

Honing their skills in the wilderness and learning the methods of warriors, they did not have an inkling of the raid until they returned to the smoldering remains of the village. The memories of the charred bodies littering the scorched area continued to haunt Marragesh's dreams from time to time, horrific visions he could never forget.

He still felt a burdensome guilt that he had not been there to defend the village, even though not one Trogen caught within it had survived the attack. In that one dreadful day, he had lost his mother, father, a brother, and two sisters. He was the last sibling left alive, the only one who yet carried the blood of his strong-hearted father and mother.

"How can we stop them?" Jarun asked, a forlorn lilt to his voice. "We will not run, but how can we possibly counter them?"

"We should use what they do not think we have. They rely on their sky warriors for ground and air. This night, we should lure them into a trap," Marragesh said firmly. "It is time we stop training, and use the Harraks in open battle. Let them come thinking it is as before, and then let us unleash hell upon them."

"Use the Harraks?" Jarun queried, and Marragesh could hear the thick disbelief in his tone. "They have never been taken into battle. They are unproven in combat. It has not been that long since they learned our commands."

"We have no choice. Tonight we need them, or our kind will be slaughtered," Marragesh replied tersely.

"You speak of a trap?" pressed Jarun, still looking unconvinced.

Marragesh nodded. "We might be able to draw them to attack the settlement of Grandthir. They will come on the ground, and through the air, as they always have. They will think we will fight only on the ground. We must pick our moment, and then we can strike a heavy blow they do not see coming."

"What do you seek to do with the Harraks?" Jarun asked.

"Rise into the skies to challenge their warriors above, warrior to warrior," Marragesh said. "We need only distract them and obstruct them. Our warriors on the ground will only have to worry about the Elven raiders on foot."

Marragesh knew the Elven tactics well enough. They would swarm a settlement on foot, from all directions, while striking with a force of sky riders that would proceed to harass any Trogen defenders.

Many of the sky riders would land their mounts, and use them on the ground like cavalry, while others would remain in the air. Any Trogens that sought to flee would be chased down, ensuring that all within a targeted village would be slain by the time a raid concluded.

"Even if there is wisdom in what you say, how can you be certain our chieftains will follow along with such an idea?" Jarun asked. "Even Uzod."

Marragesh hesitated for a moment, as some shadows of doubt slipped into his mind. He was a newer warrior, as was Jarun and most of the others who were part of the first group of Trogen sky riders.

What he was proposing involved full cooperation, from the clan's great chieftain, to other warriors of high stature, especially those regarded as war chieftains among their kind. Before the idea could even be presented to other Trogen leaders, it would need the full support of Uzod himself.

"There is no other way, Jarun," Marragesh said. "If we do

nothing different, we will endure a storm of bloodshed. I cannot let that happen."

"You remember what happened to the Thunder Wolves," Jarun countered, dredging up the widely lamented tragedy. "Uzod has been careful to hide our training."

The older chieftain had been cautious, as all training flights on the Harraks had been kept far away from the shoreline, where Elven eyes could espy them from afar. Once the Elves knew of the Harraks, there was little doubt that they would seek to kill them all.

Marragesh was well aware of the implications, in unveiling a force of Trogen sky riders. Yet something had to be done that night, or a great many Trogens would die.

"I remember, Jarun, but we must fight in the skies one day. This night is as good a time as any," Marragesh said.

"It is a good night to become what we have trained to be," Jarun replied, showing the first sign of agreement.

"Then let us wait no longer here," Marragesh declared, relieved as he saw Jarun's embrace of his proposed course of action.

Jarun fell in alongside him, as he headed in the direction of the settlement. With long, rapid strides, Marragesh made for the hut closest to the byre.

Circular in construct, its walls were of wicker and mud plaster, with a steep-pitched conical roof of thatch. A hide flap covered the entrance, and the two Trogen warriors drew to a halt before it.

"Uzod," Jarun called, before pausing. "Marragesh has come. It is an urgent matter. An Elven raid approaches our shores."

Sounds of rustling came quickly from the other side of the

flap. A moment later, the hide covering was pulled aside, revealing an older Trogen warrior. He eyed the two warriors outside his hut impassively, and limped forward, using a tall, thick staff of timber to assist his movements.

A grizzled, burly Trogen, Uzod was a veteran of many skirmishes and battles with the Elves. Over his rough-spun woolen tunic and hide jerkin, he wore the silvery pelt of a Sea Wolf, which designated him as one of the elite war chieftains of the Trogen clan.

Such pelts were rare and precious, as they were only taken from the bodies of dead Sea Wolves that washed up on Trogen shores. Many Trogens believed that such pelts were bestowed on the clan in a mystical way by their sea patrons, a sign that the oceanic creatures found the clan worthy of the sacred relationship.

Uzod eyed Marragesh and Jarun closely. "An Elven raid approaches?"

Marragesh nodded. "A very large one, a great many vessels."

Other than a glint in his eyes, Uzod showed no outward reaction to the dire news. "Then we must warn the settlements, and ready ourselves to fight, wherever we can. We will greet them with iron in our hands and fire in our hearts."

Jarun cast a sideways glance to Marragesh, who had found that he was hesitant to venture his thoughts to Uzod. He was a newer warrior, far removed from the rank of one who wore a Sea Wolf pelt. It was not his place to give war counsel, even if he felt strong conviction in his idea.

"Speak," Uzod growled impatiently. "I can see that you hold something of a strong nature inside. It is not the Trogen way to restrain a conviction. This place would not exist if I had silenced myself."

"You know that I am just a newer warrior," Marragesh said, after a moment's hesitation. "But my heart says that we should confront them in the skies, this very night."

Uzod's eyes widened slightly, and it was plain that he had not expected such a response. "You, Jarun, and the others who have taken up the cause of flying are brave warriors, but what you suggest would be an embrace of death. The Elves would outnumber us heavily in the skies, and their riders have had untold years to master their skills in flying. We have only just begun to gain mastery of the Harraks. It would be like a group of uninitiated Trogens engaging in battle with a much greater number of veteran Trogen warriors."

"All who go up into the skies would likely die," Marragesh said flatly. "But maybe not those on the ground. An attack by our sky warriors would take the Elves by surprise. If we could draw them to a place of our choosing, and attack them in strength, it is possible that our sky warriors would gain enough time for those on the ground to fight a more evenly matched battle. We have never fought in such conditions, so do we really know what that outcome would be?"

Uzod grew very quiet, and Marragesh could tell nothing by the stony expression on the warrior's face. Marragesh had imparted his idea, and the reasoning behind it. He could do nothing more. The rest was not up to him, and he silently awaited the verdict of the older Trogen.

After some time had passed, Uzod began to nod slowly. He

spoke in a low, purposeful tone, "There is truth to what you say, Marragesh. They would never expect to be challenged in the sky. And if the ground is left free, our fighters there have a greater chance to fend those pale-skinned bastards off."

"They will not be able to direct their forces on the ground, and they will not be able to attack from above," Jarun said. "We may not be able to drive them from the skies, but we can take some of their advantages away."

"If our sky warriors can fight well, and cause confusion in their airborne ranks," Uzod said.

"We can," Marragesh said.

Uzod nodded again. "Each sky warrior must make their own choice. I will not command them to do this, as it will be a flight into certain death."

"With your favor, I will ask them myself," Marragesh said.

Uzod then looked away, and Marragesh could see the older warrior's mood taking a swift downturn. He could see the fingers on Uzod's hands squeezing tighter where they held on to the walking staff. When he looked back towards the two younger warriors, the frustration on Uzod's face was unmistakable.

"I should be asking this, and I should be taking a mount into the skies this night," Uzod said heavily. "The choice has been taken from me."

Marragesh and all of the sky warriors knew the old Trogen could not take to the skies, and likely never would again. He had paid a costly, bitter price for his vision, having taken a long fall when a feisty Harrak female, the matriarch of the Harrak clan being trained, had thrown him from the saddle shortly after leaving the ground. Fortunately, Uzod had survived, but the injury to his back and right leg had prevented him from riding again.

Ever since then, the Trogen sky riders had taken to securing themselves into saddles fitted with special straps and buckles. No Harrak was taken into the air until it was well-used to carrying riders along the ground. A harsh lesson had been learned, but it had been one that undoubtedly prevented other Trogen deaths.

"It was no fault of yours, and we would not have anything to confront this Elven raid with, were it not for you," Marragesh said, in consolation. "If you had not sought to harness the Harraks, our lands would be as vulnerable as before to the Elven savagery. Because of you, we have a chance to spare many Trogen lives tonight."

Uzod held Marragesh's eyes for several long moments. At last, the older Trogen nodded slowly. "My heart will remain heavy, but I thank you, Marragesh, for trying to soothe an old warrior's heart."

"I will do you honor in the skies, Uzod, as will Jarun, and all the warriors who are willing to go with me," Marragesh said.

"I have no doubts about that," Uzod said. "But you will still need me for passing along the word of what you seek to do. Coming from me, the war chieftains and Granthir will be much more likely to cooperate. Do you understand this?"

"Yes," Marragesh answered.

"Then our fliers must be used as messengers, without delay," Uzod said. "We will gather up the others, so you can address them."

Leaning on the staff, he reached down with his left hand to

where a horn was hanging at his side. Bringing it up to his lips, he inhaled and loosed a long, deep blast that resonated throughout the outpost.

In moments, Trogens were hurrying swiftly from every direction, emerging from huts and the trees at the edges of the outpost. They hastened towards Uzod's hut, gathering at the sides of Marragesh and Jarun. All carried weapons, as Trogen warriors maintained a constant state of preparedness.

When all of the Trogens were assembled before Uzod, the old warrior addressed them. "This night, all of you face a choice. It is yours to make … each and every one of you."

The Trogens looked to each other, their faces carrying traces of confusion.

"The Elves are coming to kill our kind, as they always have, but this night their hunt can be resisted in a way they do not expect," Uzod continued.

He went on to explain Marragesh's concept. Looking at their facial reactions, it soon became obvious that most, if not all, supported the idea.

Uzod made it very clear that the Trogens had a free choice, to go into the skies or stay back. There was not a single warrior that did not volunteer to undertake the mission. Once consensus had been attained, the sky warriors were all dismissed by Uzod, to gather their weapons, saddles, and harnessing together.

Marragesh's hut was on the far side of the settlement. It was rather austere, but it was the place he had called home for some time. A melancholy feeling descended upon him as he neared the entrance.

The hide flap was shoved aside as a squat, four-legged creature with dark, lustrous fur trundled out of the hut. Its two rounded ears were perked up, as the creature raised its head to look upon Marragesh. A frosting of silvery fur graced its short muzzle.

While possessing some significant differences, the Gulobar were smaller cousins of the huge Forest Wolverines another Trogen clan was named after. Long ago, the Gulobar had somehow been domesticated by the Trogens, though as ferocious as they could be, few Trogens could fathom how that had been accomplished.

As Marragesh looked upon Teltas, he though about how the Gulobar were not spared the blades of Elven raiders either. Many fell each time a Trogen settlement was annihilated in a raid.

Marragesh set one knee on the ground, and rubbed the Gulobar's head affectionately. To the Trogen's eyes, the creature had saddened eyes as it gazed up into his face. The enormity of what he was about to embark upon struck him profoundly as he looked into the face of the Gulobar.

"Live, Teltas. Just live," Marragesh said, rubbing his forehead against that of the Gulobar. The creature emitted a rumbling vocalization of contentment.

The burly creature rolled over onto its back, exposing a broad white patch on its chest. Teltas loved being scratched in that spot, and Marragesh obliged his loyal companion, feeling his heart grow heavier with every moment.

After visiting with Teltas a little longer, he proceeded into his hut, and gathered up everything he would need for the coming flight. He did not go to the pen containing the Harraks until he had arranged for Teltas to be given into the care of a young Trogen who was living at the settlement. An orphaned youth named Cressir, he had been adopted by the sky warriors after miraculously surviving the last Elven raid.

Cressir promised Marragesh that he would take great care of the Gulobar. Looking away from Teltas for the last time was one of the most difficult things Marragesh had ever done.

His heart was aching with emotions as he walked away from his hut that night. Gulobar, like Banca and Yallan, were not Trogens, but they had become genuine family to Marragesh in the times following the raid destroying his home village.

***

Marragash carried his weapons, a saddle, and harnessing out to where Yallan stood, a younger male Harrak that harbored a fiery spirit. The creature gazed attentively upon him as he approached, its triangular ears erect, and head raised, as if it sensed the momentous nature of the situation.

Many other Trogens had entered the pen, heading towards their Harraks, but for Marragesh the entire world had narrowed down to just him, and his steed. After setting the weapons and other implements down, Marragesh patted the Harrak on the neck, stroking the beast's fur for several moments. The Trogen leaned his head against the coarse outer fur of the Harrak, taking in the musty scent that he always found welcome.

"This night, you carry me on a flight to Elysium, Yallan," he said, in a low tone. "But I want you to survive this night. When my spirit flees this world, do not linger. Seek refuge, and live onward."

The Harrak turned its head and nuzzled Marragesh. As with Banca, a bond had formed between rider and steed, and Marragesh knew the Harrak sensed the bittersweet feelings churning inside of him.

He had sensed the same thing with Banca, who he had visited just prior to going into the pen with the Harraks. The Amnoros seemed unusually agitated, and not because of the close proximity to Harraks.

It had tried to follow Marragesh when he walked away. He had left instructions with a couple of other Trogen youths living at the outpost, who would be remaining behind with Uzod. As with his Gulobar, Banca would be seen to when the sky riders departed on a flight that would have no return.

After he ruffled the Harrak's fur for another few moments, he worked to secure the saddle and harnessing. There was not much to get in place, as the low-profile leather saddle rested just forward of the wings, atop a blanket fashioned of Amnoros wool that prevented chafing for the Harrak. Accustomed to the sequence, Yallan remained still all throughout, as the Trogen tightened buckles and straps.

He took up an extended lance, and pulled himself up into the saddle when he was finished. Sitting tall astride his mount, he took a deep breath. His longblade sat comfortably in its hide sheath, and he had a large, single-edged knife in another sheath at his waist, affixed by hide thongs to his narrow leather belt.

Looking around, he saw that most of the other Harraks were saddled up with riders on their backs. Several were looking towards him, clutching their weapons in readiness.

Without Uzod accompanying them, Marragesh was given authority over the band of sky warriors. As such, he was the first to take to the air, after a few last items were discussed and the signal to depart was given.

Yallan charged forward and leaped upward with a burst of muscle power. The night air rushed over Marragesh's broad, short muzzle, as he began to ascend on the wings of his steed.

Marragesh pressed Yallin with haste, alerting two smaller settlements of the looming Elven danger. The other sky riders were doing likewise, spreading out and warning several other villages of the Sea Wolf Clan about the impending raid.

He could feel the fear that his reports sparked in those who he spoke with. Both of the settlements were within close range of the coast, and readily assented to Marragesh's urging for them to make haste for Granthir's principle settlement.

***

When the Elves finally arrived at the northern shores of Trogen territory, disembarking their galleys and heading inland, they discovered a vacated land. Trogen scouts watching from afar sent along word that the Elven force was pushing deeper into the Trogen lands, as they came across empty village after empty village.

The Elves' Lavion sky steeds swept all throughout the area. Concealed Trogen scouts watching the patterns of the Elves recognized it when the raiders became aware of the large concentrations of Trogens gathering at Granthir's great settlement.

Both in the air and on the ground, the Elves were funneling straight towards the Sea Wolf clan chieftain's settlement. Just as Jarun had suggested to Uzod, the Elves were taking the bait set out for them.

The Trogen sky riders had gathered much earlier by the chieftain's settlement, sequestered under heavy cover. It was of critical importance to ensure the Elves had no inkling of the Trogen's newer capabilities with sky steeds.

Several Amnorosen were employed in the harrowing task of luring the Elves deeper, the daring Trogens riding the burly steeds drawing them towards Granthir's settlement. Posing as startled scouts, the Trogens raced for the encampment, bringing a wave of Elven warriors in their wake. Thirsting for slaughter, the Elves had no forewarning of the existence of Trogen sky riders.

***

Their bone-white skin was largely concealed underneath their iron helms, tunics, and leggings. Lightly armored, they wore hide jerkins over their tunics, and carried spears, longbows, and the lengthy, curving single-edged blades that had ended so many Trogen lives. Moving swiftly, and noiselessly, they flowed lithely through the trees as they approached the outskirts of the large Trogen settlement.

The rustling of their attire was no greater of a disturbance than the light breezes jostling the leaves. The Elven raiding force would have gone undetected and caught the Trogens by surprise, were it not for the foreknowledge of the defenders as warned by Marragesh.

As it was, Marragesh, Jarun, the sky riders, and a large number of other Trogen warriors watched the Elven approach from midway up the slope of a rise close by. Anger swelled in him as he watched them converging on the settlement, knowing they would have no restraint about letting Trogen blood flow.

Several of the Trogens on foot began to pull back on their longbows. As the creaks of bending wood began to percolate through the area, Marragesh could see the eagerness within their eyes to begin the attack.

"Hold!" Jarun urged them, in a low voice. "We must strike them in the right moment."

"The right moment? They are within reach of our arrows," hissed a huge Trogen named Gundohar, a war chieftain of the Sea Wolves, who Marragesh had learned was the leader of the warriors on foot.

"Let them draw in their sky warriors," Marragesh responded, in a non-confrontational, respectful manner. "We can only gain a chance to deflect their sky warriors from you if we are able to catch them by surprise. If we succeed, it will mean they will not land their sky steeds to ride upon the ground, and they will not strike at you from the air."

Gundohar's face looked strained with tension, but after a moment he nodded. "We will hold back."

Farther below, the Elves fanned out, and took up positions surrounding the village. At the center of the circular, thatch-roofed huts, a very brave throng of Trogens warriors faced outward, with weapons at the ready. A foreboding silence hovered over them, as all were well aware of the threat closing in upon them.

Once the encirclement of the settlement was complete, an Elven warrior raised a horn to his lips, and blew out a deep, resonant note. It echoed all throughout the surrounding rises, carrying high and far.

Fathoming the purpose of the signal, Marragesh felt the blood accelerate in his veins. The Elf's summons was exactly what Marragesh had been counting on.

"The sky riders will come now. Be ready," Marragesh told Gundohar, and the Trogens around him. "The ones on the ground will not attack yet. Not until they are supported from the air. Let the sky riders draw near."

Though Gundohar still looked irritated and impatient, he stayed the hands of his warriors, to Marragesh's great relief. He knew it was not an easy thing for the veteran Trogen, a vaunted war chieftain, to trust a young, inexperienced warrior at such a precarious moment.

Looking into the skies, Marragesh waited with expectation, not taking his eyes away from the velvety, star-strewn canopy for a moment. Like a dark cloud sailing across the skies, a large force of Elves mounted on Lavions came into view. Well over a hundred and fifty strong, it was a force Marragesh and the other Trogens riding Harraks could not hope to match.

Marragesh could see the Elven riders were gathered into four distinct groupings. Each cluster would be led by an Elven warrior riding a male Lavion, while the other steeds in a given throng would all be female. Though rarer, there were occasions when two male Lavions ruled over a pride, resulting in a pair of the larger, thick-maned beasts at the forefront of a cluster.

Outnumbered almost three to one in terms of winged mounts, Marragesh was not dissuaded in his course. The Elves were coming with the conviction that they would go uncontested in the skies. But this night would be different, even if the resistance ultimately loomed as hopeless.

For the first time, the Elves would be challenged in the sky, no matter the cost. They would be met blade to blade, and would have to fight their way into the village.

The Trogen warriors fighting on the ground would not be harried from the air at the outset of the fighting. Nor would they be plagued by Lavion riders on the ground, as the Elves consistently used a portion of their sky mounts as cavalry.

On the ground, the Trogens enjoyed strength of numbers. Gundohar's force could possibly drive back the Elven raiders, if the efforts of Marragesh and the other Trogen sky riders could purchase them a little time.

The Elves were used to overwhelming, lopsided fights. Staunch resistance would throw them into a scenario they were not used to, and perhaps their reaction would be to the Trogens' advantage.

The four throngs of Elven riders drew closer, and the moment was at hand. Raising his lance, his eyes blazing with intensity, Marragesh cried aloud, loosing the momentous signal that all of the Trogens had been waiting for. "My brothers, into glory ride!"

The other Trogen sky riders lifted their weapons, shaking them vigorously and hailing Marragesh fervently. Their faces had a determined, iron-like cast, as they took up the reins of their steeds for the unprecedented flight.

"Yallan, to the skies!" he called to his steed, using heels and reins to convey his wish.

The creature bounded forward, and launched itself powerfully into the air. Its wings built upon the momentum gained by its bursting strides, flapping robustly and pulling its body upwards. Tucking its legs to its underside, the Harrak maintained a steep angle of incline.

One after another, the other Trogen sky riders took off from the ground in Marragesh's wake. In a few moments, the entire force of fifty-three mounted sky warriors was ascending towards the Elves. The riders gradually guided their mounts in closer, tightening up the formation as it ascended.

The Trogen sky riders were badly outnumbered, but Marragesh blocked the thought out of his mind as they climbed higher and higher. It felt as if he was soaring into the heart of night, as the sky sparkled with its raiment of stars. The shadowy forms of the Elves hovered in place, a deadly cloud waiting to receive the upstart Trogens, who dared to challenge their dominion of the skies.

Without any prompting from its rider, Yallan picked up speed as Marragesh spearheaded the Trogen contingent. He sensed the other riders flying close to him, but he kept his eyes steeled to the incoming formations of Elves.

Faintly, he could hear the Elves calling out to each other, as they took notice of the unexpected throng rising to challenge them. There was urgency to their tones, and Marragesh knew the Trogens had taken them completely by surprise. He could not understate what was occurring. The airborne domain the Elves assumed to be theirs in its entirety was about to be contested for the very first time.

The contingent of Harraks leveled out their flight before the two sides came together. Picking up the scents of the Lavions, the Harraks barked and accelerated, as always showing no reticence to engage their hated adversary. Marragesh felt Yallan's surge, and knew the steeds would fight as furiously as their riders.

Marragesh could see the leader of the Elven cluster before him, demarcated by the huge male Lavion he rode upon. A thick golden mane framed the face of the Lavion, as it spread its jaws and erupted with a defiant roar. The air was filling with the feline growls and cries, as the Lavions readied to engage the Harraks.

With Marragesh at the fore, the Trogen force drove into the heart of the broad Elven formation. Lavions swiped their big claws, even as Harraks snapped their thick jaws. Weapons were thrust and slashed, as the two sides flew through each other.

The Trogens, with their condensed throng, were like a spearhead penetrating a broad body. The Elves could not take advantage of their larger numbers, at least not just yet.

A couple of loud cries indicated that first blood had been drawn in the unfolding sky battle. Marragesh looked around, and saw one of the Harraks near him with an empty saddle.

He looked down just in time to see the diminishing form of the warrior who had been riding the steed, as he plummeted towards the ground far below. It was a terrible thing to witness, as nothing could even be attempted to save the doomed Trogen.

The warrior had made the lethal mistake of leaving the special straps anchoring him to the saddle unsecured. No matter how many times Uzod had admonished certain warriors, they stubbornly felt they needed to be as freed up as possible, to effectively wield their weapons. The falling Trogen was one of those warriors, who had not heeded Uzod.

Marragesh swiped his spear blade in raw fury at a couple of Elven warriors, but missed them by a wide margin. He gnashed his teeth in frustration, passing beyond the far end of the Elven force. Banking Yallan to the left, be brought the steed into a tight arc, intending to come back around for another pass.

He did not have to worry about chasing down the Elves, as two enemy warriors angled their steeds to come directly at him. He roared a battle cry at them, leveling his spear in an underhanded grip using both of his hands.

His Harrak yelped, and Marragesh cried out, as the two Elves grazed both rider and steed with their curving, finely honed blades. Fear clenched him, until he realized that the Elven blade had only taken some fur and a little skin from Yallan's right hind flank. The Elves passed unscathed, one of them moving his head to the side just in time to avoid a rapid spear thrust from Marragesh.

The first exchanges confirmed what Marragesh suspected. The Elves were faster, and far more balanced in wielding their weapons from the backs of their steeds. Every advantage possible lay with the Elves, from skills to sheer numbers; except for one.

The Trogens were defending their homeland and lives, and their hearts were unshakable as they fought against the invaders. In the chaos of battle, an indomitable heart could offset shortcomings in other areas.

Marragesh continued forward, and waded back into to the

thick of the fighting. Sometimes he found himself side to side with another Trogen, and sometimes he was left to himself.

The sounds of beating wings, growls, barks, and cries surrounded him. Everything was instinct and reaction in the swirling fight, and his spearblade began to find openings. Sometimes, he caught an Elven warrior by surprise, and once a Trogen warrior felled an Elf about to attack him unawares from behind.

As Marragesh had foreseen, the steeds continued to beset each other with lethal intent. When a Harrak's jaws could find the throat of a Lavion, another Elven rider was eliminated from the fighting, but more than one set of Lavion jaws found the throats of Harraks.

The Lavions were larger, stronger, and faster than the Harraks. The advantages the Lavions held were played out right before Marragesh's eyes as he saw one of the big males envelop a Harrak, overpowering and mortally wounding it in a couple of heartbeats. The Trogen rider on the slain Harrak was condemned to a long descent, and the bone-shattering death that would follow.

The Lavion and its rider had to turn a little to face an attack by another Trogen, positioned on the farther side from where Marragesh was. Reacting, Marragesh dug his heels in and made for the rider on the big male.

Hurtling towards the Elf from the side, Marragesh struck fast and truly, burying the long iron head of the spear into the upper back of the raider. The Trogen could not pull the spear free, and had to let go, lest he be ripped off the back of his own mount. Without hesitation, he reached down and pulled his longblade free.

Yallan's rear haunch had been raked with claws in a parting swipe by the male Lavion as they flew past, but the enemy steed was left with a dead rider on its back. Yallan's speed carried Marragesh well beyond the edge of the fighting. As they turned around to come back, he chanced a glance towards the fighting on the ground far below.

***

Far down below on the ground, momentum had been stolen from the Elven raiders from the outset with the abrupt emergence of the Trogen sky force. Without the support of their airborne comrades, the Elven warriors on the ground found themselves in a battle that was much more evenly matched.

A sizeable group of Trogens mounted on Amnorosen worked their way around the upper slopes until they were on the other side of the village from Gundohar's warriors. After a few horn signals passed between the two groups they descended in a thundering charge.

The massed warriors from the hillside, Gundohar bellowing at their lead, swept down from the front. Without Elven sky steeds alighting on the ground and becoming a cavalry force, the Amnorosen could be utilized effectively. They were skittish and fearful in the presence of the massive Lavions, which was the reason that the few attempts to use them before as ground mounts ended in disaster. Without the Lavions around, there was nothing to shake the Amnorosen's nerves.

Some of the Elves on the perimeter of the village shifted

to defend against the host of warriors on foot and the multitude of Amnorosen calvary. The Trogen warriors in the center of the village reacted swiftly. Including many great warriors that dwelled in Granthir's settlement, they moved forward to attack a couple of thinner segments in the ring of attackers.

A brawling melee developed, as the skill and speed of the Elves was pitted against the fury, power, and numbers of the Trogens. Fighters from both sides fell, but it was the Elves who swiftly became dismayed, as they were not used to suffering casualties on such raids.

The coordination and ferocity of the Trogens kept them off balance, and without their sky steeds providing eyes above, they found it difficult to grasp the course of the battle. They were denied the elements that they had come to rely on during raids, and the effect on their morale was potent.

One of the first-born races of Ave, the Elves did not age or grow sick. Death's touch within their ranks quickly spurred fear. Added to the pervasive confusion, it was not long before the Elven leaders began to orchestrate a fallback, though the defenders were not about to give them a moment's rest in the fighting.

Seeing the Elves begin to pull back elicited a deep-toned roaring from the Trogen ranks, a chorus that rose far into the skies to where the fighting still continued.

***

Marragesh's lance blade dripped thickly with Elven blood, but the outcome of the sky battle was clear to all involved. The end of the fighting was drawing near. Looking around, Marragesh saw that only a handful of Trogens yet survived, each isolated warrior being hunted down by groups of Elves.

A Lavion closing in on the rear of a Harrak lashed out with its right paw, ripping into the right haunch of the Trogen steed. As the Harrak reacted, banking sharply to the right, the Elven rider thrust a lance into the Trogen's body. The Trogen slumped forward, the reins falling out of his hands as he dropped his longblade.

Marragesh cried out, and steered Yallan towards the slayer of his comrade. The Elf deflected the slash of the incoming Trogen's spear blade. The two traded heavy blows, as their steeds strove to wound each other.

Fury pouring from his eyes, Marragesh cried, "Fall to hell!"

He drove his spear into the open maw of the Lavion, yanking it back just in time as the creature wings ceased flapping, and it began hurtling towards the ground. The shriek of its rider faded as the Elf was dragged downward, trees and rocks waiting below to break its extensive fall.

Marragesh fought onward, with no shortage of opponents as the Elves swarmed all around him. He deflected strikes, countered with his own, and fought with desperation. Looking around and gauging the situation, he saw that another Trogen was down to the right. He guided Yallan into a steep glide, racing for his fellow warrior and pulling the Harrak up into a hover as they neared.

"Let us stand together!" Marragesh called, to alert the Trogen to his presence.

When the rider turned his head, Marragesh saw it was Jarun. They were the last two Trogens left in the skies. As fate would have it, they were a fair distance from the nearest Elves, though their enemies hemmed them in on all sides like predators circling their quarry.

"This night is a good night to die," Marragesh said with a grin between heavy breaths, with full conviction in his heart.

Yallan bobbed as a strong breeze buffeted them. Marragesh glanced downward, and could see the forms of Elves fleeing swiftly through the trees on the ground.

The sight was everything he had hoped for. They were in full retreat, and not one hut in the village had been set on fire.

"It is such a night," Jarun agreed, returning the smile.

"The village stands," Marragesh said, savoring a moment's satisfaction.

"Then we have been measured, and measured favorably," Jarun replied. "It is all a Trogen warrior can ask, yes?"

"It is, but let us send another Elf or two to hell, before we walk in the Elysian Fields," Marragesh said, a flare of intensity in his eyes.

"I will see you there, Marragesh," Jarun said firmly. "Soon enough."

Loosing fierce war cries that caused more than one Elven warrior to hesitate, the two Trogens spurred their Harraks at a group of Elves who had gathered in front of them. Marragesh felt exhilarated as he clutched his longblade. There would be no return from the charge, and he prepared to meet the end; with determination, and without regret.

He cleaved into the Elves on the back of the Harrak, a tempest of fury as he struck out again and again with his longblade. One

Elf cried out as Marrageh's blade opened a gash on its arm, and another winced as it deflected a weighty blow.

While he did not have the range that a lance afforded, Marragesh was much more proficient with a Trogen longblade. His skill was demonstrated as he slew an Elf following a flurry of strikes, parrying and counterstriking with a fluid rhythm.

To his right, an Elven warrior speared Jarun's mount, driving the blade deep into the Harrak's chest. The creature hovered just long enough that Jarun was able to spring free from the saddle. Casting his longblade aside, Jarun flung himself at the Elven warrior, who had a look of shock and dismay as the Trogen fell upon him.

The Lavion could not hold up two riders, and immediately began tumbling down out of the sky. Marragesh heard another battle cry from Jarun as they plunged downward, and knew that his comrade would not lose his hold, taking his opponent on a final descent.

The courageous act drove Marragesh into a maddened frenzy. His eyes burned with hot tears, as all the emotion within him finally broke free. The blood in his veins spiked to a boil, as he roared defiantly into the night.

He beheaded a female Lavion with one blow, dooming its rider to a lethal plunge, and then engaged the Elven warrior positioned just beyond. Crying out his fury, he blocked two strikes, before rolling off a third and wounding the enemy fighter. The Trogen was so enraged that he did not feel the Elven blade nick his own arm, opening a new trickle of blood.

Hacking with all of his might, he battered the Elf's blocks with his heavy longblade. His steed reared back suddenly, as it parried with the Lavion, riders and mounts alike fighting furiously.

As Yallan dropped back down, Marragesh brought his blade rushing forward. The air rang loudly with the clang of the impact, as the Elf got his own curving, single-edged blade up just in time.

An opening was created, and Yallan lunged forward and chomped down onto the lower half of the Elf's face. The Elf screamed in agony, the shock of pain leaving the enemy warrior vulnerable to the torrential blow Marragesh then levied. Still gripping the sword, the Elf's severed arm fell towards the ground far below.

"For my father, mother, sisters, and brother," Marragesh growled. "For all in my village!"

A volcanic fury engulfed him, as the anguish and sorrow of that terrible loss was transformed into crackling power, flowing like lightning through his limbs as he struck. The whoosh of his blade accompanied the separation of the Elf's head from its neck.

Marragesh pulled Yallan away from the headless body, and sought out the next opponent. Three more enemy warriors would fall before Marragesh finally suffered a mortal wound, as an Elven blade cut deep, splitting his side open. Blood gushed from the wound, as searing pain enveloped him.

He felt darkness steadily coming over him, his mind growing dizzy as the blood poured out from his body. Time seemed to slow to a complete halt, each breath he took an exquisite luxury.

Perhaps there was nothing at all, at the end of life's journey. Sounds fading, and his sight ebbing steadily, a part of Marragesh felt a terrible dread as his life slipped away, immersing into an ocean of blackness.

***

He did not see Yallan turn, the Harrak's eyes blazing with rabid anger as he fell upon the Elven warrior that had slain Marragesh. The raider was engulfed in the Harrak's storm, and the jaws of Marragesh's loyal steed found the soft flesh of the Elf's throat.

Clutching haplessly at its torn throat, as its lifeblood gushed out, the Elf was plummeting towards the ground a moment later. In the tumult, Yallan had managed a vigorous slash on the Lavion, tearing deep into the flesh at the base of its right wing.

The wing rendered useless, the Lavion could no longer maintain flight. Screeching and flailing, its good wing beating uselessly, it fell like a stone dropped from a cliff's edge.

As if Yallan remembered Marrageh's spoken desire, far back at the Harrak pen in the outpost, the steed tucked its wings in close and dove for the ground. No Elves gave chase, and the Harrak finally neared the tall pines and other trees below. Spreading its wings into an extended glide, it slowed until it found an open stretch of ground, landing a few moments later.

Some time later, a few Trogens would come upon Yallan, as they gathered up the steeds surviving the heroic clash in the skies. In the depths of night, there were no Trogen witnesses to Marragesh's actions, as every last warrior who had gone up to challenge the large Elven force had fallen.

Yet for years afterward, there was one creature living among the Trogens who knew the truth of it all. Some said it was why Yallan would carry no other rider, in all the years remaining to him. Many believed it was the creature's way of testifying to the great heart within Marragesh.

Uzod made sure that the creature was well-cared for, and the Harrak would become a part of the next group of Trogen sky riders, in a way. Siring many robust offspring over the years that followed, hale steeds that carried Trogen warriors into the skies to defend their lands, Yallan's bloodline would go onward.

***

Blackness and silence encompassed Marragesh, but only for the blink of a moment. A blinding light shattered the ebon morass, as an invigorating warmth permeated his being. He had never felt more aware or alert, and wondered at what was happening to him.

Sweet floral scents flooded his nose, as the voice of Jarun cut through the stillness, brimming with excitement and happiness, "Are you ready to stride the Elysian Fields? Are you ready to fly once more, my brother? Then come with me now, our journey begins!"

A joy Marragesh had never felt before flooded the Trogen who had given his life for his kind. What had been taken was returned to him a hundred-fold, as his vision cleared and a wondrous sight was unveiled before him.

His mother, father, sisters, and brother were among many Trogens standing before a dazzling vista. All were waiting to greet him, as he began the first moments of an incredible adventure that would have no ending.

A Touch of
Serenity

A Touch of Serenity

"Wisdom, compassion, and courage are the three universally recognized moral qualities of men."
-Confucius

The body thudded into the mixture of silt, clay, and shell bits, joining the macabre throng already lumped within the unfinished section of the Wall. Chung-Li Ch'uan kept his face still, though he was not so numb to the sight of the dead being buried within the Wall that he remained unaffected.

His stomach churned, and Ch'uan had to look away as one of the guardsmen barked orders at the bone-weary laborers to keep working. The deaths were never easy to bear, no matter what expression he presented to their overseers.

They were an unsettling, daily occurrence that had to be endured. Deeply troubling to Ch'uan, the frequency of the deaths had risen considerably since the Emperor's high-ranking minister Cao Qiu had arrived to supervise the construction.

The unfortunate man who had died would soon be covered

with more loess. Eventually, laborers would be tamping everything down using long-handled wooden hammers, until the surface became hard-packed.

A layer of bamboo would be set down, more loess would be introduced above that, the hammers would begin pounding, and soon another layer would begin to take form. At the top, bricks would cap the many levels of compacted infill, the latter encased between two facings of kiln-hardened bricks. When the laborers were finished with the section of wall, there would be no traces indicating the Wall's nature as a grave for so many who died in its making.

An earlier Divine Emperor had ordered the construction of the Wall, connecting some earlier rampart fortifications marking boundaries. Countless multitudes had toiled in heavy labor for decades as the barrier grew and took shape.

Rising hundreds of feet into the air, it was thick enough that six mounted warriors could ride abreast along the crenellated top of the Wall. It now stretched for hundreds of leagues from the eastern sea deep into the west, and lengthened by the day.

Thousands upon thousands had died in the building of the Wall already, and thousands more would undoubtedly perish before the great task culminated. No consideration had been given to the conscript laborers, or the families they came from. Their bodies were unceremoniously added to the Wall's bulk, as the work proceeded without hesitation.

The Wall, in the view of Ch'uan and so many forced to work upon it, had the presence of a huge, snaking tomb that cleaved the verdant lands of the Empire of Heaven. It stood as something far more abhorrent than it could be something to take pride in.

He hated that wall with a bitter passion, as it encased the body of his own brother, Shimin. The cruelty of several guards had visited a brutal end to his brother's life.

Shimin had tried to intervene on behalf of another man, who had dropped from fatigue and remained inert, about to be killed where he had fallen. The small act of mercy was rewarded with a barrage of heavy blows from the pitiless guards.

Ch'uan could not get the battered, bloodied image of his brother's lifeless face from his mind. It proved to be a deep scar that the passage of time did not lessen, the shock of it all so great that ever since he could only remember the grisly mask of death.

Memories of his brother in the fullness of life, a good-humored man who laughed often before the sorrowful days on the Wall, were fleeting and ephemeral. To Ch'uan, the bludgeoned face of his brother served as the cold image of reality, and the smiling one nothing more than a far-faded dream.

Yet there was nothing that Ch'uan could do about any of it. He remained a landless peasant himself, without wealth or influence of any kind. He could only hope he survived long enough to be freed from the harsh labor, and eventually allowed to return to his own village.

The command finally disseminated for the laborers to cease working, as the sun's light ebbed to the cusp of twilight. Ch'uan trudged along in the loose, staggered column of worn-out laborers making the long walk back to their sleeping quarters. Every time he made that walk, he found it difficult to imagine he could last through another day.

Little to no conversation took place amongst the laborers. It took an act of will just to move forward, as exhausted as they all were. Ch'uan trudged, riddled with aches, and his skin had acquired more than a few new scrapes and cuts during the day.

The only consolation he had centered around the fact that he was not one of those cursed to transport loess all day long. Baskets full of the mixture were affixed to each end of a pole, the latter balanced across the backs of the porters. The weighty burdens left their mark in the stooped forms of many men in the column, including a pair near to him.

Ch'uan took his eyes away from his companions, and gazed at the looming rises around them, eyeing the Wall where it ran along a lengthy ridge towards the east. It always proved hard for him to envision that the wall culminated in the sea, so many leagues away.

Ch'uan wondered how far the Divine Emperor intended to extend the Wall westward, with the occasional offshoots cresting mountain spurs. He doubted the barbarian tribes in the north, the stated reason for the Wall, could reach so far west. But he was just a peasant, and did not know all the possible threats facing the Empire of Heaven.

***

Chewing and the smacking of lips accompanied the group of laborers in the dim space, as the drops of light rain pattered outside their quarters. Ch'uan did not miss the absence of conversation, as he had nothing to say to the others with him.

They were bound in the solidarity of extreme weariness. Slivers of rest and sustenance were the only goals most of them harbored anymore.

Ch'uan was not oblivious to his companions or the plight several were facing. Again, he took notice of a particular man seated near him, and felt a tugging pity. Zhang An looked to be around fifty years of age, his weathered face creased with fear, pain, and fatigue. His back undeniably failing, he had already been beaten harshly by the merciless guards.

Ch'uan knew it to be likely that the man would soon be added to the Wall's grisly material. In truth, if it were not for Ch'uan, he already would have been long before.

"Here, for your strength," Ch'uan said gently to Zhang An, offering the man half his own rations; as he had most every evening for quite some time.

The older man looked up into Ch'uan's face. Zhang An's eyes glistened, as Ch'uan tipped over his small bowl. His callused hands trembled as Ch'uan poured some millet gruel out into his own vessel, as if each little bit carried a notable weight.

Ch'uan would have shared all he had, but he knew that to do so would be suicidal. He could never hope to last a day if he weakened himself too much.

The guards were not above killing a laborer outright, if the impetus came to them. He had witnessed such barbarity often enough, including with his own brother. More than once, he had wanted to scream watching a man flogged until life fled his body. The laborers were expendable, and replaceable, in the eyes of their ice-hearted overseers.

Ch'uan watched Zhang An scarf down the additional food, hoping that it would help the man live another day. For all the talk of the Emperor's benevolence and divinity, only hardship and cruelty reigned among the peasantry. Ch'uan could only hope that the men from Zhang An's village were soon dismissed and allowed to return home.

The peasants were given no indicators when such a turnover occurred, but it seemed that since the new minister Cao Qiu had come almost no contingents of laborers had been given leave to return to their homes. If anything, the ranks of the laborers were swelling, to the point that ramshackle, makeshift quarters had to be hastily constructed to house the influx of new workers.

A short time after the meal had finished and he had returned to his sleeping quarters, Ch'uan stared up at the ceiling, listening to the groans, sighs, and moans of the other laborers packed within the congested space. The thick stench of sweat and other unpleasant bodily odors filled the air, prompting Ch'uan to breath through his mouth. It was a miserable environment, one he and the other workers were subjected to every day, with no sign of an end to the ordeal.

The other voices would begin soon enough, as they always did within the depths of night. Ch'uan tried to block thoughts of those whisperings from his mind, as no sense derived from building up anxieties over what would come to him anyway.

There were problems enough to occupy his mind. He wondered if this nightmare would be the only life he knew, day after day, week after week, and perhaps year after year. The thought of that possibility daunted him to the core.

Ch'uan had not yet reached the point of resignation that so many others succumbed to. He knew the hollow look of a man who had come to terms with the drudgery. Sapped of will and worn out, such men surrendered to an existence where their spirits barely flickered inside them. Ch'uan hated the thought of himself ever reaching that kind of hopeless state, but he knew it was not impossible.

He wondered at the wisdom of the Gods. If they truly existed, they certainly permitted heartless, rapacious men to be born into the privileged lives of emperors and soldiers. Even more distressing, they allowed so many kind-hearted souls to find themselves trapped within a battered, suffering existence, one that only death would liberate.

Many of the men, especially the newer arrivals, would pray fervently to the Gods in the dark of night, but Ch'uan had long felt in his heart that the divine beings were entirely deaf to his pleas. Those who prayed and those who did not would be roused together at dawn to begin their arduous labors; and a few of both kinds of men would not be returning the following evening.

The more Ch'uan thought about everything, the angrier he grew. The rising ire did not bother him, as in a way it let him know the flame of life still burned potently within his heart.

Getting to his feet, and stepping carefully through the mass of prone workers, he decided to go for a stroll in the woods nearby. It would be better to contend with the coming voices while breathing fresh, cool air, instead of the dank, thick air pervading the sleeping quarters of the laborers.

The rains outside had drawn to a stop, and the ground had

not gotten too soft to make footing uncertain. As always, Ch'uan found it easy enough to slip by the guards and make it into the trees unnoticed.

The taste of the crisp woodland air refreshed him, and a cool tinge clung to the evening's touch. The smell of pine a welcome change, Ch'uan savored every bit of the atmosphere, but he did not remain alone for long.

"Please…"

"We are lost…"

"Help us…"

"Have mercy on us…"

"Save us…"

The voices had arrived, soft but distinctive. The words trailed off into the night, but all of them held the same pleading quality.

The tones of the disembodied voices always brought a feeling of heaviness to Ch'uan's spirit, but he did not know what to do about them. He had begun hearing them not long after he had arrived to work on the Wall.

At first it was just once voice, and then two. As time passed, the number increased, until now he estimated dozens, if not a hundred different voices beseeching him each night.

Ch'uan could not understand their purpose, but knew the voices could only mean one of two possibilities. The possessors of the voices were spirits, or he was losing his grip upon his own mind. Neither option harbored any degree of comfort, or easy resolution.

"Go farther… go farther this night…"

The latest voice, stark and more insistent, contrasted with

the pleading tones of the others. Something faintly familiar about the voice nagged at him, but he could not place the feeling.

"Go where? How can I help you?" Ch'uan responded in a low voice.

Though doing so always made him feel awkward, he had tried many times to reply to the voices, but there was never any indication that his own words were understood. A one-way conversation, no invitation was ever extended to Ch'uan in his questioning.

"*Go farther... you will see...*" the stronger voice stated insistently. "*Trust my words...*"

"Do you hear me?" Ch'uan asked, a little frustrated.

"*Go farther ... go farther now...*" the voice persisted.

Ch'uan shrugged, and started forward, his hempen sandals sinking into the rain-softened ground. No compelling reason existed for him not to walk a little farther.

A part of him had the urge to keep striding onward, and never turn back. Yet if he did so he would be deemed a fugitive, and could never again hope to return to his village.

Ch'uan passed deeper among the towering pines. He was already encompassed by the shadows that were supposed to contain malevolent beasts and other specters, which he had always believed were unfounded tales meant to keep the workers firmly in line. Ch'uan had never encountered anything remotely threatening during his nighttime treks along the tree-ornamented mountain slopes.

There were undoubtedly wild beasts in the mountains, but most probably sought to avoid him. Ch'uan stood willing to risk the few that were an actual threat for some peace of mind, and a relaxing walk that took him away from his onerous world for a little while.

"Go farther … " the strongest voice continued to urge him.

"Leave me alone, I am going farther," Ch'uan retorted, growing irritated.

"Go farther …" came the voice again, a moment later.

Ch'uan just shook his head, and continued stepping forward, enjoying the pine-scented, woodland air as he entered an area he had never crossed through before. He hoped that was enough of a response for the disembodied voice.

***

Ch'uan's sandals scuffed on the pine needles and dirt as he halted suddenly, freezing in place as a huge form manifested from the shadows. Terror swarmed him, as the world appeared to spin. On four great paws, a massive tiger padded towards the spot where Ch'uan stood, a sword-bearing man astride the predator's back.

The presence of a man upon the tiger did nothing to ease Ch'uan's spiking fears. If anything, it added more anxiety, as he knew at once that he faced someone of great power. Not even the emperor's ministers rode upon tigers.

Unable to say a word, Ch'uan backed up slowly, his anxiety welling up quickly. The brawny tiger fixed its mesmerizing gaze upon him, while the noble-looking rider stared quietly, with a solemn expression that told Ch'uan nothing of his intentions.

Ch'uan noticed a number of jars affixed to the low saddle on the tiger, as well as a few suspended from the belt circling around the man's waist. His mind grasped for firmer purchase, so troubled that he could not recall anything that would help him fathom the identity of the figure mounted upon the tiger.

"Escaping?" the man finally asked, in a calm tone that melded smoothly with the gentle breezes.

Ch'uan shook his head, unable to speak. If the man served the Divine Emperor, he knew he would be punished severely for straying so far into the woods; if not killed outright and made an example of.

"I am not with the Divine Emperor, if that is what you fear," the man stated, as the tiger strolled a little closer. The creature loomed tall enough to stare right into Ch'uan's face. His breath accelerated as the tiger neared to within a handful of paces.

"I ... just needed ... a walk," Ch'uan finally managed to reply, wrestling with the feelings of panic spiraling inside.

"Enough devils gather around this wall, in the guise of men," the rider said. "It keeps me very busy. I will not let Feng Po get everything he desires here."

Ch'uan's eyes widened, caught by surprise at the words. He knew Feng Po to be a powerful Wizard who could command the winds, a being also reputed to be able to assume the form of a dragon. Feng Po was anything but benevolent, and the open mentioning of the dangerous Wizard only made him more nervous.

"You know of Feng Po, then?" the man asked, his dark eyes narrowing.

Ch'uan nodded.

"Then know I am Chang Tao Ling," the rider announced. "And

be assured I am no friend of Feng Po."

Ch'uan's eyes widened. Chang Tao Ling was a legendary exorcist, a Wizard said to be able to capture evil spirits who had taken possession of humans. For Ch'uan to see such a mythic figure right before him boggled his mind.

"So you have heard of me?" Chang Tao Ling asked, with a trace of bemusement underlying his words.

"Yes," Ch'uan answered, nodding.

He could not believe that a great Wizard would take time to talk to a mere peasant, or even acknowledge the existence of a lowly commoner in the first place. Wizards were beings concerned with the greater troubles of the world, from everything Ch'uan had been told.

"You are very talkative," Chang Tao Ling chided, after several moments of silence passed.

"I ... do not know what to say," Ch'uan replied, in a low tone, forcing the words out. At the least, it was an honest reply that reflected his thoroughly rattled state of mind.

"It is no easy life for those such as you," Chang Tao Ling replied, with an air of sympathy. "The way of things in this world is crueler far more than it is kinder. Evil men flourish while the compassionate suffer. This hard truth about the world has not escaped my eyes."

"I will do everything I can ... to survive ... and return to my family," Ch'uan said, finding a strand of mental clarity.

"Choosing to live requires courage," the Wizard stated. "But what brings you into these woods, where you risk death unnecessarily? Is it not forbidden for those who work on the Wall to walk these slopes?"

Ch'uan hesitated, as thoughts of the strange voices rushed into his head. Speaking openly of the voices to the Wizard was the last thing he wanted to do.

"I ... I often find it difficult to sleep. I seek fresher air," he finally replied. He had not lied, but he had skirted around the phenomena that visited him with regularity each and every night.

Chang's eyes narrowed further, and his expression grew more somber. "But there is more, yes? I can see it written plainly enough upon you. There is something you are not telling me."

Ch'uan did not respond, feeling increasingly nervous under the heavier scrutiny. He feared talking to a Wizard known for exorcising demonic powers, as perhaps something was amiss within himself. A normal man did not go about hearing disembodied voices on a regular basis.

"Spirits ... but not ones from the hells," Chang said slowly, as if discerning something. "They speak to you often. And it is they who brought you out a little farther this night. I believe I am right about this ..."

The Wizard's keen insights stunned him. Ch'uan had the unsettling sensation of being naked before the Wizard; feeling as if all of his thoughts were laid bare for the other's examination.

Unable to deny the truth, he confessed to Chang. "I ... do not know what they are. To me, they are just voices."

"We all have different gifts, whether Wizard or human," Chang replied. "It would seem you have a gift that has brought many who no longer belong in this world to you."

"To hear voices is a gift?" Ch'uan asked, tentatively, more

than a little surprised at the claim.

"Yes, even if you feel it is a curse," Chang responded. "And it would seem there is purpose behind our paths coming together this night. I am on my way to a council of great importance, and had you been even a few moments later we would never have met."

"I … do not understand," Ch'uan replied.

"I have come to see purpose in the most unexpected of things," Chang said. "I have learned to trust my instincts over the years I have traveled across Ave. It is not chance that brings a man who can hear the voices of troubled spirits to me on this night."

"What do they want?" Ch'uan ventured hesitantly, hoping for some answers at last to the questions vexing him for so many days and nights.

"I do not yet know, but I trust we were supposed to meet this night," the Wizard replied, a little enigmatically.

"I wish I knew," Ch'uan said, with an edge of weariness.

"Come with me, and we will seek to learn more," Chang Tao Ling responded. At a nudge from the Wizard, the huge tiger lowered its body to the ground. He then added, "Do not worry about the guards, I will see to it that you are back by dawn."

Ch'uan's eyes reflected astonishment as he looked upon the prone tiger, perceiving the intent of the Wizard. "You … wish me … to ride the tiger?"

Chang Tao Ling nodded, a faint smile resting upon his lips. "We will get to the council faster that way, and there is little time left before it begins. Climb up behind me. He will not harm you."

Ch'uan willed himself to approach the tiger. It took a little effort to get up behind Chang Tao Ling, but after several moments he found himself seated behind the Wizard.

The tiger lifted off the ground, handling the additional weight with ease. Ch'uan could feel the powerful muscles of the beast between his legs as it strode across the ground.

He felt awkward, having never ridden so much as a horse before. When the tiger picked up its pace he could not help grabbing onto the robes of the Wizard, to steady himself. Ch'uan tensed up immediately, hoping he had not transgressed.

The Wizard must have sensed his sudden anxiety, telling him at once, "Do not worry yourself so much, Ch'uan. You are not going to hurt me by holding onto my clothing. And I do understand it is not every day you have a chance to ride a tiger."

Ch'uan could not help but grin as the Wizard laughed merrily. The two continued on their way to the council, and as Ch'uan settled down he was left to his thoughts.

The world seemed to have turned itself over. He had gone from pungent, overcrowded sleeping quarters to riding a tiger behind a legendary Wizard. Even more amazing, all of it had occurred before the moons of Ave were even halfway through their nightly journey.

Not about to bemoan the turn of events, he knew something extraordinary was happening. Though still deeply nervous, Ch'uan determined himself to take in the unprecedented experience as much as he could.

Ch'uan loosened his grip on the robes of the Wizard, and gazed around at the trees while the tiger carried him through the towering sentinels. He realized then that the voices had gone completely silent.

***

Ch'uan and the Wizard rode the tiger out of the trees and into a moonlit clearing, where four figures were gathered. They cast a distinctive air of prominence, which Ch'uan sensed the moment that he set his eyes upon them.

His curiosity prompted him to look around at the four individuals, but his fears compelled him to keep his gaze from lingering overlong on any one of them in particular. There was no need to ask Chang Tao Ling about the nature of the others.

Ch'uan knew that he was among individuals of great power, and he felt entirely out of place. Anywhere else, even laboring on the Wall, would have felt far more comfortable of a place than did the clearing with its august group.

A pot-bellied, cheerful-looking man in long blue robes stood a few paces to Ch'uan's right, next to a tall, broad-shouldered man of harder countenance. The second man had luxuriant attire, with a beautiful robe of finely-brocaded silk, and Ch'uan wondered if he had come from the Divine Emperor's court.

To their right, cross-legged upon the skin of a tiger, sat a brawny figure with an adamantine expression. The visage of a tiger adorned his black robe, and he bore a great sword. To his other side rose a slender man, whose expression appeared as relaxed and peaceful as the seated man's looked intensive.

All of them looked in the direction of Ch'uan, as the great tiger lowered to the ground for the two riders to dismount.

Ch'uan's knees felt weak as he climbed down and felt the hard ground beneath his feet once again.

Almost at once, a feeling of trepidation came over him. He harbored a little soreness from the ride, but the physical discomfort did not bother him. The sensation he had experienced when meeting Chang had returned even stronger; that of his most intimate thoughts being laid entirely open to examination.

Chang Tao Ling remained near to Ch'uan, who kept a stride's distance in back of the Wizard. With smooth grace, the tiger rose up and walked over to the edge of the trees. Turning about, the massive creature set its body back down, and joined its stare with the others at Ch'uan. The collective weight of the gazes pressed in and rendered him highly uncomfortable.

"Who else would join our council this night?" the man on the tiger skin queried, in an even tone. He cast a brief glance over to Chang Tao Ling.

"One who would ask our help, on behalf of a great many," Chang Tao Ling announced firmly, looking to each of the others. "One who has been given a great gift."

"Then make us known to him, and ease his discomfort," the serene-looking, leaner figure stated. He extended an amiable smile at Ch'uan.

Chang Tao Ling nodded, and proceeded to introduce the other figures to Ch'uan. The heavier-set individual to Ch'uan's right, went by the name of Fu Shen, the taller one Tsai Shen, the hard-looking man on the tiger skin Kuan-Ti, and the peaceable figure Shou Lao.

Just as Ch'uan expected, all of them were Wizards, akin to

Chang Tao Ling. The thought that he stood in the company of no less than five beings he had only heard about within incredible, fantastical tales both intimidated and inspired a sense of awe within him.

If the stories were to be trusted, the individuals around him had walked the world ever since the dawn of creation. They were said by many to be the first-born, drawing breath in Ave before even the Great Dragons had set foot onto the surface of a pristine, uncorrupted world.

The thought was staggering to contemplate. Ch'uan wondered what such individuals could possibly want with a landless, mortal commoner such as him.

"What is his gift? Kuan-Ti asked, after the introductions were finished.

"He can hear the voices of those who belong in another realm," Chang Tao Ling answered. He looked to Ch'uan for a moment, before continuing. "I have pondered his gift while we rode here together. I saw a great many who had followed him out to the mountain, and guided him farther this night, such that our paths crossed.

"They were drawn to him because of his gift. There is also the nature of his spirit. These lost ones are desperate spirits, and his own spirit shines in the darkness to their vision. He is a beacon to them, and they have gathered in number, clinging to desperate hope in their confusion and sorrow."

Ch'uan was astonished at the revelation that Chang Tao Ling had seen something, and known about it the entire time they had traveled. He wondered why the Wizard had not spoken a word to him of the vision, but he did not doubt that Wizards had solid reasons for their decisions.

Yet the idea that droves of spirits had hearkened to him was quite unsettling. He had no idea why he would attract them, or what they hoped to gain from him. Nothing more than a conscript laborer whose body could well become fodder for the Wall on any given day, Ch'uan held no special authority or power.

"We can sense his nature here, for ourselves. But what about the nature of these others? These 'desperate spirits', as you call them," Shou Lao asked calmly. "What did your vision tell you?"

"None are destined for the hells," Chang Tao Ling answered firmly. To Ch'uan's eyes, a weighty sadness came over the Wizard. He closed his eyes, and a sorrowful expression arose upon his face. His voice carried deep sympathy as he continued, "If only your powers could return what was taken from them, Shou Lao."

As if an understanding passed between the two Wizards, Shou Lao shut his eyes, and his face mirrored the melancholic look upon Chang Tao Ling's. Somberly, he stated, "Yes, Chang Tao Ling, I sense a part of the same evil that we have gathered to face. The wickedness is woven with the plight of these spirits who have followed this man. I do wish my arts could return what was stolen from them. But I am afraid they are well beyond my power."

Ch'uan could not make complete sense of the words, but there was no mistaking the grave nature of the situation involving the voices. An unmistakable air of tragedy surrounded the situation regarding the spirits.

He wondered how the voices he had been hearing could possibly be intertwined with the concerns of powerful Wizards, but he had no mettle for arguing with beings who counted their years in millennia. With vast ages of experience and deep wisdom, they saw everything in a different light. It would be foolish not to defer to their understanding of the matter.

"We know our purpose, Shou Lao," Fu Shen stated. He then turned to look at Ch'uan. "What kind of help do you seek, Ch'uan? What would you ask of us? Speak openly here, without fear. No harm shall come to you."

Ch'uan swallowed and took a breath, contemplating his response. Part of Ch'uan thought about the voices, but he found that another part of him thought of Zhang An.

He recalled the older man trembling earlier that evening as he accepted the gift of a small portion of millet gruel. The man's weathered face had held surprise and gratitude in the wake of Ch'uan's gesture. It was as if he had given the tired, elderly man a pile of gold, not a half-portion of his ration.

A thought struck him deeply, as he recalled the old man's reaction. The desperation Ch'uan always heard within the voices and saw in the face of Zhang An were of the same essence. Something intrinsic connected the voices and the older man, and Ch'uan glimpsed that relation just in time to respond to the Wizards.

"If ... if I could ask for anything ... I would ask if something can be done to help those who would soon fall in their labors," Ch'uan replied, his voice sounding thin as he addressed the august Wizards. "I ... I can endure, myself, and there are many young men who can ... but some will not survive another day.

"No mercy is shown to those who cannot continue working.

I would do whatever I could to ease the pain of spirits. But I also wish to ease the pain of those suffering in this world."

Ch'uan sighed deeply, and finished his response with a tone of resignation, "I do not know how to aid spirits, and as a poor man I can do so very little for the living."

A ponderous silence fell over the clearing. Looking past Chang Tao Ling, his gaze searched the faces of the other four Wizards, but he could read nothing from their stoic expressions. He had answered them with full honesty, but doubted that the worries of a commoner mattered to such powerful, ancient figures.

"I wish I was free to break the power of this self-proclaimed Divine Emperor," Kuan-Ti said in a low, tense voice that had the air of a growl. "But Feng Po and many others of our kind support his wickedness. Open war would bring devastation to your family, and the families and villages of all who dwell in this land."

"I most wish for mercy upon those soon to fall," Ch'uan said deferentially, eyes downcast. "If nothing is done, many will continue to die, and be buried within that terrible wall. I would do anything to stop that, even if it meant I must give my own life."

"And these voices? Would you seek to help those who they belong to?" Fu Shen queried pointedly.

Ch'uan nodded. "I ... do not know who they belong to. I do not know what brought them to me. But if they are the voices of spirits, they are spirits who are seeking help. I feel they do not wish to cause any harm. If it were in my ability, I would help them find rest."

"Chang Tao Ling, you are sure they are not of the hells?" Tsai Chen asked in a somber tone, looking away from Ch'uan. "Of this we must be certain, beyond all doubt, or we will destroy what we have gathered to do."

Chang Tao Ling nodded, his expression grim. "Of that, I am most certain. Transgression of justice holds them back from crossing into the higher realms. These are lost spirits, not ones corrupted with wickedness that would see them taken to the hells."

Tsai Chen nodded thoughtfully, and said nothing further, looking content with the answer. A weighty silence fell over the gathering again, and it appeared that each Wizard was immersed within their private thoughts.

"Could not his request be added to our own task?" Shou Lao asked the other Wizards, after some time had passed, his voice sounding as gentle as his appearance. "Could we not do something that aids those who suffer on the Wall, and those who call to him from between realms?"

Glances were cast between the Wizards, and Ch'uan's curiosity rose, wondering at their purpose. After a long pause, they all looked back to Chang Tao Ling and Ch'uan, as if a consensus had been reached.

"Perhaps there is a way," Kuan-Ti said. His gaze narrowed to Chang Tao Ling. "To see if there is one, we must now speak of the purpose for this council. Chang Tao Ling, you are certain a demon dwells inside the body of the warrior Bai Wei"

Chang Tao Ling nodded. "I am most certain. A demon very powerful indeed. This demon now acts directly in the world and must be stopped. If it gains the authority of a general under the emperor, it will unleash a hellish war within this world."

Listening to the Wizards talk, Ch'uan was surprised at the

mention of Bai Wei. The warrior, though certainly a figure of great renown, was not the prime authority. Cao Qiu held that status, the direct representative of the Divine Emperor in the region where Ch'uan and the other peasants wore themselves down laboring on the Wall.

Yet to Ch'uan it did not matter who held the higher authority, as the results were the same for those such as himself. Cruelty and indifference were the bitter fare served to the conscript laborers, whose blood and sweat flowed in the building of the damnable edifice.

"If only we knew what else Bai Wei is doing now. Demons do not rest," Kuan-Ti said, with a tone of impatience. "Where is she?"

"She has been summoned to this council," Tsai Chen stated. Her children have been watching Bai Wei, Cao Qiu and everyone else around them. Do not worry, Kuan-Ti. She will be here."

"I have sensed a greater evil, an affront to Heaven itself, underneath the works of Cao Qiu," Kuan-Ti replied. "A dark sorcerer is one matter, but the fact that a demon inhabits the body of Bai Wei only raises the danger of what may be happening as we speak."

"Demon or sorcerer, power wielded in this world requires a source," Tsai Chen stated.

"There is a source," Shou Lau said. "Like nothing we have faced in this land. It resembles a sickness to the body of a living being. It grows and consumes, and out of this darkness those who work evil can draw power. It is a poisonous well that grows deeper by the day, fed by a wickedness that thrives under both sun and moons."

"We have all felt its presence," Chang Tao Ling said dourly, nodding. "And I suspect it is the Wall itself. It has been turned to the service of darkness."

"The Wall is a place of blood and sorrow, but it is simply a wall," Fu Shen said, and Ch'uan caught a trace of incredulity in the Wizard's response. "What makes this wall something more than what it appears to be?"

"I believe the building of this wall has been turned towards a much darker purpose," Chang Tao Ling said. "I have-"

"-Ah! She has come!" Fu Shen exclaimed, interrupting Chang Tao Ling as he looked past him and Ch'uan. "We will not have to wait long for answers."

Ch'uan turned to see what had attracted the Wizard's attention. Revealed in silvery beams of moonlight, the most beautiful woman Ch'uan had ever set his eyes upon walked out from the shadows of the trees, and continued into the midst of the gathering.

Graceful of movement, her long robes of bright red with golden ornamentation flowed with her statuesque form. Padding along with her was a pair of cats, one to each side. One had black and white fur, and the other brown. There looked to be nothing extraordinary about the pair of cats. Both were no different than those existing all across the Empire of Heaven.

There was something very different about the woman's eyes, but she remained too far away for Ch'uan to see exactly what caused the anomaly. She took notice of him fairly quickly, resting her gaze for a moment upon Ch'uan before looking to the others in the assembly. She exhibited no change of expression, giving

Ch'uan no indication of what she was thinking.

"I am sorry for my late arrival," she announced in a smooth, mid-toned voice. "I had to wait for a few of my children to return and tell me what they have seen."

"We understand," Fu Shen replied. "The more we can learn, the better prepared we will be to confront the evil that is rising."

"Yifan Zhang, what have you learned from your children?" Kuan-Ti addressed the comely woman.

"My children have gathered the information you seek," she replied. "Bai Wei is in league with the powers of hell. He must be a great sorcerer, for he has found a way to make use of the deaths from the building of the Wall. The Wall has become a place of sacrifice."

"Sacrifice?" Kuan-Ti asked, his eyebrows and pitch raising slightly. "The Wall?"

Yifan Zhang nodded. "Blood sacrifice. Rituals most powerful are made possible with the strength fed by the deaths happening every day on that wall. One is being conducted this very night. Bai Wei is gaining great power, and is able to open a portal between this world and the next."

"Though this portal opens into hell itself, I imagine," Tsai Chen stated.

Yifan Zhang nodded again.

"As I feared and suspected," Chang Tao Ling said, shaking his head slowly. He looked back to Yifan Zhang. "And there is more I must tell you. We are not facing just a man. A demon dwells within the body of Bai Wei."

Ch'uan could see that the news both surprised and bothered

Yifan Zhang greatly, as worry crept into her countenance. She looked to the faces of the other Wizards.

"Then the power being wielded is even greater than I thought," she said.

"Yes, much, much greater," Chang Tao Ling concurred somberly. "A demon has turned the sorrow and death on the Wall into something that can be harnessed for the working of great evil."

"We must not delay then," Kuan-Ti said, urgency resonating within his voice. "We cannot spare even a moment. Who knows what Bai Wei is bringing through that portal, and into this world? It must be closed immediately!"

"Will Li Wu assist?" Fu Shen asked.

"Yes, with many warriors," Kuan-Ti responded. "He is ready at any hour should I ask."

"But so many will die if you bring Li Wu into this. Are we not enough to confront this evil?" Shou Lou asked Kuan-Ti.

"Even with a force of warriors at our side, we may not be strong enough," Kuan-Ti replied dourly. "We will need all the strength we can muster to oppose this kind of evil."

"I may have some additional help," Fu Shen replied.

"We will need as much help as can be found," Kuan-Ti responded. "Let us not delay any longer."

A pained expression spread on Shou Lao's face. "What must be done, must be done."

"Do you know where Bai Wei is conducting these rituals?" Kuan-Ti asked.

"Yes," Yifan Zhang answered. She glanced down to the cats

flanking her. "My children have watched from the shadows, and speak of the horrors they have witnessed. They know where Bai Wei is, and it is not far from here."

Kuan-Ti rose to his feet with an air of urgency. "Then we must do what we can to put an end to these horrors."

A little panic and fear came over Ch'uan, watching himself being swept up into the affairs of Wizards. The talk of a demon, blood sacrifice, and a portal to hell rattled his every last nerve.

Yet another part of him did not want to walk away from what was happening. Something momentous loomed nigh, and Ch'uan felt in his heart that he had to remain on the path he now walked on.

"Staying with us?" asked Chang Tao Ling in a lower voice, as the other Wizards began to move. "You will not be forced to take this risk."

"If I may," Ch'uan replied, feeling dread even as he committed to go with the Wizard.

"You may join with us," Chang Tao Ling responded. "Though there is much to do before we move to confront Bai Wei."

Ch'uan nodded, following Chang across the clearing in the direction of the tiger. In moments, they had mounted up again and were heading off with the others.

***

Peering downward from high up on the mountain slope, a chill came over Ch'uan as he beheld the spectacle within the open meadow. It was difficult to trust his own eyes, but the fear he felt was real enough.

Accompanied by well-armed guardsmen, several figures draped in the colorful attire of nobility were arrayed behind a man who stood a few strides ahead of them. Ch'uan did not have to ask to know that he looked upon Bai Wei.

Bai Wei was positioned a short distance before what looked to be a large rift in the air itself, through which a light fog, or perhaps smoke, drifted steadily. He called out to something beyond the portal, in a language that Ch'uan did not understand.

A few heartbeats later, a number of brutish creatures began emerging through the portal. Broad, hideous faces leered at the small group of humans as the newcomers lumbered forward. It was clear that the beings were of great height, as they towered over assemblage gathered in the meadow.

Each of the burly creatures had extensive locks of dark hair, and they were garbed in what looked to Ch'uan's eyes to be skirts made of straw. The creatures had weapons, carrying wide, single-edged blades that were much shorter in proportion than a sword, but larger than a knife. In a short span of time there were at least a dozen of the hulking things standing before the portal in a cluster.

Ch'uan could not believe what he saw before him. Monstrosities of an otherworldly origin were coming into his world. Ch'uan now understood the great impatience that Kuan-Ti had displayed back at the assembly of the Wizards. A terrible danger was manifesting that very night.

A low growl came from the tiger, who crouched by Chang Tao Ling, to Ch'uan's right.

"Not yet, we must wait for Kuan-Ti," Chang Tao Ling said,

stroking the fur of the muscular tiger. "He is coming."

Ch'uan wondered how much longer they could afford to wait. The portal still gaped open, and Bai Wei continued chanting.

As if to underscore Ch'uan's worry, four more of the bulky ogres trudged through the portal to join their brethren in the meadow.

"He ... is bringing an army of those things through," Ch'uan whispered to Chang Tao Ling.

"He has gathered far more power than I imagined, to be able to do something such as this," the Wizard replied. "This is a transgression of the natural world."

The pensive look upon Chang Tao Ling's face looked anything but comforting to Ch'uan. The Wizard appeared to be in a state of deep worry, and Ch'uan perceived that the extent of Bai Wei's power had been unanticipated. Anything that could cause such a degree of concern and trepidation in a Wizard was something Ch'uan knew had to be feared.

Ch'uan nearly jumped upwards when a white cat pushed through the undergrowth near to him. The feline mewled softly, staring at Chang Tao Ling with its green-flecked, golden eyes.

A look of relief passed across the features of the Wizard. He faced Ch'uan, and said, "Kuan-Ti is here. It is time."

***

At a loud cry from Kuan-Ti, the forces gathered on the slopes surged forward. Brandishing weapons that gleamed in the moonlight, the mass of warriors flowing downward made the mountainside itself appear to be sliding towards the meadow.

The human entourage with Bai Wei and the throng of ogres turned quickly at the outburst. A raw, primal shout of rage came from Bai Wei as he glared hotly at the approaching attackers.

He moved swiftly towards the forefront of the group of humans, followed closely by the infernal troop he had just summoned from hell itself. Bai Wei and the ogres formed into a stout line facing the mountainside. The guardsmen attending the richly-attired humans took up positions in front of them, weapons in hand.

The attackers reached the bottom of the slope and raced forward across the meadow, loosing a host of battle cries as the sides drew closer together. Kuan-Ti, wielding his great black sword, charged several paces ahead of the force and leaped into the line of hell-spawned ogres. His blade slashed and stabbed with lightning fury, and two of the huge monsters fell to the ground dead.

The swarm of attackers engulfed the ogres, but blood rapidly spilled as the big creatures fought back using their tremendous strength, greater speed, and enormous size. The humans stabbed and hacked desperately, but many began to fall.

The ogres swept their blades with rage-driven might, sometimes killing two humans with one blow. Screams of the wounded and cries of the dying resounded, filling the night air as the battle raged.

Even Kuan-Ti found himself hard-pressed after his initial onslaught. No longer were the ogres on the defensive. Facing off with three of the brutes by himself, Kuan-Ti's blade whipped about to thwart the flurry of strikes coming at him.

Riding behind Chang Tao Ling on the tiger, Ch'uan's heart raced as they sped down the mountain and streaked towards the battle. He continued watching the fighting around Kuan-Ti until they drew close, his attention engulfed as he looked up into the horrid visages of ogres directly before him.

Large, glistening fangs shone from within their capacious maws. A pair of the creatures squarely blocked Chang Tao Ling's path to Bai Wei.

The Wizard's tiger aided in the fighting, swiping a paw and opening a huge gash on the arm of one ogre that had barely missed the Wizard with its blade. The ogre roared in pain and recoiled, as its comrade sought an opening to strike at Chang Tao Ling.

The tiger nimbly leaped backward as a large blade cleaved the air where it had been an instant before. Planting its broad paws in the ground, the tiger roared at the ogres. Undaunted, they held their ground, and loosed guttural cries back at the tiger and the two riders mounted on its back.

Ch'uan could see a stalemate developing fast between all the combatants, and every moment of delay resulted in more death among the attackers. He could see Bai Wei fighting hard beyond the ogres. To his eyes, Bai Wei looked to be close to Kuan-Ti in skill with a blade. The warrior's sword flashed coldly in the moonlight, leaving flows of crimson in its wake.

The well-dressed group of humans farther behind the ogres then began shouting and gesturing frantically at the sky. Even their guards looked distracted. Ch'uan craned his neck upward to see what had caused the sudden commotion.

Racing down from the skies was a creature that Ch'uan had

only heard of in tales from his childhood. He forgot to exhale, stunned by what he saw above.

In those tales, dragons were always guardians and protectors, fearsome adversaries of the wicked. Ch'uan hoped that the creature hurtling downward, nearing the meadow, was no different in nature.

As it sped closer to Ch'uan's position, he gained a clearer view of the creature's body. The dragon's head, broad with extended jaws, held echoes of the form of a horse. A pair of horns resembling those of a stag rose up to either side of a distinctive lump atop its head.

The lengthy, serpentine body of the dragon had four legs that were currently tucked firmly into its sides. Each leg ended in five sharp claws, mirroring those of a bird of prey.

Ch'uan tensed as the dragon streaked directly at the area where Chang Tao Ling, the two ogres, and Bai Wei were fighting. The dragon streaked right over Chang Tao Ling, Ch'uan, and the ogres, swiftly dipping down and snatching up Bai Wei with its front talons. The warrior's sword tumbled out of his hands and fell to the ground in the tumult.

Carrying the immobilized warrior through the air, the dragon turned about in a tight arc and came back. Dropping Bai Wei in an unceremonious heap before Chang Tao Ling, the dragon continued forward, immediately assailing the pair of ogres that had been facing off with the Wizard.

The creatures shrieked in agony as they were bathed in a stream of white-hot fire. Wreathed in brilliant flame, both tottered about for a few paces before they fell heavily to the ground.

Neither moved as the fires blackened and consumed their flesh, permeating the air with a terrible stench.

Bai Wei tried to rise to his feet, but found himself batted down with a heavy swipe of the tiger's paw. Only the fact that the claws of the tiger were retracted spared the warrior a terrible mauling. The blow had some effect on the warrior, as Bai Wei looked to be highly disoriented in the aftermath.

Chang Tao Ling was not extending Bai Wei a mercy, Ch'uan realized. For reasons that only the fabled exorcist knew, the Wizard kept the human body alive to deal with the demon dwelling inside.

The dragon had meanwhile returned, and landed upon the ground, taking up a position in front of Chang Tao Ling and Bai Wei. Rushing to the aid of Bai Wei, and unfazed by the fiery deaths of their companions, a small group of ogres broke away from the sprawling melee and converged on the dragon.

The dragon's ferocity was something to behold, its lengthy jaws snapping and claws glittering as they lashed out with tremendous speed. Even massive ogres were little match for a dragon, and three of the former were brought down gruesomely, in a matter of moments.

The swift bloodletting instilled caution in the remaining two attackers. One managed to open a small gash in the side of the dragon, but the two lasted only a few heartbeats longer than their brethren, before succumbing to the dragon's fury.

The dragon reared up, glowering over the pulverized bodies of the ogres, its gaze engulfing the emperor's emissary and the others with him. Their backs were to the portal, with nowhere to run. Nothing in sight could stop the dragon, and abject fear filled their faces.

Behind the dragon, Chang Tao Ling and Ch'uan had dismounted from the tiger. Chang Tao Ling withdrew the sword crafted from the wood of a peach tree, breaking into a loud chant as he strode up to Bai Wei. Ch'uan held back, staying clear of the others as he awaited the signal that the Wizard had instructed him about while they were on the mountain slope.

Still dazed from the tiger's blow, Bai Wei could muster no effective defense against Chang Tao Ling. The Wizard drove the wooden sword far into the warrior's body, eliciting a shrill cry from the man.

Chang Tao Ling kept up the chant, releasing his hold on the wood. Bai Wei struggled to get up, but the tiger moved forward and used its forepaws to slam the warrior flat on his back against the hard ground.

The Wizard calmly took up one of the jars affixed to the saddle of the tiger and opened it. Returning to Bai Wei's side, Chang Tao Ling held the jar near the warrior's head as he continued chanting loudly.

To Ch'uan's eyes it looked as if Chang Tao Ling leeched tendrils of black smoke from the body of the enemy warrior, but he knew it to be something else entirely. More and more of the dark substance drew forward, funneling into the jar. At last, a few final wisps were pulled from Bai Wei's body and sucked into the container.

"Now, Ch'uan," the Wizard called out to him. Signs of strain were appearing on the Wizard's face as he held onto the jar, which visibly shook.

Ch'uan moved forward with a small jar that Chang Tao Ling had given him, and began repeating the words that the Wizard had recently taught him. He had only memorized the sounds, as the words themselves were from the strange language that Chang had used to begin the exorcism on Bai Wei.

"They are here," Chang Tao Ling remarked curtly, as he clutched the large jar tightly. Signs of great strain wracked the Wizard's countenance.

From every direction, small, faint tendrils of what looked to be black smoke meandered through the air and entered the jar in Ch'uan's hand. It was as if some force from within the jar pulled the slithering wisps out of the night.

Ch'uan observed the phenomenon in a state of amazement. The event did not come as a surprise, as the Wizard had explained what to expect. Ch'uan knew that the tendrils were the anger, confusion, and disharmony from the spirits who had been beseeching Ch'uan.

The ethereal bile was being leeched out from their spirits and collected in the jar. Spirits in a much more purified state were left behind.

When there were no more traces of activity with the smoky tendrils, Chang Tao Ling told him insistently, "Put your jar into this one, now!"

Ch'uan hustled over, cradling the small jar protectively. Carefully, he placed his jar into the mouth of the larger one, as the Wizard had instructed. The air around the jar was frigid to the touch, and Ch'uan drew his hand back quickly after setting the other vessel inside.

Chang Tao Ling capped the large jar immediately, setting it on the ground and backing away. The vessel shook even more violently, cutting a jittery dance across the ground.

"Let the wicked one choke on his own fumes," Chang Tao Ling muttered dourly, staring at the jar while Ch'uan watched anxiously from behind him.

With a deafening crack of thunder, the jar shattered into bits. A huge mass of the black, smoky substance exploded into sight from the ruins of the jar. The amorphous manifestation hovered in the air for several heartbeats, before speeding quickly towards the portal, rushing into the rift.

Ch'uan looked back upon the warrior's body, lying on the ground, and saw lifeless eyes staring upwards. The demon had had been overcome, but a question remained.

"What of the spirit of the man?" he asked.

Chang Tao Ling shook his head. "I do not know. It is beyond my ken. Whether the Heavens have mercy or the hells claim him is not made known to me."

"Why did the man not survive?" Ch'uan asked.

"The demon inside had too great a hold over him," Chang Tao Ling said. The Wizard turned his head and looked off in the direction of the portal. "Keep your wits about you, Ch'uan. This night is not yet over."

Ch'uan peered at the emperor's men clustered near the portal. All had witnessed the demon's flight from the world, and they still faced a powerful dragon.

Even the guardsmen standing before the imperial representatives looked dismayed. Outright panic shone from many faces, guard and noble alike; only one figure among them maintained a posture and expression of full composure.

An old, white-bearded man within the entourage shuffled forth, shouldering his way through the thin screen of guardsmen. With an angry look on his face, the old man held out a large sack, glaring towards the dragon. With a grating outcry, he opened the bag.

"Feng Po!" shouted Chang Tao Ling, and Ch'uan heard the sense of alarm and shock within the Wizard's voice.

The grass in the meadow flattened as a tempest loosed from the bag stormed across it. In scant moments, Ch'uan was knocked from his feet, landing flat on his back.

Combatants from both sides were thrown forcefully to the ground, and only the remaining ogres, the dragon, and the Wizards were able to keep to their feet. At the center of the clearing the winds coalesced into a cone of power, one that could be seen with the dust and debris caught within its grip.

As the cyclone continued building size and strength, the white-bearded man thrust his arms forth, at the dragon. The swirling winds lashed out with tremendous speed. Caught up within the bindings of the wind, the majestic creature was overwhelmed and propelled high into the sky.

Ch'uan watched in horror as the dragon's body followed the course of a towering, arching pathway, driven along relentlessly by the Wizard-controlled winds. After reaching a lofty height, the dragon's body curled around and began plummeting.

Faster and faster the dragon fell, as the winds unleashed from the bag exercised merciless force. The ground shook underfoot when the dragon finally struck the surface. The ill-fated creature's body went limp, looking misshapen and undoubtedly shattered in an instant.

Several cries broke out, and Chang looked back to see the nobles and their guards scrambling to their feet and scattering outward. Eyes everywhere were drawn in the direction of the old man with the sack, and even those fleeing kept glancing over their shoulders.

Keeping his eyes on the spectacle, Ch'uan rose from the ground, feeling a strong urge to run away. Every instinct within screamed that something very dangerous was coalescing.

Shrouded in a fell light, Feng-Po's body began undergoing a transformation into something of great size. Lengthy and serpentine, several aspects of the form assumed reflected those of a dragon, but the monstrosity's head was much more akin to that of a carrion bird. Ch'uan noticed the creature had three talons at the end of each leg, further distancing its appearance from natural dragons.

The ghostly light ebbed as the metamorphosis concluded. The beast lumbered forward, roaring in fury as everyone in its path scrambled desperately to get away. A few of the men from the attacking force met with terrible fates, shredded or crushed whenever the beast could get hold of one of them.

In swift fashion, the beast's claws and hooked beak were slathered in blood and gore. Its baleful gaze swept over all in the meadow, and lingered malevolently wherever it espied one of the Wizards. To Ch'uan's eyes, the beast that was once Feng-Po seemed to be daring the other Wizards to come at him.

Worsening the situation, it then became apparent that Feng-Po retained full control of his faculties in the dreadful form, as the creature began speaking in a deep, grating voice. The words were in another tongue, similar in cadence and sound to the ones used by Bai Wei when he had called the ogres forth from the portal.

In the aftermath of the words, a few ogres trickled in from the surrounding chaos and gathered behind the monstrosity. Ch'uan looked across the meadow, and then back to the ogres. Only five of their infernal kind had survived the fighting, and now the dragon-sized beast shielded the remnant.

In a strange way, Feng-Po held the appearance of an animal from the wild protecting its offspring. The defensive posture taken by the massive beast formed a bulwark against the battlefield victors. A standoff bristling with tension set into place.

Not all of those who had come to stop the dark ritual remained inert. Kuan-Ti charged across the blood-soaked ground, but even he could not fight past the beast to get at the ogres, coming dangerously close to being maimed himself. The beast kept its body squared at Kuan-Ti, as it began backing away from the field of battle with the ogres protected behind it.

Behind Ch'uan, Chang Tao Ling leaped to the back of the tiger. The huge cat bounded swiftly in the direction of the beast. Ch'uan could see Tsai Chen hurrying in from another area of the meadow, and then quick movements to the left revealed Shou Lao hastening across the ground as well.

Ch'uan turned his attention back to the fight between the beast and Kuan-Ti. He flinched as the beast slashed at Kuan-Ti and raked the Wizard's skin, opening rivulets of blood and casting him to the ground. It proved fortuitous that the beast concerned itself more with its retreat than finishing the fight, as it continued moving away instead of pressing its advantage.

The other Wizards reached the place where Kuan-Ti and the beast had fought. They took up positions around the wounded Wizard, while two attempted to strike at the beast, or get around it to attack the five remaining ogres.

It was all to no avail. Though not powerful enough to reverse the course of the fighting, Feng Po could not be overcome, showing to be too strong and fast in the bestial form he had taken.

His purpose looked firmly set on salvaging the lives of the five ogres as he continued backing away. When the group reached the trees at the edge of the clearing, the ogres turned and trotted into the shadows, while the beast kept his eyes fixed upon the Wizards.

"Know that this night will bring a harvest in the ages to come," the beast thundered in words that could be understood by all. Loosing one final roar, brimming with rage, the creature turned at last and entered the cloaking dark of the woods.

Ch'uan's gaze riveted to the spot where the creature's lengthy tail snaked into the darkness. He hoped it was the last he would ever see of the monster.

***

The survivors of the battle were not given long to recover and gather their thoughts in the aftermath of the beast's departure. Wizards and humans both quickly turned their attention back to the portal, as a soul-freezing roar blared out of the rift.

Gigantic wings spread wide from its back, a huge, shadowy being loomed within the large gateway. "Let none interfere! I lay claim to what is ours!" the dark figure thundered furiously, its deep, commanding voice filling the meadow.

Ch'uan blanched, knowing all of the Wizards combined would not be able to contend with the being's infernal might. Deep inside, he knew he witnessed an entity far greater in power than the dragon, Feng Po, or any Wizard. He broke into a run, and headed swiftly for Chang Tao Ling, reaching the Wizard close to where Kuan-Ti had been wounded.

He took immediate confidence from the Wizard's apparent lack of alarm. Chang Tao Ling and the other Wizards were staring quietly at the portal, and there was no indication of immediate danger. The Wizards showed no sign of either fleeing or taking up defensive postures.

"We cannot stop what is coming," Chang Tao Ling said to Ch'uan with a tone of grim resignation. "We could not interfere if we wished to. The demon comes for one who belongs to hell."

Ch'uan followed Chang Tao Ling's gaze, looking to the imperial emissaries. One of them looked particularly distraught at the ominous development.

"Cao Qiu, you are summoned!" the demon's voice boomed.

Sounding weak and pitiful, the emperor's high-ranking minister cried out, "Noooooo!"

"You failed to see those who were watching us," the dark entity thundered from the portal. "Your soul was already forfeit. You were allowed to remain in this world to serve my purpose. You have failed, and deserved torment awaits you!"

The minister backed up and tripped over himself in his fear and haste. His face filled with raw panic, as he looked around hurriedly.

"Hold him! Or know that you will all be dragged to hell!" bellowed the demonic entity at the group surrounding the minister.

Men who assiduously obeyed every order of the emperor's minister cooperated immediately with the demon's command. They grabbed hold of Cao Qiu, who struggled desperately against them, but could not get away from their firm grasp.

The minister looked back to the portal and emitted a bone-chilling cry, brimming with terror and hopelessness. Ch'uan turned his head, peering at the rift, and his heart froze.

Emerging from the portal were a pair of fearsome, bestial figures. Each had the body of a heavily-muscled human male.

Their heads were those of animals, as one had the head of a bull, and the other a horse. They were titanic figures, even taller than the ogres, and both carried weapons in the form of lengthy pitchforks.

Fires burned within their eyes as they stepped into the world of the living. The creatures glared hotly at the Wizards and humans, and their expressions reflected pure malice. Their heavy footsteps thumped upon the ground as they trod towards the forsaken minister.

As if not wanting to come into contact with the monstrosities, the men holding onto the minister mustered enough strength and willpower to fling him forward. The old man tumbled down to his knees before the ox-headed creature of the demonic pair. The entity swiftly reached down with its free hand, and seized Cao Qiu roughly.

Screaming hysterically, the man twisted and flailed, unable to slow his plight as he was dragged unceremoniously across the ground. The ox-headed being paid the hapless man no heed, pulling him through the portal after the horse-headed creature had crossed first. A suffocating blast of heat filled the meadow as the hellish portal vanished from sight.

Nobody spoke for several minutes, as a somber disquiet filled the air. The evil had been overcome, but not without a terrible cost. Bodies of the slain littered the meadow, including the broken form of the dragon.

Ch'uan found the atmosphere surreal as he looked across the meadow. Looks of relief were on the faces of many of the men in the force brought by Kuan-Ti, while confusion and a little fear was in evidence among the imperial entourage.

Ch'uan knew he would need a long time to sort everything out, regarding what he had witnessed. He could never go back to the state of mind he had before this night. Ch'uan knew the experience had permanently changed the way he would look on the world in the years to come.

Soft breezes flowed through the air, building into powerful winds that brushed the grasses of the meadow low. Ch'uan felt something familiar within the cool gusts, just as he heard the voices again.

"Thank you..."

"Bless you..."

"We are...free..."

A buoyant smile came to Ch'uan's face. He could feel the

joy surrounding him, in the stream of jubilant voices expressing sentiments of thanksgiving and happiness. A cascade of rapturous celebration swirled around him, and he basked in pureness of the elation he sensed from the unseen multitude.

"They are here with you now, and they are now able to go onward," Chang Tao Ling said, from astride the great tiger, having padded over to Ch'uan's side. "You are being given a great tribute. They delayed their journey to heaven, and have come here to thank you. You should see their faces, Ch'uan. The blissfulness they have is like the light of the sun. It is the kind of beauty that transcends this world."

Ch'uan smiled warmly up at the Wizard, whose eyes glistened with powerful emotion. "I wish I could see them, but I can feel their happiness."

Chang Tao Ling did not reply at first, but the joy on his face radiated even brighter. His voice took a gentle tone, when he spoke again, "Now is not the time to talk, Ch'uan. Listen now ... just listen. You are about to receive a precious gift."

Ch'uan became puzzled by the response, but only for a moment, as a distinct voice came to him, above all the others.

"My brother, I thank you."

Ch'uan's heart pounded hearing the unmistakable voice of Shimin, his brother who had died so terribly upon the Wall. Emotions swirled within Ch'uan, and he blinked back hot tears as he listened to the voice on the winds.

"I am free now, as are the others. You have done so well, Ch'uan. Heaven is calling. I can go now."

The winds picked up in strength, and the voices faded steadily into the distance. Ch'uan looked up again towards Chang Tao Ling, who still carried an expression of resplendent joy. He was staring off, with a faraway look in his eyes. Suddenly, the Wizard squinted, as if blinded by a swell of brilliant light.

"It is magnificent, Ch'uan ... so very beautiful," Chang Tao Ling said wistfully, looking to be on the brink of shedding tears. "Know without doubt that they have all found their way home."

Ch'uan said nothing in the wake of the profound experience. Powerful emotions still flowed through him, and he did not stop staring into the space where he had heard his brother's voice come from, even when he heard light footsteps from someone drawing nearer, on his right side.

"Well done, Ch'uan," Shou Lao said, in a low voice, putting a hand upon Ch'uan's shoulder.

"I wish I could have seen him," Ch'uan replied. "But I know he has found his way home."

"You will, one day, Ch'uan," Shou Lao replied. "Know in your heart that you will see him again."

"You are part of a wonderful victory this night," Chang Tao Ling added, after several peaceful moments had passed.

"Yes, many have been freed," Shou Lao said. "Those who have gone to the heavenly realms beyond, and those in the times to come, who will not be taken up by the evil of Bai Wei or Cao Qiu. Their wickedness has been brought to an end."

"I am a simple man, but I am not fooled into thinking the Wall has been stopped," Ch'uan replied in a more somber tone to Shou Lao, as he looked out into the night.

Shou Lao glanced over to him. When he spoke, his voice

had a gentle aspect, but the words were clear enough. "No, what happened tonight will not stop the Wall from being built. Others will come on behalf of the Emperor. The labor will resume in time, but do not think that a great victory has not been gained. Many more will live, who would have died if this wickedness had not been ended."

"A terrible evil has been overcome," Chang Tao Ling said. "Do not underestimate that, Ch'uan. And many now walk in the fields of Heaven, because of your bravery tonight."

Ch'uan smiled back at the two Wizards, and took heart from their words. He thought again of his brother, and no longer did he recall a mask of death. This time he saw Shiman's face resplendent with life; filled entirely with merriment and laughter.

***

The work upon the Wall had been cast into disarray by the downfall of Bai Wei and the emperor's minister, Cao Qiu. Everything ground to an immediate halt.

Without any guidance, the remaining guards offered no opposition when the Wizards advised that all the workers be dismissed, and allowed to return to their homes and villages. The acquiescence of the guards was in their best interests, as Ch'uan strongly suspected that something much to their detriment and chagrin would have transpired had they refused.

Most of the conscript laborers left the Wall immediately, eager to be as far from the sorrowful place as they could. A few lingered, and among that small number was Ch'uan.

Of those remaining, some wanted to bask for a moment in their sudden liberation, while others, mainly elderly individuals, wished to recover some strength before setting out for their homes. Ch'uan's reason for staying had more to do with the state of his heart.

He sat with his back to the structure where he had spent so many sleepless nights. Sitting with his head bowed, his heart filled with a new sorrow. All the joys from the previous night's triumph were dampened by the news that had greeted his return.

Zhang An had passed away during the previous night.

Ch'uan had returned with one personal desire burning above all others within his heart. He had wanted to tell the old man that his suffering was over, and that he could go back to his family. He remembered vividly how the older man's eyes sparked when speaking of his grandchildren, which made everything all the more painful.

Zhang An stood at the forefront of his mind when Ch'uan had petitioned the Wizards for help, and when he had risked life and limb going into the fray in the meadow. To be denied the chance to bring such wonderful news to Zhang An seemed such a cruel twist of fate.

The sweetness of the victory had been wrenched from Chuan's heart. He clenched his fists, feeling the bitterness clinging inside.

Ch'uan then felt something soft brush slowly against his legs, and took notice of a small cat at his side. Reaching down, he gently stroked the cat's light orange fur, eliciting a contented purr from the feline.

The sound of footsteps approaching prompted Ch'uan to look upwards. He took in the sight of Shou Lao, who had a tranquil smile on his face.

"Such courage among men, and such compassion to others must be rewarded. Your brother has gone forward, and has petitioned One far greater than I," Shou Lao pronounced. His smile grew broader. "So has Zhang An, who will never be in need again, and who will never forget your kindness."

Strong emotions welled up swiftly in Ch'uan at the words, and his eyes began to glisten as he pondered what Shou Lao had just said. As raw as his feelings were mourning the passing of Zhang An, the Wizard's tidings struck him in a deep, heartfelt way.

"It has been made known to me that you can go onward," Shou Lao continued, after a little time had passed. "You may join your brother, and Zhang An, this very day, should you choose to do so."

Ch'uan said nothing at first. The implications were staggering to contemplate. He was being offered a chance to leave the world and all of its evils and corruption far behind.

Yet he would also be leaving many others behind, victims of terrible injustices similar to those his brother and Zhang An had suffered. He would also be leaving many members of his family, and would not be there to help them if shadows should fall over their lives.

Ch'uan knew in that moment he had gained a much different perspective on things. Even if he still remained a peasant, he held something very special inside, and he knew he stood far better prepared to face the trials and ordeals of the world.

"I can only tell you what my heart says," Ch'uan said, after a short period of silence had passed. "I do not wish to go just yet. If there was a way, I would choose to use what I have learned, to help others struggling in this life."

Shou Lao nodded, and his expression hinted that he was very pleased with Ch'uan's answer. "I somehow knew you would say that."

"I have no wealth, or influence, but perhaps there is a way I can bring comfort to others," Ch'uan stated. "I cannot return to what I was before. I just wish that I had the strength of body and the time to travel far and wide. I feel a desire to search out those such as Zhang An, wherever they are in need."

"I could extend your years upon this world with the power I have been gifted with," Shou Lao replied with a bright grin. "But something very rare has been granted you this day, Ch'uan. Something precious and divine."

As he spoke, powerful rays of light manifested at his right side, the overwhelming brilliance causing Ch'uan to shield his eyes. As the intensity of the light receded, Ch'uan blinked his eyes, and looked to see a woman of incredible beauty standing before him.

The lady smiled down at him. Speechless, Ch'uan beheld the aura of light that emanated from her body. Her white, silken robes glowed with the otherworldly luminance, and he felt both shy and awkward, not knowing how to respond.

The woman handed him what looked to be a peach, but it was no fruit gleaned from the natural world. Its surface glowed with a soft light, and no blemish of any sort could be found upon it.

The fruit felt light in his hand, and a soothing warmth passed from where it touched his skin, spreading throughout his body. He held it carefully in his palm, again unsure of how to react.

"Eat of this fruit, and you shall walk the world as long as you desire," the woman told him, her voice melodious, bestowing her words with the quality of a harmonious song.

Ch'uan did as the lady asked. He raised the fruit to his lips and bit into it.

A tremendous joy filled him as the sweet juices filled his mouth. The fruit's taste exceeded far beyond anything that had graced his mouth before, and it brought along with it a clear revelation within his mind.

He knew his ultimate destination, beyond a shred of a doubt. Ch'uan understood at once that he had been granted a miraculous gift.

Following the revelation, an extraordinary feeling of peace and contentment infused him. Uplifting and invigorating, the sensation made him giddy with a child-like feeling of wonderment.

He looked up to thank the woman, wondering who the lady was. With a flash of blinding light, the woman disappeared from his sight, leaving Ch'uan with Shou Lao.

Ch'uan looked over to Shou Lao with a mystified expression. The Wizard laughed merrily, gazing down upon him.

"Come, let us walk together," he invited. "Before you even ask, no, I cannot explain everything about what just happened. Your brother and Zhang An must have touted you strongly indeed before the Court of Heaven. It is not every day that Hsi Wang Mu leaves Heaven to visit a human, and bring him a celestial gift."

Ch'uan knew he would never forget that feeling of pure

serenity as he got back up to his feet. He walked at Shou Lao's side, as the two strode away from the laborers' quarters and proceeded in the direction of the looming mountains.

They walked together in peaceful silence, as Ch'uan reflected upon everything he had just experienced. A new road lay ahead for him.

Bathed in the light of a new day's sun, a resplendent smile bloomed upon his face. The expression conveyed joy, courage, and peace. Quite a few others would come to behold that expression in time, as Chung-Li Ch'uan would bring a touch of serenity to a multitude of lives in the long ages to follow.

Moonlight's Grace

Moonlight's Grace

"Sometimes the heart sees what is invisible to the eye."
-H. Jackson Brown, Jr.

Brigit walked to the edge of the meadow and raised her head upward, peering into the depths of the twinkling skies. The first of the two moons now crossing overhead, the orb appeared full and immaculate as it gazed down upon Gael.

No clouds marred the gilded cloak of night. A vision both wonderful and vast to look upon, the bejeweled skies were not the reason she had come.

Brigit gave a radiant smile as Finnian emerged into sight, stepping out from the cover of the trees. Even as a burst of joy flowed throughout her, a bitter sadness welled up within her heart.

The conviction of her love for Finnian was steadfast, but many other things seemed so far away. Brigit wished she had the powers of a mystical druidess, or had gained the friendship of the undying Wizards who had adopted Gael as a home. As it stood, she was just a young girl who stood no chance of overruling her powerful father, in the one matter that meant more to her than anything else in the world.

Not the tallest or the brawniest young man in the area, Finnian nonetheless towered above all others in her eyes. His compassionate spirit shined in times such as the one when he had nursed an injured young squirrel back to health in the seclusion of the woods; when most other boys and young warriors would have killed the creature without a moment's consideration.

Finnian had suffered being pummeled more than once by the toughest lads, but not because of weakness, or anything that attracted others to pick on him. Rather, he had stepped in more than once to prevent the strongest from preying upon the weakest, bringing the ire and attention of the bullies to him. He had endured a few beatings, but always made the would-be tormentor earn it, leaving a few marks of his own on their bodies in the forms of bruises or swollen eyes.

Every incident that set Finnian apart from the usual path of boys proceeding into manhood endeared him further to her. The examples too numerous to count, they made him the most handsome lad Brigit had ever known, even if there other young men existed whose physical appearances prompted all the other girls and younger women to swoon.

Finnian drew near, having crossed the open ground. His dark hair fell in thick, rolling locks to his shoulders, and his smile still carried a hint of the boyish nervousness she always found so adorable.

"Brigit," was the single word that Finnian said as he walked up to stand before her. Whenever he spoke his name to her in that tender way it conveyed so much to her, carrying depths of meaning that echoed in the soft, warm look filling his eyes.

She took his hands into her own, and lost herself for a moment within his hazel eyes. In gentle fashion, she drew him in to her, and her lips searched out his. A sense of peace spread through her body and all cares fled as the two shared a long, lingering kiss, their witnesses the two moons far above.

A warm tingle ran through her body. The deep kiss carried the promise of so much more. An urge to draw him down to lie upon the loamy earth right there and then tugged at her.

It was all she could do not to give in to the feeling. Everything within her sought a consummating union with the young man she loved so dear.

A warm smile glowed upon her face as their lips parted. Moonlight glistened on the surface of his eyes, and she beheld him in tranquil silence for a moment.

"Finnian," she whispered. "Why don't we just run as far as we can, this very night."

He smiled at her words, the curling shock of dark hair adorning the right side of his face swaying as he shook his head. "If it were just a matter of our hearts, we could make it to the farthest ends of Ave. But I fear that it is not the only thing to consider," he replied, in a low voice tinged with regret.

Brigit could sense his frustration and sorrow, and the same emotions churned within her. She knew he would have loved nothing more than to leave with her. There was nothing for him to lose, as he owned no cattle, nor was he destined to be the head of a family of prominence.

In a dark, cruel twist of irony, his genuine love, and an abiding concern for her well-being, served as the reason he would not depart with her. The great chieftain Murchadh was her father, a man of renown who could call a host of warriors to arms. He possessed a bountiful herd of cattle envied by chieftains all across Gael. While not the High King of Gael, Murchadh was not far removed in esteem or authority.

It was not inconceivable that Brigit could become a great Queen of Gael someday. The stories of her beauty had traveled far and wide, reaching the ears of many great families in the emerald land. Tales of her striking green eyes and lustrous red hair had piqued the interest of more than one high-born young warrior; the kind that became kings.

The subject had been one of the very few things Brigit and Finnian ever argued about. She insisted she could care less about how many cattle she had, or how prominent she was deemed to be. Finnian had not disputed her in that regard, but spoke instead of how many people would benefit from her compassion if she were to someday become a queen.

Even if she did not marry one who became High King, she would still become a wealthy, influential matriarch, and would never endure the travails of poverty. Fate had bestowed her at birth with the promise of a bountiful future. It was no mystery that Finnian did not wish to take her away from that destiny.

Foolish or not, Brigit knew, in the most intimate depths of her heart, that she would cast aside a place as queen or matriarch if she could have Finnian. Yet the choice did not reside with her, as her powerful father would never accept the young man as a proper suitor. The knowledge was a bitter companion to live with, one she cursed often as she lamented the ways of the world.

"Can we change the stars? Can we find ourselves in a different world?" she responded with a gentle tone, a glisten coming to the surface of her eyes. "Maybe we can fade with the mists into another time and place."

"I wish it could be so, Brigit. I wish with all my heart," Finnian said, his voice beginning to choke up, and his eyes glistening from more than moonlight. "But the All-Father saw fit to have me where I am, and He has blessed you with abundance. Even if I do not understand it, and feel sorrow about this each and every day, it is not for me to protest. You must honor these gifts, as precious few in this world receive them."

"But they say it matters not whether one is a king or the poorest of men in the eyes of the All-Father. All are His children, the priests say. Is that not so?" Brigit asked. "And do not they also say the least shall be the greatest, and the greatest the least?"

"Another world, one with different stars," Finnian replied, sadness thick in his voice.

Brigit pulled Finnian tight to her, and buried her head against his chest as she sobbed. She could feel the trembling in his body as they stood together in the night, mourning the barriers life had placed in their way; walls that could not be overcome.

***

Brigit walked with a soft step across the timber span reaching to the palisade-encompassed crannog. Something splashed a short distance away, the winds rippling the surface of the waters she crossed over.

There was no sense attempting evasion upon her return. The protected cluster of huts was well-warded at night. Beasts and faerie-folk alike presented threats in the dark, among things even worse, and Murchadh's warriors were assiduous in their duty.

Brigit could see their shadowy outlines as she neared the other end of the bridge leading into the fortified area. The spear-bearing sentries, Donal and Rory, nodded, and did not impede her access, recognizing her at once.

"Brigit, your father would not be pleased at this," Donal said with a disapproving air. Though dark, she could see within her mind his stern expression, crossed with a deep scar.

It was no secret that he regarded her nighttime forays as ill-conceived trysts, and he never ceased admonishing her. But she never tired of reminding him about a few things either.

"And your wife would not be pleased to learn of your familiarity with Devorgilla, yet I say nothing. Can you not extend me the same courtesy?" Brigit retorted to the older warrior, her voice amiable while she conveyed her threat.

At times, the guards needed clear reminding of what she knew of them. The things that she knew about the sentries were the only things protecting her nighttime excursions.

"Aye, you know I extend you the same courtesy. It is only my concern for your safety that makes me try to get you to see that these night sojourns are unnecessary risks," Donal replied, and his words rang with truth.

Like all men, virtues as well as flaws rested within his heart.

She knew that his care for her well-being was genuine.

"And I appreciate your concern, but my business is my own, Donal," Brigit said, her voice sounding more firm. Rory, the younger of the two men, said nothing as she nodded to them and continued onward, heading into the body of the crannog.

The huts remained silent as their occupants slumbered, and no one stirred as she neared her own dwelling. Brigit slipped inside the structure, silent of step, but her entrance did not go unnoticed.

"Brigit where have you been?" a soft voice emerged from the shadows.

"A walk into the woods, on a beautiful night," she responded.

"The dark of night shrouds many dangers," her mother responded, in a cautionary tone.

"As the light of day falls upon such," Brigit replied.

"Your father would have you confined for these night walks of yours," Gormlaith said. After a pause, she added, "Even more so, if he knew who it is you encounter on these walks ... and who draws you out from the protection of the crannog. You are lucky that he is away."

"I cannot change my heart any more than I can stop the sun from rising, or the rain from falling," Brigit replied, with an edge of defiance.

Gormlaith nodded slowly from the shadows, and a melancholic air drifted into her words. "You remind me very much of myself, when I was your age. Murchadh has been very good to me, and I have grown to love him, but he is not the only one that held my heart. Do not think I do not understand."

"Then you know why I cannot turn away," Brigit responded,

more softly.

"I know, my beloved daughter ... I know," her mother answered, her voice heavy with regrets.

***

Two days later, as night spread across the land, Finnian took up a small hand axe and set out through the woods. On this night, he would not be meeting with the woman he loved, but great purpose inspired by Brigit burned within his determined heart.

He followed the course of the Shadow River, knowing it would lead him on a direct path to the war band assembled from his home region. Well-rested, his step spry, Finnian kept to a brisk pace. The musty scent of damp woods filled his nose, as his lungs drew in the cool air.

Though the Midragardan raiders in their sleek longships plied the rivers during their deadly forays into Gael, Finnian had no worries about running into the fierce seafarers. Murchadh had called his warriors together because the raiders harried Gael again, but the Midragardans would be somewhere ahead of the war band's position.

Finnian kept his wits about him as he strode through the dark forest, his mind settled to his course. Just one way existed to gain the approval of Murchadh; one distant, slim chance of acquiring his blessing for marrying Brigit.

Somehow, someway, Finnian had to acquit himself more than just favorably on the field of battle. He had to show himself to be a man worthy of Murchadh's daughter. He had no viable path to accumulating wealth, but he could fight.

It was a fool's chance, Finnian knew, as he was not a trained warrior. His skills lay in farming, not wielding weapons of war. Yet no other possible way for a poor young man to prove himself existed in the eyes of a powerful chieftain.

The thrill of adventure and fear of the unknown contended within the core of his heart. The night deepened as he trekked the moon-dappled woods, covering more than a league without incident. Shadows undulated as chill breezes swept through the trees, and every leaf rustled like thunder in Finnian's heightened state of alertness.

"Who walks the woods this hour?"

The sharp query halted Finnian in his tracks, as much as did the cool iron edge of the spear pressed against the flesh of his throat. Finnian's heart beat faster, and fear reflected in his eyes as he looked to the dark figure. The only thing staving off panic were the words spoken in his native tongue, eliminating the worry of a Midragardan standing in the shadows before him.

"I ... I'm Finnian, of Murchadh's people," he managed to respond.

"You fool! Had you been coming from any other direction I would have slashed your throat!" the sentry growled.

Finnian recognized the voice. "Niall?"

The spear blade was replaced with a large hand clutching his throat tight. The strength of the grip conveyed the ire of the other man, as he hissed, "I should give you another beating right now, Finnian."

"And ... I promise ... I will leave you ... in a weaker condition

... to fight ... the Midragardans," Finnian gasped through his constricted throat.

He glared at Niall, discovering some resolve in the wake of the other man's threat. Though he struggled for breath, he set his mind to fight, and prepared to break the other man's hold.

Niall shoved Finnian backwards. "Then we'll wait until after we see the Midragardans back to their longships."

Finnian nodded, sucking in a full breath through his freed throat, and glowered at the larger figure. "That we will, Niall."

"What are you doing here?" Niall asked him, with an air of incredulity.

"I come to fight for my people, no less than you," Finnian replied in a terse manner.

"You will die the first time a Midragardan comes at you! What do you know of the ways of a warrior?" Niall riposted with a mocking edge. "Are you ready to face a veteran raider wielding sword, axe, or spear?"

"We shall see," Finnian replied, mustering as much conviction into his voice as he could.

"No, we will not, because you are turning back now!" Niall said.

"I am not!" Finnian countered, adamant.

His left hand balled up into a fist as his ears picked up the footsteps of others being drawn by their commotion. In a few moments, several other figures came into view, all bearing weapons.

"What is it Niall?" came Rory's voice, the first of the warriors to reach them.

"Farmer boy here says he wants to fight the raiders," Niall answered, derisive in tone.

"He wants to lose his head to a raider's broad axe, more like," a burly warrior named Diarmait said.

"Finnian?"

The deep-toned voice caused all the others to fall silent. A tall, broad-shouldered form stepped into sight, and Finnian could feel the weight of the man's gaze falling upon him.

"Yes," Finnian answered in a low voice.

"What foolishness is this? You wish to die?" Murchadh thundered, his voice rippling with ire.

"I ... I wish to defend our people against the raiders," Finnian responded, his words sounding thin in contrast to the chieftain.

"You wish to die, lad. This is no game. Blood is about to flow, and many of us will not live to see another night," Murchadh stated. He glanced upward for a moment. "Bah! Dawn is almost upon us, and the raiders are nigh! Go home, Finnian. Go home now!"

Murchadh was the reason Finnian had come, but all thoughts fled his mind as the chieftain glowered at him. Words would not sway the other man, and Finnian's low status guaranteed that no others would even try to plea on his behalf. Frustration, a sense of futility, and a wave of resentment filled his heart.

His upper lip quivering, a mix of emotions running through him, Finnian said nothing more, and turned away from Murchadh. His right hand gripped the handle of his axe tightly, as his steps crunched upon the woodland surface.

Hearing low laughter behind him, most likely from Niall,

Finnian bit back surges of frustration and embarrassment that threatened to break his composure. Everything in him wanted to lash out and scream his rage towards the observers.

Somehow he kept moving forward, holding fast to one singular thought. He could not openly defy Murchadh, but he was not about to return home.

After dawn lightened further upon the horizon, turning the skies from blue-black to paler shades, and the shadows began to recede, Finnian came to a stop. He gathered his resolve, feeling the damp touch of morning upon his skin.

Cognizant of the fact that he was about to defy the express decree of Murchadh, he saw no other way. Returning back home would only serve to bring more shame, and do nothing to further his desperate cause.

In that moment, it seemed as if the entire world had arrayed against him. With a deep breath he turned around, and hurried back in the direction of the chieftain and his men.

***

Atop a low rise, the small timber buildings of the monastery served as a bright, inviting beacon to the Midragardans. Most of the buildings sparse in furnishing, the ascetic monks had no interest in accumulating wealth. Yet valuable treasures were there to be taken.

The raiders descending upon Lóchrann Monastery were well-aware that altar pieces of the Western Church were often fashioned out of gold and silver. Many a church vessel from monasteries perched on Gael's coastline had found its way onto longships during the initial raids.

Word had spread quick enough about the monasteries, and it was not long before many more longships were drawn towards the land of the Gael. Even more troubling, the raiders came in ever greater strength, sometimes in fleets carrying several hundred warriors.

Lóchrann Monastery, a heavenly light to the people of Gael, was one of the few in the region that had not yet been pillaged. Its fortuitous location, a few leagues inland from the coast, spared it the savagery befalling the other monastic sites for a time. Without any more monasteries to be found along the shores of Gael, the raiders had to press a little farther inward to slake their rapacious thirsts.

It was precisely what Murchadh had been counting on. The Midragardans entered territory that he and his men knew well. Pathways through the woods and contours in the land provided several advantages unknown to the marauders.

The warriors of Gael traversed the woodlands easily enough, shadowing the loose, extended throng of Midragardans as they marched towards the monastic site. Every step the raiders took separated them farther from the ships they had arrived in.

At least ten vessels involved in the current raid, over two hundred enemy warriors had crossed the seas. A small number of the raiders remained with the ships, but most of the force tromped across the soil of Gael; killing and looting.

The size of the force bothered Murchadh, as it would not be satisfied with the gains taken from a single monastery. Lookouts had given sufficient warning for Murchadh to muster enough men to make the looming clash close to an even fight.

The warriors of Gael crept through the woods, coming from the farthest side of the monastery. Spears and blades in hand, they awaited the signal from their stalwart chieftain.

Murchadh grimaced as he took note that the monks had not abandoned the site. It seemed that the holy men always had a death wish, remaining in place when they knew slaughter approached. Even so, he admired their courage, as they picked up tools and farming implements and prepared to defend their church.

The Midragardans started their way up the slope, some with swords drawn, others with broad axes gripped with two hands, and many with spears at the ready. The thin line of monks prepared to make their futile stand, like so many leaves about to be caught up in a gust of storm-wind. Murchadh eyed the Midragardan advance with caution, and when the force reached half-way up the slope he gave the signal.

With vigorous war cries, the warriors of Gael burst out of the woods and charged forward. They swarmed over the monks around the outermost buildings and continued onward, leaving the monks with looks of astonishment. Rolling over the top of the slope, the Gael fell upon the raiders with lightning fury.

The raiders were anything but dismayed. A zealous roar went up from the Midragardans, who looked invigorated at the recognition they would be fighting something more challenging than untrained monks.

Clangs and thuds filled the air as iron and wood embraced.

Grunts, shouts, and cries of pain followed after, as flesh was torn into and blood began to flow.

There was nobody to stop the last of the Gael defenders to emerge from the woods, a dark-haired young man holding a small hand axe. A few monks eyed him with looks of curiosity as he ran past them into the heart of the swarming fray.

***

Finnian raced through the cluster of timber huts and came to the top of the long slope. Looking around quickly, he chose his first opponent, a tall raider bearing a large round shield and spear. A look of surprise shone in the man's eyes as he glanced up and saw Finnian bearing down on him with nothing more than a small axe.

Without formal training, Finnian attempted something he never would have done had he been taught the ways of a Gael warrior. He dropped to his knees and slid right as he neared the raider, figuring that the Midragardan would expect him to engage in a more direct fashion.

The slope was not steep, but the angle lent Finnian further momentum as his body carried under the red and blue swirling pattern of his opponent's shield. Sweeping his right arm through, he hacked savagely at the ankles of the enemy warrior.

He had to let go of his axe as it lodged deep into the flesh and bone of the enemy warrior, but his attack crippled the warrior. With a cry of agony, the raider fell to the ground.

Finnian scrambled about and hurled himself at the Midargardan, desperately pummeling the man with his fists. In his frenzy, the blows were chaotic, but several landed solidly on his enemy's face.

Another warrior charged at him from behind with a broad axe, his war cry warning Finnian just in time. Fury reigned on the bearded face of the raider as he glared at Finnian straddling his fallen comrade. In a powerful arc, the Midragardan brought the honed blade within a hand's span of chopping into Finnian's neck.

Having swayed back at the last moment to avoid being beheaded, Finnian leapt up and barreled right into the warrior. It was a clumsy attack, but one that prevented the other man from using his long-hafted axe.

The tip of a spear flashed into sight, driving into the enemy warrior's body. The Midragardan emitted a low-pitched gasp, and toppled to the ground.

"Finnian, you should have gone home!" Rory snapped, holding onto the spear haft.

Finnian made no reply, snatching up the long-hafted axe the enemy warrior had been using. Though a much heavier weapon, the weapon felt much better in hand than the small axe he had arrived with.

Rory had already moved off to engage another raider, leaving Finnian alone for the moment. Many on both sides had fallen, but it looked as if Murchadh's warriors were gaining the upper hand. The fighting sprawled across the slope, with melees taking place all along the grassy incline.

Finnian eyed another pair of combatants nearby. A man named Donal, who had always been one of the kinder individuals to Finnian, was sorely beset as a huge Midragardan warrior wielding a sword pressed the attack.

Finnian sprang forward to go to Donal's aid. Leaping over fallen bodies, keeping his eyes out for enemy warriors, Finnian made his way in a curving route that brought him up behind the Midragardan. Bringing the axe head back, and gripping the haft tight, he swung with all his might

The Midragardan arched his back and grunted as the broad blade cleaved into flesh and bone. It gave Donal the opening he needed, and he wasted no time in driving his spear deep into the gut of the raider. Wide-eyed in shock, the Midragardan fell between the two men of Gael.

"Thank you, Finnian," Donal said with an expression of relief, after taking a moment to catch his breath. Donal moved quickly to get his spear back, looking around warily. His eyes widened, and a grin spread on his face. "Looks like we've gotten the best of them!"

Finnian gazed around and saw that the Midragardans were indeed falling back, abandoning their attack on the monastery. He smiled, knowing the day had been won and that he had taken part in the thick of the fighting. He had not performed any great feats on the battlefield, but he had done his part to defend his people. Without doubt, Finnian knew Murchadh would be angry that he had disobeyed, but the chieftain could not deny his courage.

The warriors under Murchadh began cheering, shouting acclaim to their chieftain, who stood tall at the center of it all. A few of the Gael began checking those who had fallen, finishing off enemies and seeking to help those of their own that still drew breath.

Finnian lingered in place, hesitant to come to the attention of Murchadh. A few of the other warriors cast him curious glances, and a couple even nodded to him, but by and large he was left to himself.

"It is not over, traitors!" a deep voice thundered, breaking the stillness and bringing immediate silence over the area. "You who have shunned the faith of your fathers! Answer for your wickedness in this hour!"

Face filled with wrath, the long-bearded, robed figure standing at the top of the slope commanded the attention of the surviving warriors. Several other men in similar attire, and also displaying lengthy beards, flanked him, but it was clear that he held authority over the rest.

He held one of the monks firmly in place, an elderly, white-bearded man that might well have been the head of the monastic community. The monk struggled in the other's grip, but the tall druid was far too strong.

A grave unease sank into Finnian. He knew he looked upon the Supreme Druid, a man said to be capable of calling upon otherworldly powers.

Though clandestine since the words of Emmanu had been brought to the land of Gael, the druids yet existed, and were feared for good reason. It was no secret they desired vengeance on those who had abandoned the old religion. There was little doubt they carried a burning antipathy towards monks of the younger faith.

"Did you think you would never answer for your betrayal?" the Supreme Druid shouted. His eyes blazed with anger. "Judgment comes upon you this very hour!"

The druid shouted in a language that Finnian did not understand. Stunned, he watched as the clouds far above the druid began to swirl, and low, rumbling thunder emitted. The cloud began to flash with pulses of lightning, and an icy wind began to course through the slope and buildings.

With a powerful shove, the druid sent the monk staggering several strides away. The monk cried out, losing his balance and falling to the ground as cold winds whipped up further.

The Supreme Druid grabbed at the sky and cried out, before thrusting his right hand towards the monk. A searing, blinding streak of lightning lanced from the sky towards the ground, engulfing the monk.

A charred husk was left in the wake of the strike, with wisps of smoke wafting off the unrecognizable body. Gasps of surprise and astonishment arose from the Gael warriors.

Finnian had never seen anyone who had been struck with lightning, but he suspected there was something more to the bolt that came from the sky. Sickened at the sight of the blackened remains of the monk, a touch of nausea hit him as the pungent scent of burned flesh reached his nostrils.

"Did his All-Father save him? No more than the All-Father will save you!" the Supreme Druid shouted with a mocking edge, a cruel smile on his face.

The druid cried out again, uttering more words in the strange language. The other druids with him took up the chant, resonant and unified in its call upon some unknown force. Filled with unease, a strange sensation came over Finnian as something powerful rippled through the air.

A frigid chill permeated the area, and the sky darkened rapidly. It was as if the things of the natural world shared the anger of the powerful druid. The winds picked up faster, and fear began to rise within Finnian as he knew something terrible was about to happen.

Horrified, Finnian saw movements along the ground and a wave of dread rolled over him. Though hard to believe his eyes, he realized that the bodies of the slain warriors were beginning to stir.

The other Gael took notice of what was happening too, as shouts filled with raw surprise and fear filled the air. Making matters worse, the reviving bodies were from both sides of the conflict, Midargardan and Gael warrior alike.

Looking to one of the fallen raiders nearby, the breath caught in Finnian's throat as he saw a fell light emerge from within the dead man's eyes. A bestial growl rose from the throat of the maimed warrior, a sound inhuman. Finnian knew he was witnessing dark, ancient arts, of a kind rarely exercised in the open.

Finnian heard Murchadh shouting in the background, encouraging the living Gael to fight back with everything they had. Hoping that the thing trying to get off the ground needed its head to govern its body's movements, Finnian took up the axe in his hands, raising it high. He hacked downward with all his strength at the exposed neck of the raider.

The blow cleaved almost entirely through, leaving the head attached by a shred of muscle and bloody skin. Finnian's purpose met, the thing flopped back down and twitched. With a hard kick Finnian completed the task, separating the head from the body, even as he heard Donal yell out a warning to him.

Turning around, he hesitated for a moment as his eyes locked with the spectral light in the gaze of the former Gael warrior shambling towards him. In shock, Finnian realized the body coming after him had belonged to Rory.

He could not raise the weapon in his hands, though his mind screamed that it was not Rory commanding the body. The thing reached back with a spear in its right hand, preparing to thrust at Finnian. The light in the thing's eyes extinguished a moment later, bits of bone and flesh flew from the spear blade driven through the back of the Rory-thing's head.

"That was not Rory. It was something evil," Donal told Finnian, after the thing fell face-first to the ground. Donal tore his spear blade free. "Do not hesitate again!"

Shaken deep to his core, Finnian nodded, as Donal turned to engage another of the risen corpses. Everything then became like a blur to Finnian as he cried out and waded into the fray with the axe.

The things getting up from the ground moved slower than they had been in life. Yet many more of the dead fighters existed than there were Gael remaining, and several more of the latter fell as the fighting continued.

Finnian swung his axe many times, and suffered no less than two painful gashes from the weapons of the undead warriors. His heart sank further, as he saw fallen Gael warriors rising up with the cold light shining in their eyes.

He could hear the faint chanting of the druids as the fighting progressed, but he could not afford to look as he swung the axe at the head of another undead warrior. The metal bit deep into the thing's neck, but it did not expire until one of his fellow Gael warriors finished lopping its head off with a sword.

A loud, piercing cry carried across the battlefield, and a sideways glance from Finnian revealed the Supreme Druid with a spear embedded deep in his chest. A short distance away stood Donal, who had managed to get close enough during the melee to hurl the weapon.

The triumph of the moment became bittersweet, as three of the resurrected bodies had been closing in upon Donal when he threw the spear. The brave warrior could not have failed to see their approach, and had used his lone weapon to strike at the Supreme Druid.

Donal was left heavily disadvantaged, unarmed with a trio of corpse-warriors assailing him. They were already upon him from three points that had him at their center, and he could not easily evade them.

Finnian cried out and started running towards Donal, but the distance was too great to help the other man in time. Fighting with the frenzy of a cornered animal, Donal landed a few heavy blows with his fists, but the dead things did not react like living men. Unfazed, they stabbed with their weapons, opening terrible wounds in Donal's body.

Seeing blood pour from Donal filled Finnian with fury as he finally reached his comrade. He beheaded one of the three undead with a tremendous axe stroke that landed flush upon its neck.

Sucking in a deep breath, Finnian yelled out in anger and brought the axe rushing back around. Arms extended and balanced on his feet, with his torso and lead shoulder in synchronicity, he swung the weapon with great force along a horizontal plane. Lodging squarely in another entity's head, the axe blade chopped right through both of its glowing eyes.

The light dimming fast, the thing teetered for a moment before collapsing. It fell at an angle that took the axe haft dangerously close to the remaining entity, stymieing Finnian from retrieving the weapon.

Backing up and thinking fast, Finnian took up the sword that the beheaded one had been holding, as the last of the three that had attacked Donal trudged towards him. The long, double-edged sword was a heavier weapon, ponderous for an untrained warrior like Finnian to wield, but there was nothing else in reach.

Though the leather-wrapped hilt was crafted with the intention of being gripped in one hand, Fillian used two as best he could. He clutched the multi-lobed pommel with part of his bottom hand, while his top pressed tight against the straight iron cross-guard.

Quicker than Finnian thought it could move, the thing jabbed towards him with its spear. Finnian slashed downward with the sword, cleaving through the lower part of its arm and severing the undead thing's spear hand.

The thing lurched towards Finnian, its otherworldly growl rising in pitch as blood poured thick from its ruined arm. It reached towards him with its remaining hand as Finnian stepped back. Gaining enough space to lift the sword Finnian brought it crashing down into the middle of his attacker's head. The thing shuddered for a moment as the ghostly light fled from its eyes.

Finnian watched spellbound, still holding onto the sword hilt as it toppled over. The weight of the body and his firm grip on the sword dislodged the weapon, though he stumbled at first, having to jerk back to keep from being pulled downward.

He cast aside the sword, stooped down, and pried the spear free from the severed hand. He grimaced as his skin touched the dead flesh, but he knew he would be quicker with the spear. The clumsy attacks and slower speed of the undead warriors were the only things keeping him alive, and he was not about to overlook any improvements he could gain.

Looking around, he saw that the four lesser druids had gathered around the body of their fallen leader. Nothing stood between Finnian and the quartet.

Finnian gritted his teeth and broke into a run. Charging at them, a white-hot anger fueled his every stride.

The druid priests turned towards him as he drew near, and what he saw shocked him. Their skin was withered and sunken, all looking to have aged tremendously since the battle had begun. Their formerly thick hair and beards were thin and wispy, strands blowing away as he approached.

The Supreme Druid, in the worst state of them all, looked to be already decomposing. Finnian's spirit recoiled in fear and astonishment as he gazed upon the increasingly skeletal appearance of the druid leader, but his furor steeled his nerves a moment later.

The aging men cried out as they took notice of Finnian descending upon them. They threw up their hands in a feeble attempt to protect themselves, but their weak efforts proved futile.

Finnian's spear blade drove into them again and again, until all four lay dead around the body of the Supreme Druid. Their white robes spattered and soaked with blood, the priests' lifeless eyes stared upward.

For a moment, he looked upon the Supreme Druid, horrified at the apparent cost the man had paid to wield such powerful forces. Down to taut, parched skin over bones, the body continued eroding right before Finnian's eyes.

Forcing his eyes away from the macabre spectacle, he looked down upon the continuing battle. Another Gael warrior fell, where he had been facing four of the undead at once. Though the druids were dead, whatever they had summoned to control the corpses still gave strength to the reanimated bodies.

A notion stabbed at him and he looked back, wondering if the druids he had slain were rising back to life. To his relief they remained in place, without any sign of light in their eyes. Looking back down the slope he saw that the fallen Gael warrior still lay inert. Finnian hoped the sorcery had been broken.

Finnian breathed laboriously, his limbs heavy, exhausted from the grave trial, but he knew he could not stop. Mustering his willpower, he began running down the hill, his heart pounding and lungs pumping.

Farther ahead, he saw Murchadh attack the four undead that had just killed the Gael warrior. Martial prowess flowed from the Gael chieftain as he brought down all of the things with his sword.

Amazed by the display, Finnian's attention was pulled suddenly towards a towering figure to the right. The huge undead warrior had been a Midragardan, with a thick, black beard, and an iron half-helm with eye guards descending from the brow at the front. His upper body was protected by chain mail from the neck down to the waist. Quite possibly, as well-equipped as the undead warrior looked, it had once been the leader of the raiders.

The entity buried its longsword into the head of the Gael fighter it faced. A shocked expression froze upon the face of the man with the split skull as he slumped down. His slayer yanked the sword free, and turned around, eyes shining with the unholy light.

The entity's eyes locked on Murchadh, who swayed in place. Having drawn closer, Finnian saw that the Gael chieftain bled from multiple wounds.

Killing the four undead looked to have taken the last reservoirs of energy out of the man. A cold smile spread on the face of the giant Midragardan entity, and it shouted words in a layered, unnatural voice that curdled Finnian's blood.

Another Gael fighter rushed the undead warrior, but the thing batted aside the warrior's attack and brought the man down with a slash that opened his throat wide. Nearly as quick as when natural life inhabited the body, the revenant moved much faster than the other undead entities. There was no time for Finnian to ponder the anomaly, with the father of the woman he loved in mortal peril.

Murchadh clashed swords with his assailant, and staggered back from the heavy force of the blow. His attacker strode forward, giving the chieftain no respite.

Finnian tripped as he reached the bottom of the slope and fell down in an ungainly heap. Ignoring the scrapes and pain from the fall he glanced up, knowing that Murchadh would not survive the onslaught. Weakened and badly wounded, the Gael chieftain was no match for the tempest pursuing him.

A robust temptation beckoned from the back of Finnian's mind. His own wounds not severe, he could lay low, and return to Brigit with nobody to refuse his heart's desire. Everything he ever wanted in life beckoned to him, with nothing to stand in the way.

Murchadh had only shown him disdain and indifference, and was the one primary obstacle to the only dream that Finnian had ever embraced. It was now within his grasp to be with Brigit for a lifetime. He thought of the children they would bring to life, and the contentment that would finally bring rest to his troubled heart.

Staying in place for just a few moments more would rid him forever of his final impediment. He could go back home and marry Brigit, and realize his soul's dream.

The impulse was not the only force tugging at Finnian from within. Another thought contended with the powerful temptation. Murchadh was Brigit's father, and she loved him. No man could dispute that he cared deeply for his family, his protectiveness of them the very thing that set him against Finnian.

Only one path resonated with the kind of spirit that Finnian was. He made his choice and got back up to his feet.

Determined to his course, he ran towards the huge undead warrior from behind. As Finnian closed the distance, the entity whirled about, swinging its sword into his side. A delirium of fiery hot pain seized Finnian, dropping him to his knees.

The undead warrior was about to strike another blow when the thing jerked upright. Head lolling to the side a moment later, its body wavered in place.

Though in agony, Finnian did not fail to perceive the abrupt ebbing of light within the entity's eyes. The undead being fell to the side, Murchadh's sword driven up into its skull from under the bottom of the half-helm.

Finnian's breathing became labored as he failed to stay on his knees, falling to the ground and rolling slowly, in great pain, to his back. The burning agony clutched his side, the anguish making him light-headed and dizzy. He had no illusions about his situation as Murchadh's face came into view above him.

The Gael chieftain kneeled by Finnian's side. For the first time in Finnian's life, there was no sign of contempt in Murchadh's face. The older man's eyes looked softer, and even had a glisten to them as he leaned close.

"Foolish boy … what have you done?" he asked in a sad tone.

"Given my love … her father back," whispered Finnian with some effort, a trace of a smile coming to his lips.

"You could have left, and gone back to her," Murchadh replied in a voice thick with emotion, with a hint of incredulity. "I was a dead man, and the battle was almost finished. You could have had her without me being there to stop you. Everything was within your grasp, Finnian."

"Had I done so … I would not be … the one she loves," Murchadh replied with more effort, as a falling sensation began to come over him. "I would have … betrayed her … and myself."

"You foolish, foolish boy," Murchadh said in a low voice, as his eyes watered.

The voice of Brigit's father grew fainter as a tremendous brightness bloomed within Finnian's eyes. His chest lifted once more, fell, and became still, as his last breath fled his body.

"What have I done?" Murchadh said, his voice forlorn. "Forbidden my daughter the man truly most worthy of her." Closing Finnian's eyes with his hand, the old chieftain wept bitter tears.

***

It took some time to muster enough resolve to return to the ridge-top, but one night, a few weeks later, Brigit made her way back to the great overlook. The larger of the two moons beamed radiantly in its fullness. It was the kind of night when she had met with him before, which made the moments all the more painful to endure.

A cavernous sorrow dwelled within, of a kind that could not be assuaged by any words from family or priests. The loss had been terrible to bear. Ever since her father had given her the awful tidings, she had descended into a pit of sorrow, soon becoming listless as her world became draped in shadow.

The sight of the gleaming river meandering underneath the moonlight, and the quiet, wooded hills lying beyond, had always looked so magical before. Now everything looked cold and empty, a wilderness uninviting.

She began to heave with sobs, as the tears welled up yet again. They were always there now, torrents of them just a scratch beneath her surface ever since word of Finnian's death had arrived.

Brigit did not know how she could possibly go on. Finnian had died in the act of proving himself to her father, and she could not shed feelings of guilt that he had ultimately died because of her.

She looked back towards the meadow, her eyes stinging with tears. Brigit peered towards the place she had always seen him emerge before. Dark shadows reigned in that area now. No matter how hard she prayed, or how fervent her wishes, he was not going to walk out from those trees ever again.

Her spirit sank further, and the tears streamed down her cheeks. She wanted to rage at the heavens during one moment, and collapse into a dreamless sleep the next. It was hard to imagine how she could ever go forward with her life.

As she stared across the meadow, she blinked her tear-filled eyes as something unexpected drew her attention. Her breath quickened as she beheld a strange phenomenon.

To her growing amazement, beams of moonlight appeared to be outlining a human figure, one who became more distinctive in form with every moment. Brigit's eyes widened further and her heart pounded faster, wondering if her grief now spurred illusions within her mind.

Drifting across the meadow like a glimmering mist, the figure seemed to take on more weight as its features continued to manifest. Brigit remained in place, stunned by what the moonlight revealed in the meadow. Astonishment filled her as the ethereal form drew closer, the identity unmistakable when the figure came to a halt.

Finnian stood before her, no more than ten paces away. He smiled with radiance, and except for the glow limning his body he looked just like he always had. The lock of curling black hair at the right side of his face, hazel eyes, full lips, and every other characteristic she cherished stood there before her eyes once again.

"Finnian?" she ventured in a low voice, half in disbelief. She wondered if she was dreaming, though if it was a dream she hoped with all her heart that it would never end.

He smiled warmly, with a peaceful, relaxed expression, of the kind that carried no trace of worry or care. "The veil has been parted this night, for a few moments. A grace for you ... and for me."

Finnian was anything but a specter. In truth, he looked more alive than ever, with merriment in his eyes and a luster to his skin.

"How ... can this be?" she asked, after a few more moments had passed, encompassed in a state of amazement.

"As I said, a grace for both of us," Finnian replied in a calm tone.

She began to reach out, and drew back, hesitant. The tears began to well up again. "I ... I want to hold you. Is ... is it possible?"

"Can you embrace a ghost?" Finnian responded with a playful grin, spreading his arms wide as he stepped forward. "I am still alive ... just in another place. But part of my heaven still remains in this world."

She wrapped her arms around him, resting her head against his chest. As she did so, all of the fears of death, and all of the sorrows that weighed her down, vanished in an instant. The sting of mourning vanquished, the hollowness that had plagued her was replaced by a fullness absent of anxieties or regrets.

Brigit hugged him tight to her, never wanting to let go. His lips softly kissed the top of her head, and his hand gently stroke her long, red tresses.

When she looked up into his face, his eyes were as tender as his touch. Their lips sought embrace and joined, and they shared a long kiss under the starry night sky.

When their lips parted, he gazed into her eyes. "I love you, Brigit … and a time will come when we will meet once again. I cannot find words to describe what I have seen … and what you will see with me one day. But you have a life yet to live. Bring your kindness and compassion to others suffering in this corrupted world."

Slowly, he pulled back from her, a smile of pure joy on his face. Tears streamed down her cheeks, but this time they were born of happiness.

"I love you Brigit … and it is a love that lasts forever," came the final words from his lips.

Finnian faded slowly from view. The last she saw of him was his face, full of peace and contentment.

A sharp pang of sorrow struck her when she was alone on the ridge-top once again. Brigit knew she would miss him always, a man who loved her in the truest sense. Yet he was right that she had to live her life.

She crossed her arms, trembling with the powerful emotions running through her. Turning about, she made her way slowly from the meadow back to edge of the overlook.

Bridget quietly stared out over the winding river and hills. The magical aspect about them had returned, but this time she perceived something else; the beautiful scene a shadow of an even more incredible reality.

As the realization came to her, she understood that a very

special gift had been given her that night, in the grace of moonlight. Brigit had witnessed the light of a world where death had no dominion.

Abounding with rapturous joy and gratitude, a bright laughter bloomed from deep within, no longer needing to grasp for hope but instead embracing the comfort of knowing. The song of her soaring elation reached to the stars on that magical night.

***

Finnian's final visit brought her a precious grace she cradled in her heart from that day forward. No longer did she need to harbor hope, as hope was something that always carried with it an aspect of uncertainty. Now she knew without doubt that the path of life went onward, extending far beyond the boundaries of the world.

As much as the gift had been brought to her, she realized from the beginning that it was something she could share with others. Brigit would not see Finnian again during her remaining years of life upon Ave, but the consolation he had given her would be multiplied a hundred-fold; for she would go on to live an incredible life, and become one of the most storied figures in all of Gael.

Winter's Embrace

Winter's Embrace

"A man of courage is also full of faith."
-Marcus Tullius Cicero

Manfred did everything he could to keep the bone-rattling chill out of his mind as the loose file of horses proceeded through the pine and birch trees. No sign of the heathens had been found yet within the sprawling forest, despite the contingent of knights, sergeants, and Order servants having traveled for three full days into the heart of enemy territory.

Thankfully, the snow was not too deep, and did not impede the brawny stallions, palfreys, and pack horses. Most of the latter were a shorter, stocky breed native to the region, whose hardiness in austere conditions was well-proven.

While the palfreys were carefully tended in their own right, it was the state of the expensive, highly-trained war horses that had to be watched most of all. A winter campaign's hardships could exact a heavy toll on the strongest of battle-hardened mounts. Every experienced rider and handler of horses knew the signs to look out for, and all were assiduous in keeping a watch upon the Order's exceptional war stallions.

For the time being, all of the horses were faring well. A significant distance had been covered under clear, sun-brightened skies, which evoked an unsullied sheen from the surface of the snow-cloaked ground.

The tales of what happened in the woodland depths helped distract Manfred from the bite of the deep winter. Macabre stories abounded regarding the strange rites and practices the heathens engaged in.

Even human sacrifice was said to be taking place regularly within the shadowy woodlands, which to Brother Manfred was the worst transgression of all. There was no question such blood rites enabled powerful sorcery, something all members of the Order of the Sacred Lady had to be wary of.

The heathens had forced the hand of the Order with a recent spate of raids upon the newer settlements. They had taken many captives, including a number of young, unmarried women.

Whispers of a powerful leader called the Undying had also reached the ears of Johann von Richtenberg, the Land Master for the region where Manfred served. Joined with the pervasive rumors of human sacrifice, the taking of captives, especially in light of the fact that many of those abducted were young women, prompted swift, decisive action from the Order.

Knights, sergeants, and others serving the Order from no less than three commanderies rallied for the excursion. After gathering at the Land Master's formidable Black Eagle Castle, they set out together with the unified goal of eradicating the heathen threat near their borders.

The wind's fangs sank into Manfred's face again, as another icy gust whipped through the column. The barrel helm he wore served well enough against weapons, but was not effective against the chill. Ventilation holes and eye openings alike let the frigid assault through to his skin.

A part of him wanted to dismount and walk alongside his palfrey, for no other reason than to summon the bodily heat that physical motion would bring. He knew that was not an option, as the warriors of the Order had to get as far as they could before stopping for the night.

Manfred eyed the brother knights and sergeants ahead of him, wondering at the thoughts within each of their minds. The strike into heathen territory was laden with risk, but the Land Master had set about the campaign with an air of great urgency.

Manfred fully understood the situation with the captives and tales of human sacrifice, but he and many of his fellow brother-knights sensed something else deeply worrying the Land Master. For the normally cautious, calculating man to order such a large force to issue forth from the high walls of Black Eagle Castle, and then lead them far beyond the usual range for a punitive raid upon the heathens, there had to be something he perceived as a grave, imminent threat to the Order and all the new settlements.

Manfred often pondered the source of the Land Master's worries, the figure called the Undying. Wild tales of heathen sorcerers in the forests always abounded, but the bits and pieces Manfred had gleaned about the Undying indicated something much more than the usual sorcerer.

If the things he had heard uttered around firesides could be believed, then this particular sorcerer was said to be impossible to kill. A younger version of Manfred would have laughed the claims off as entirely outlandish, but experience with the darker things of the world had brought him enough wisdom to assume nothing.

***

As the shadows grew longer, the column was ordered to a halt. The brother-knights, sergeants, and others dismounted, as the command to make camp was disseminated to the far end of the line. Shelters had to be erected, steeds attended to, and equipment checked.

With honed discipline, the men from the Order of the Sacred Lady saw to their assigned tasks. It did not take long for the animals to be cared for, and everything necessary for a night's encampment to be set in place.

Manfred's first priority resided in seeing to the needs of his war horse, a large black stallion named Firestorm. He was gladdened to see the horse in favorable spirits, where it was quartered in a special, well-protected area of the camp arranged for the particular care of the Order's war stallions.

Trained as a battle steed for knights, and bred for size, strength, and speed, a premium war horse required experienced riders and knowledgeable handlers. While Firestorm could be temperamental with those assigned to care for the stallion, Manfred's relationship with the brawny horse was generally harmonious.

Over the past few years, he had formed a solid bond with the steed. Firestorm became more at ease with the knight's presence, and the current evening was no different.

Speaking gently to Firestorm, Manfred spent extra time grooming and petting the stallion. He took heart from the look in the creature's eyes, which was healthy, full of vigor, and even a little affectionate. Satisfied that Firestorm was holding up well on the campaign, he then procured some quality oats, and fed the hardy steed out of his hand.

After checking with a few of the attendants assigned to the care of the horses, Manfred was confident that all was in good order concerning his primary battle mount. He then left Firestorm in the camp section with the other war horses, and went to prepare his own tent.

A lower, steeply-pitched style with a ridge-pole, the tent took little time to assemble. It was anything but luxurious, but it would keep out the worst of the elements should a bout of wind and snow break over the forest that night.

As campfires were lit and food was being prepared, Manfred finally broke away from the activities involved with pitching camp. At a relaxed stride, he made his way towards the outer edge of the newly-erected mass of tents.

A few of the men were already sitting by themselves and whittling away, a sight Manfred was well-used to on a campaign. Putting sharp blades to wood, they engaged in one of the few pursuits of amusement allowed a brother in the Order.

Manfred wondered what kind of woodcarvings would take shape that evening, given the different kind of mindset prevailing during a campaign. The activity was not one that he had ever taken to, though he wished he had more interest in it, as the diversion certainly would help him pass the time.

He pulled his sheepskin, outer cloak tighter, over the white surcoat with its telltale, black Spear of Emmanu woven into the front. Manfred carried his barrel helm along at his side, giving his face a little air, despite the worsening cold. His wavy, dark locks were short-cropped, in alignment with the Order's dictates, but his beard was full and dense, serving to provide some protection against the harsher elements.

Light yet filtered through the trees from the dying sun, but it would not be long before the woods were shrouded in night. The rising moons and the layer of snow on the ground would grace the men of the Order with enough ambiance to see for a fair distance, but the presence of threat was thick within the frigid air. Aside from the whistling of the winds, like some sepulchral voice crying out in a ghost land, there was nothing but an uneasy silence permeating the still forest.

Manfred was no fool. He knew the heathens were out there, somewhere, among the trees. By now they were well aware of the Order's presence within their forested land.

Boots crunched upon the snow as someone walked up slowly behind him. A sideways glance revealed the garb of a full brother-knight of the Order to Manfred's eyes, though the other figure was just then reaching to remove his helm.

Manfred said nothing, and kept gazing outward. His warm breaths came as little bursts of grey with each new exhalation, only to dissipate swiftly within the embrace of the evening chill.

"What is it, Manfred? Do you sense the heathens are near?"

The youthful voice identified the speaker easily enough. Only a month before, Lothar had been raised to the status of a full brother in the Order. Now, the young man was on his first campaign as a brother-knight.

Manfred found it hard to believe that he once felt the eagerness and exuberance reflected in Lothar's face and voice. That time now seemed so distant and faded, even if it had only been eight years since he had been raised to the status of a brother-knight himself. With what Manfred had been through, spanning from the blistering heat of the Sun Lands to the wintry territories west of Ehrengard, even a small number of years spent as a full brother-knight seemed a lifetime.

The youth standing at Manfred's side did not have enough experience to know that campaigns were not grand adventures to be looked forward to. They were times to be survived, and a brother-knight on a campaign could not afford to relax the least bit until surrounded by high castle walls once more.

"Nothing particular. Not yet at least," Manfred replied.

"They are out there, I just know it," Lothar replied, staring off into the trees. "Probably watching us right now."

"I am certain of that," Manfred responded firmly. "They would be fools not to have an eye on an adversary within their lands. Have your sword at hand, and keep your wits about you at all times. We take enough risk removing our helms."

"I will, Manfred, you can be assured of that," Lothar replied quickly, in the tone of a young man wanting to placate a mentor or superior.

Manfred kept his face turned away from Lothar, acting as if

he was looking off to the right. He could not stifle the grin that came to his face.

He was still a rather young man himself. Yet here he was, feeling like an old, scruffy dog in the company of an eager pup.

The image that came to mind was undeniably comical, and he did not mind the bit of relief that the humorous thought provided. Anything that lightened the heart a little during the rigors of a campaign was welcome.

Once his expression had settled, Manfred looked towards Lothar. Curly-haired, square-jawed, and with bright blue eyes, Lothar had a strong appearance. It was also one that would have gained him the favorable attentions of women with ease. His commitment to chastity as a brother-knight was undoubtedly a significant one.

The youth would have temptations of all sorts over the course of time, even beyond the dangers of a campaign. Whether at risk of feeling like the old dog or not, there was one piece of advice that Manfred could not iterate often enough.

"If you listen to just one thing I say, ever, then take what I say now to heart. Commit all things to prayer, for there are always things we have no control over," Manfred said. "We will need the All-Father's Grace to return home, or to enter Palladium if we do not. No prayer is wasted, Lothar. Not a single one."

"I do commit all in prayer, and I know in my heart that we must always seek the guidance of the All-Father, especially when we take sword to hand," Lothar replied earnestly.

For a young knight, Lothar already displayed an encouraging degree of wisdom. Manfred knew there were those in the world who found it hard to reconcile the idea of merging a warrior's path with a monastic one, but his own time in the Order of the Sacred Lady had revealed it to be an absolute necessity.

From protecting pilgrims traveling in the Sacred Kingdom to confronting the purveyors of blood rituals in snow-filled forests, the Order served a necessary purpose in a world where evil spared no weapon or tactic in its onslaught against the innocent and defenseless. There was nothing good or holy about doing nothing to protect the vulnerable from certain violence. He knew in his heart that Emmanu Himself would not have stood idle if He came upon victims beset by violent attackers. Neither would Manfred or any of his fellow brother-knights.

The danger lay in making sure that emotions were kept firmly under control, and certain boundaries were not crossed in the executing of the Order's duties. It was an easy step to become the very monsters that knights like Manfred sought to protect others against.

Human emotion had its merits, but in swift fashion it could overwhelm good reason and judgment. Manfred had witnessed that often enough to develop a healthy vigilance towards his own self-control.

"What of this Undying?" Lothar asked, with a little trepidation in his voice. "I have heard some of the others talking of this man ... if he is a man. What do you know about him?"

"I know as much as you do," Manfred replied evenly.

Like the rest of his fellow brother-knights, he only knew the rumors about the Undying, but the claims made about the heathen leader were deeply unsettling. Yet it did little good to speculate, as dwelling upon fears only served to feed rising anxieties.

"They say he cannot be killed," Lothar said with an air of amazement, echoing the primary fear held by the brother-knights towards the Undying. "Even a Wizard, who disease or time cannot touch, can be slain by violence. Yet this Undying is still said to be a man. How can that be so? How can he endure what even an immortal Wizard cannot?"

"I do not know," Manfred responded. He then looked towards Lothar, and his voice took on the tone of an instructor. "And it does no good to worry yourself about these rumors. Whatever the Undying is, or is not, it cannot be changed by your anxiety or fear. Turn your mind to other things, until we can learn more."

Lothar nodded, though Manfred doubted the young man would cease contemplating the fantastical rumors. Once given free reign, the imagination was a difficult thing to regain control of.

"What else do you think is out there?" Lothar inquired, after several quiet moments had passed.

"There is much we do not know about what lies in these woods. But we will find out. I am sure of that," Manfred answered grimly. He cast a final glance into the depths of the woods, and then turned towards Lothar. "But for now, let us get some food and rest, while we still can. Rest, above all, is a precious thing on a campaign. Heed my words Lothar, learn to take advantage of every moment of it that you can get."

"I will, Manfred," Lothar replied, a hint of a pup in his inflection. Manfred patted him on the shoulder, and turned for the camp.

Lothar strode along with Manfred, and the two joined with

several other brother-knights and sergeants in sharing a light evening meal. Everyone pressed as close as they could to the fire, as the night took on an increasingly icier chill.

Not much was discussed between the men, other than a few minor matters pertaining to equipment needs and camp duties. A little news was gained as the veteran woodsman serving as their guide through the region stopped to talk with them.

A convert with no love for the heathens, — having had his entire family slaughtered in one of their raids — he indicated they were not more than a day from finding a large heathen settlement. The news came as a relief to Manfred. The longer it took to engage the enemy, the more taut the nerves would become on the men, especially those with less campaigning experience like Lothar.

Manfred could already sense the rising edge in his fellow brother-knights. They were in the heart of enemy territory, and the heathens could strike at any moment without warning.

Even with a well-ordered watch arranged at the camp's perimeter, everyone remained highly guarded. Such tense conditions instilled a constant wariness that tended to dampen lighthearted camaraderie.

Following the repast, Manfred begged leave of the men and went to pray in solitude. He said a few extra prayers for Lothar, beseeching the All-Father that the young man would return from his first campaign unscathed.

When finished, he made his way through the camp to his tent. Crawling into it, he pulled his cloak tight over his body. Stretching out, Manfred settled down to go to sleep. Despite the relentless cold, he slipped into dreams soon enough.

***

The next day dragged on laboriously, enough that Manfred began to wonder whether they were chasing after ghosts. As with the last few days, there was no sign of the heathens.

Yet the frigid air was omnipresent and could not be evaded, even for a single moment. As had happened the previous day, Manfred would have rather walked alongside his steed for the comfort that some exertion would bring, but the Land Master had been firm about the men conserving their strength. Obedient, he was condemned to sitting idle in the saddle, and enduring the mounting effects of the cold.

He listened to the metallic rustlings, snorts and whinnies of horses, and the tendrils of wind grazing his iron helm. At the least, the sky was a little more overcast, so there was not as much of a glare from the snow as the previous day, except when the sun broke out in open pockets between cloud masses.

A distorted outcry, caused by an arrow to the throat of a sergeant near the front of the column, heralded an ambush as the heathens finally made their presence known. The forest erupted all around Manfred, as wild-eyed heathens emerged from concealment and swarmed from every direction towards the line of warriors.

Horses reared and kicked, and knights and sergeants shouted urgently as a tempest of fury beset the long, narrow column. The Order's attendants, trained to fight as infantry, hurried to dismount and take up their weapons and shields.

Manfred swiftly brought the triangular shield hanging across his back around to the front. He gripped the leather holding straps on the backside firmly with his left hand.

Honed steel gleamed in the sunlight as he slid his sword blade free of the leather scabbard at his waist. With sword and shield at the ready, he took quick assessment of the attackers charging in.

Armed primarily with spears, maces, and axes, most of the latter of a short-hafted variety, the enemy warriors were largely unarmored. Their shaggy locks and beards flowed back, buoyed in the air as they ran hard towards the column, their churning legs kicking up tufts of snow.

As the heathen fighters closed with the warriors of the Order they attacked with zeal, shouting at the top of their lungs with hatred burning within their eyes. A few displayed skill at arms, but a great many fought wildly, and recklessly, and while their strikes held considerable strength they were blocked or evaded easily enough by a trained brother-knight or sergeant.

Manfred hacked and slashed with vigor at the heathens nearest to him, quickly cutting a pair of the enemy warriors down. Resorting to defensive instincts whenever a heathen tried to come up from behind, his mount lashed out viciously with its hooves, connecting solidly more than once. After only a short spate, Manfred and his horse had sent more than a few of the heathens on their way to the afterlife.

Cries, grunts, and gasps filled the air, along with the sharp, metallic clanging of weapons, as the fighting surged into a frenzy. The screams of wounded horses also pierced the melee, as the battle-maddened heathens did not spare the mounts of the knights and sergeants.

Firestorm collapsed suddenly underneath him, an enemy spear driven deep into the creature's side. He was thrown clear by the toppling steed, and fell fast, hitting the ground hard. His shield flew free in the tumult and slid on the snowy surface, stopping just out of his reach.

The throaty yell of an attacking heathen warned Manfred just in time to bring his sword around. Gauging his strike by the shout, his blade was guided true, the tapered end cleaving through the exposed throat of a dark-haired, long-bearded warrior.

The man's axe was already raised high overhead, though it never made the descending strike. Gurgling and wide-eyed in shock, the heathen fell to the ground clutching his throat, dropping his weapon to the ground.

Manfred did not see another heathen dashing towards him from the side. The stocky man held one of the maces common to the area. Its elongated timber haft was capped with a bronze-cast head, the latter featuring short, protruding flanges all around its circumference.

The design of the weapon channeled great force into its small area of impact, as the bronze head landed on the side of Manfred's helm. He had just begun moving to get back up when the blow rang in his ears like thunder. Only the shifting of his head kept the blow from being lethal.

Even though the mace head did not strike the helm flush, the blow was still heavy enough to cause his sight to blacken, as he spiraled down into the depths of unconsciousness. There was no time to panic over his entirely defenseless condition as he crumpled to the ground, losing the grip upon his sword.

***

A throbbing headache greeted Manfred as consciousness finally returned to him. At first, he could see nothing, until he cleared the facing of his barrel helm free of the snow that was caked thickly upon it.

His heart sped up as he recalled what had happened to him. Left to the fickle mercies of fate, he had somehow survived the fighting. Yet something was terribly amiss, as he was lying on the snow right where he had fallen after losing consciousness.

Nobody had harmed him further, or come to his aid. If the men of the Order had been the victors in the fighting, Manfred hoped he had not been left for dead.

He doubted that possibility greatly, as the men of the Order would have carefully checked every body of a brother knight, sergeant, or other man serving the Order on the battlefield. Likewise, the heathens, if they had triumphed, would have made absolutely sure that any of their enemies who still drew breath was either violently dispatched or taken captive.

Manfred lifted himself up slowly, and his aching body cried out at once, causing him to wince in the harsh clutches of the throbs wracking his joints and muscles. He listened for any indication of people nearby, as he began to look around.

A little disoriented, he paused, squeezing his eyes shut for a few heartbeats. Opening them once more, he blinked a few times in rapid succession as he sought to regain his full focus.

Everywhere that Manfred looked the bodies of heathen warriors and men from the Order of the Sacred Lady were strewn across the ground, along with the bulkier forms of dead horses. Crimson streaks and pools decorated the white cloak blanketing the forest floor.

It was a dismaying scene to take in, but there was no time to ponder it. Manfred quickly realized he was not alone, his heart leaping with a surge of fear-ignited alertness.

Large, four-legged denizens of the forest were everywhere, engaged in a grisly feast. No distinction was being made between heathen or faithful, man or horse, as flesh was flesh in the eyes of ravenous wolves.

A low, rumbling growl from behind yanked Manfred's attention. A very sizable black wolf, no more than twenty paces away, startled from its feeding by the knight's movements.

Manfred glanced down, relieved to see that his main weapon had not fallen far from him. Keeping his eyes on the wolf, he leaned forward and grabbed the hilt of his sword. Slowly, he got to his feet.

The golden orbs of the wolf remained fixed in his direction, as the menacing growl continued from the beast's throat. Its hackles raised, the wolf's triangular ears flattened against its head. Blood-soaked, shaggy muzzle baring a formidable, lengthy set of fangs, the wolf bristled with hostility.

Under his breath, Manfred uttered a prayer to the All-Father, recognizing his terrible quandary. He took one step, and then another, moving in a direction where there were no bodies in his path.

The journey of a few hundred paces seemed to be a campaign of leagues and leagues. At any moment he expected the beast to charge him, or others of its ilk to turn their attentions to the last human left alive within the midst of the carnage.

Yet step after step, no attack came. But the sense of danger remained as thick as ever, as the wolf's posture did not change, nor did its hostile expression.

The only advantage Manfred had was that there was plenty of food to go around for the wolves that took no effort or risk to acquire. Even the wolf seemed to prefer avoiding an unnecessary confrontation, remaining firmly in its place as Manfred carefully continued out of the area.

He did not turn around until he was entirely removed from the wolf's sight, and that of its companions, but even then his nerves teetered on edge. Removing his helm for better hearing and visibility, he tucked the iron headgear under his left arm.

Trudging away, he was also weighed down by the thought that he was entirely alone, with no food or mount, and had only his sword for protection. If the wolves opted to hunt him down, he knew he would be a dead man.

Further, the immediate danger from the wolves had shielded him for a few moments from an even more terrible burden. Now that he was alone and surrounded by an uneasy silence, it could no longer be kept back from his mind or heart.

An avalanche of interior sorrows began breaking loose inside. Without other distractions, he began thinking of the many brothers he had lost in the battle, in addition to the sergeants and attendants he had come to know well.

He thought of the horses too, dutiful, loyal creatures that he cared greatly for. When the ambush came, he had been riding upon the palfrey given to him at the start of the campaign, and knew it had fallen from an enemy spear.

Manfred had not witnessed the fate of his war horse, Firestorm, and he had not had any time to find the creature's body. But he could not see how his steed could possibly have survived the battle and aftermath. Even if Firestorm had escaped the fighting, it would not have been long before the wolves discovered a horse wandering alone within the forest they hunted.

It was not the kind of end that his cherished steed deserved. Firestorm had conveyed him through the worst of situations, time and again.

As cold as his environs were, it could not stop the hot tears from welling up and rolling down his exposed cheeks. The enormity of all the loss bared down on him without mercy in the frigid, empty silence.

Tears trickling down his cheeks, he willed himself forward, his steps crunching against the unsullied snow. The only thing he could do was keep moving.

Returning to the battlefield soon was not an option. In all likelihood, the wolves would occupy the battle site for some time to come, with a source of food so plentiful.

A darker part of Manfred hissed that he was still as good as dead. He knew that sepulchral voice would grow louder, as he worked to push the dour notion from his mind.

He was isolated in pagan-held territory, with nothing but the clothes, armor, and weapons adorning his body. It did not take much thinking to realize that his chances of surviving and getting back to Order-held territory were far from optimal, but a steely resolve grew within his heart. Manfred was determined not to succumb lightly.

Looking to the trees, Manfred espied a large raven perched on the boughs of an oak tree. The creature was quietly eying him with its dark, alert gaze.

He knew very well what such birds feasted upon. Ravens gathered in the aftermath of battles for the same reasons that wolves did.

"Not yet," Manfred growled in a low, defiant voice towards the winged scavenger. "My heart yet beats, and the blood still flows through my veins. You will find no meal here."

Just saying the words aloud girded his spirit, though it appeared as if the bird understood. Spreading wide its black wings, it took to the air, disappearing into the depths of the forest.

Manfred pressed onward. After awhile, the daylight gradually began to dim, prompting him to search out a suitable location to begin making preparations for the night. It did not take him long to identity a capable site.

First, he fashioned a crude shelter out of some pine boughs at the base of one of the towering, evergreen trees. He knew he was in for a cold night, but at least the chilly currents of air would be stymied with the makeshift, layered cover. Further, he had always found the scent of pine comforting, providing another sliver of consolation as the wintry night began taking root with the onset of twilight.

Manfred gave no thought to his empty stomach. There was little benefit in dwelling upon what he did not have, and could not get, at the moment.

His mail hauberk with the extended arms culminating in mail mittens would remain on his body for the time being. So would the mail chausses protecting his legs, and the additional iron plates, encased in layers of linen cloth hanging from leather straps over his shoulders.

The decision on whether to shed his protective armor in exchange for increased speed and stealth in the forest was looming, but he intended to avail himself of as much protection as possible for the first night spent by himself in the heathen wilds. The threats from both heathens and wolves were far too fresh within his mind to take any kind of chances. He did choose to keep his helm off for the benefits of better awareness and comfort, though he kept it within arms grasp.

As darkness fell, he kept thoughts of the relentless cold at a distance as he focused his mind on prayer. Yet in the loneliness, other things began to haunt and torment his thoughts.

Vivid memories of the brother knights who had set out with him on the campaign began parading through his mind. Each and every image stung his heart, as he would never share their company again in the world he still had to endure.

No man was perfect, but in the balance he knew most of his brothers in the Order were of solid character. A couple of them he deemed as close friends.

Manfred could not count the times he had discussed the mysteries of the All-Father with Kunos. He could see the man's blond-bearded face smiling broadly, displaying the good humor that always seemed a constant for the spirited brother-knight.

Then there was Hermann, whose iron-hard discipline and

dedication at arms had helped Manfred become a much better fighter. The burly knight appeared as grim as Kunos seemed lighthearted, but the generosity of his heart shined just as brightly.

Thinking of those friends evoked tears of mourning in the darkness. There was nobody to see Manfred weep, and he felt no shame in lamenting the loss of his friends and brother-knights. In moments, trails of sorrow streaked his cheeks and beard.

It spoke to the inequity of life that so many good, devout men were left in the wintry cold as fodder for the bellies of wolves. Nothing seemed right about the ends they had all met, and Manfred could only trust that he would have a different perspective if the All-Father allowed him to cross into Palladium one day.

It staggered Manfred to think that he was the only one out of the entire force sent on the campaign to survive the battle. So many of the men were much stronger in faith than him, or had given so much more to the cause of the All-Father. Why the Creator of life had seen fit to allow Manfred to be the only one to survive defied all of his efforts at reason.

Then again, the All-Father allowed men and women to exercise their free will in life, and even the choices made in the heat of a furious battle had consequences. Perhaps those choices, made by all involved in the fighting, had allowed fate to select him in some manner.

That he had been spared death was miraculous in itself, though it was also possible an even crueler end neared. He shoved the latter thought out of his mind quickly.

As far as he was concerned, Manfred was going to do everything he could to make sure he had survived for a good reason. The first thing he resolved to do was make it back to the lands held by the Order, and endeavor to bring a force back to properly inter whatever remains could be salvaged of the fallen knights and other men of the Order.

As the wind picked up outside and the night matured, fatigue finally overwhelmed his exhausted body. Reddened eyes fluttering closed, feeling hollow, and with his mind weighed down heavily with the memories of those he had lost, Manfred finally drifted off into the merciful embrace of a dreamless sleep.

***

The new day greeted him with an icy touch. As his eyes flickered open, he groaned in discomfort. Manfred's entire body felt like one continuous ache.

Slowly, he crawled out from the shelter and squinted in the radiance of the sunlight reflecting off unblemished snow. Gritting his teeth, he got to his feet.

He decided to keep his armor on for the first part of the day, at least until he had a better idea regarding what kind of threats he might encounter in the area. The wind whistled through the trees, but other than that lonesome sound a sustained quiet encompassed him.

After a brief deliberation within his mind, Manfred opted to head south and east. The direction would take him away from the battle site, and also begin what he hoped would be a long, looping return back to Order-held lands.

Moving generated body heat and his rested muscles, though

sore and stiffened from sleeping upon hard ground, were ready for some use as he trekked across the snowy land. His body limbered up soon enough, but there were a few approaching needs to consider.

Manfred kept his eyes open for any opportunity for food, but he was most interested in putting increasing distance between himself and the mass of lupine predators gorging themselves on the corpses of his slain brothers. The numbers of wolves he had witnessed undoubtedly covered a substantial range of hunting territory to keep fed.

There was no question he was still well within that dangerous area. It would be a long while before he could begin to feel some confidence that he had crossed beyond the outer boundaries of the wolves' hunting grounds.

At least going thirsty was one thing Manfred did not have to fear. Many rivers and streams crossed the heathen lands, and even if there were no channels of water to be found there was always the snow itself.

Eventually he would have to eat, but for the present he knew he could endure for at least another day or two with an empty stomach. Fortunately, towards the end of morning, he came across a river. He heard the flowing water before he saw it, and picked up his pace until he reached sight of the glistening currents.

Striding out from the trees, he approached the bank of the river and took a survey of its characteristics. It was not a particularly broad channel of water, but it was not one he could attempt to ford. It was far too deep to traverse without getting soaked, which in the biting cold would be nothing short of suicidal.

The promise of fresh water still drew him to the edge, where he freed his hands from the mail mittens covering them. Stooping down, he set his helm upon the ground.

He paused, feeling the frosty, moist air washing across his face, as a breeze swept over the water and enveloped him. Manfred cupped his hands, and scooped up the cold liquid.

Hunger gnawed inside, but he reminded himself again that he could persist for a while yet without food. Water was not something he could go without for long, and he imbibed several handfuls, feeling its icy trek down his throat. Some of the water escaped his hands, and trickled through his beard.

His thoughts turned towards figuring out a refined course of action. Wandering without a firm destination would not serve him well. He had to get some sort of specific bearing, even if it was a desperate one.

Manfred knew he was moving away from the battle site and in the general direction of the east. If he walked long enough, he would be assured of ending up in lands controlled by the Order. Yet the distance needed to reach a particular castle along the boundary of heathen-held lands could mean many extra days spent alone in the wilderness.

Each additional day would be one fraught with risks. He had enough wilderness experience to know that things much more dangerous than wolves and heathens lurked in the remote parts of the world. It was one thing to be forewarned of dangers in lands he knew well; quite another to be roaming through unknown regions.

No matter the route, he had to find a safe passage back to the lands warded by the Order of the Sacred Lady. While Manfred could not fend off a hundred wolves by himself, he could return with a large force of brother-knights and others; to try and give the remains of the slain a proper burial.

"A monk warrior ... alone in this land?" a smooth, feminine voice sounded from close behind him. "It is not a sight I often see within these woods. You have strayed far from your castles."

Manfred whirled around into a fighting stance at the voice, his hand instinctively going to the hilt of his sword. He had not heard a single sound of approach, and could not believe he had let his guard down to such a degree.

"Do I look like a threat to you?" the speaker continued, without any hint of alarm at Manfred's swift reaction and defensive posture.

Long ebony locks framed a beautiful face, with lively, dark eyes that carried a sparkle of amusement. Her light skin was unblemished, and the hint of a smile played about her full lips. She gazed upon Manfred with unmistakable interest and, notably, no fear.

The woman was tall, almost matching him in height. She carried herself with a confident posture, and was draped in a lengthy cloak of black fur. There was also a harder edge about the woman; one that warned him at once not to underestimate her.

When he made no immediate reply, the trace of a smile played further about her lips. "Or maybe appearances can deceive, after all."

"I ... I did not notice you, until now," Manfred finally replied, hesitantly, relaxing his grip on the sword hilt.

She spoke the tongue of Ehrengard fluently, something not

commonly encountered among the heathens dwelling in the wilderness. Only a few of the forest-dwelling pagans possessed command of any Ehrengardian words, and even then only a smattering.

"Wondering how I speak your tongue, monk-knight?" she asked.

Manfred nodded, as there was no use denying her query. He knew the incredulity he felt was openly portrayed in the expression on his face.

"I am not like the ones you war against in these woods. I know many tongues, and have traveled far in this world," she replied, when it was clear no immediate reply from Manfred was forthcoming.

"Who are you?" Manfred asked, after a few heartbeats.

"My name is Zora," she replied. She then continued, in the air of a declaration. "I serve no kingdom, no empire, and no master. My will is my own. I live in the way I see fit. I ask no one's protection."

The more he was in her presence, the more he sensed a great strength abiding within the woman. Whether she was a warrior or a sorceress, he could not yet tell, but he was not about to provoke her. His instincts warned him against such a course.

"I am sure you do not wish to spend another night out in these woods, and I would think some warm food and drink would do you well," she continued. "The place where I reside is not far from here, and you can have your fill, and gather your strength."

The eagerness must have shown in his eyes, as the woman laughed amiably, flashing a set of well-aligned teeth. Manfred could not deny how strikingly attractive Zora was, but he knew he could not afford to be distracted by her comely appearance.

"Well, are you afraid of a lone woman in the woods?" she queried, with a wolfish grin.

"No, I am not. And I thank you for the invitation, Zora," Manfred responded politely. "It is something I did not expect to receive when I started out this morning."

"Then we should not tarry," Zora replied. "Nor should you spend much more time at this riverbank. You would be dead soon, had I not approached. You should know that I have already saved your life once. I would back away a few steps from those waters, if I were you."

Her eyes looked past him, and he followed her gaze out towards the center of the river. Something large was moving just under the surface, stirring the dark waters.

The sight of the unnamed thing compelled Manfred to back up several steps as Zora had suggested. His heart pounded more swiftly in his chest, wondering how close he had just come to disaster.

"Always looking to take the unwary into its embrace, and it is always hungry," she said, staring for a moment longer to where the sizable entity swam along the surface, drawing a little closer to the bank.

"What manner of animal is that?" Manfred asked, his eyes remaining fixed upon the creature.

Zora glanced back to Manfred. "Animal? That is no creature of flesh and blood. That it is out in the sun shows that it is ravenous for the blood of a man like you."

Manfred cast a wary eye back to the water, and took another step back. The thing in the water created a big splash, as if it were angered at the woman's words, and then there was no further sign of it.

"You do not know these lands. I do, and if you are wise you will listen to me," Zora stated firmly. "Come, I will take you to my dwelling. There you will receive food and rest."

Manfred followed Zora away from the river and on through the trees. At her lead, they continued at a modest pace for a while, until they came to a clearing in which a small edifice fashioned of logs had been erected.

Several paces in front of it sat a large, stone-ringed fire pit, hollowed out of the ground. To the right of the cabin stood the opening to a timber structure sheltering some kind of pit or cellar beneath the surface.

Without pause, Zora proceeded to the front door of the cabin with Manfred following close behind. He saw no signs of anyone else, or anything to indicate the woman had not told him the truth. To all appearances, she did indeed reside alone.

A few carvings had been rendered along the doorway, but what they were Manfred could not tell. The woman was not forthcoming with any explanations as she led him through the entrance.

Inside the cabin, the furnishings were simple and purposeful, with a stuffed pallet, several coverings of hide, a rather spacious stove of baked clay, and an assortment of other practical implements and tools. A timber chest and some clay jars were lined up on one side. In some ways the sparseness reflected the kind of life Manfred was used to as a brother-knight.

There were only a couple of small windows filled with panes of mica, and the interior was murky, even in broad daylight. The nature of the cabin's construction would seal off the worst of the frigid winds, but Manfred doubted the environs were very comfortable unless the stove was burning a full load of wood.

As she showed him around her dwelling, Manfred continued to be wary of the woman. He could not fathom why Zora was acting so at ease around him; a large, foreign warrior who she did not know.

It was no secret that warriors often took advantage of women when on campaigns. Either she knew what kind of commitment brother knights of his order made, and trusted him to keep it, or there was another reason that had more to do with the woman herself.

The fact that she exhibited no signs of trepidation was a stark warning in itself, to a degree that Manfred knew he had to keep his guard up until he knew more about the situation. Living in such a harsh winter environment was not easy for a village community, much less for a single person.

Yet everywhere he looked, he could still see no indications of there being anyone else. All of the furnishings continued pointing to the truth of the woman's claim that she lived on her own.

"I am impressed," Manfred said, looking over to her.

"How so?" Zora asked, casting him a quizzical look.

"That you survive by yourself in such a place. It is no easy thing to endure a winter in this region," Manfred replied.

"I have a little assistance," she replied enigmatically.

"The heathens," Manfred said, before catching himself. Not wishing to cause unnecessary offense to his benefactor, he quickly added, with a little awkwardness, "I mean ...the ones who attacked my column."

"I have no time for that rabble, and they have learned it is very wise not to bother me," the woman said cryptically, an edge creeping into her tone that told Manfred there was no love lost between her and the heathens. "No, what help I have is more native to these woodlands."

"What do you mean?" Manfred asked, feeling unease at her response.

"It is not important right now," Zora replied. "What is important is that you let me prepare you some food. I am sure you are famished."

"I am sorry, but I must know," Manfred stated, a little more insistently. "Or maybe I should be heading onward."

A harder look crept into her dark eyes. "I want this to go as friendly as possible. But if I were you, I would not entertain any thoughts of leaving without my blessing. You are to stay here for now," she stated firmly to him, with the air of a command.

Zora's response, and the abrupt change in her demeanor, flooded him with alarm. There was no hint of jest about her. She clearly meant what she said, and at least believed she could enforce her words.

"Why would you not allow me to leave?" he asked, avoiding the issue of whether she could truly stop him or not. "What threat do I pose to you?"

"You are no threat, but you may be very useful," she replied.

"But come here, so that you may know I do not speak idly. What I show you is for your own benefit, as when you leave these grounds I intend for you to walk with my friendship and protection. Anything less is not something you wish to risk."

She gestured for him to go over to the entrance. Slowly, he walked to the opening of the cabin, and looked outward.

His heart froze, as his eyes fell upon the huge black wolf he had encountered at the site of the woodland battle. There was no mistaking it as the same creature, from the shaggy muzzle to its golden, piercing gaze.

Compounding the matter, the creature was accompanied by several other large wolves, grays, blacks, and even one of snow white. Dozens of others stood farther back, hidden in the trees. It was as if the horde of wolves he had seen at the battle site were now gathered in full just beyond the clearing.

Zora stepped up to his side, and said in a low, even voice. "I could have had you killed where the others had fallen. I could have you killed now, if I so wish."

There was no tone of boast within her words. They were stated as simple truths, ones that Manfred could not dispute as he stared out towards the mass of wolves.

"Let us not dwell on this any longer. I do not want threats to govern our interactions. Just know that while you are under my blessing, no harm will come to you," she said, walking outside. Zora glanced back towards Manfred, and gave him one more warning. "But do not think of departing, unless I give you leave myself."

As she walked into the area before the cabin, the wolves melted back into the trees. Zora went about getting Manfred some dried meat, bread, and cheese to assuage his hunger. The simple fare tasted wonderful, and he consumed every crumb.

They talked a little more, and he told her more about his order and the reasons for the campaign. To his relief, she continued to display a great distaste for the heathens and their practices. It became abundantly clear she shared none of their beliefs.

He did not learn much more about her, except that she had a friendship with a Wizard named Morana, who sometimes traveled through the area. Manfred believe he had heard the name mentioned before, but could not recall anything about the particular Wizard.

As Zora explained it, Morana was in many ways a mentor to her. She also mentioned other Wizards with whom she held amiable relations, including one named Vesna, and two more that she referred to as the Morning Star and the Evening Star.

Zora seemed very content with the kind of life she lived, but it still eluded Manfred as to why she would have such an interest in him. He knew there was a definite purpose, as signs of it were rife within the looks she gave him.

He just hoped it would not be much longer before he found out the reason. The sooner he could address whatever the situation was, the sooner he could leave with her blessing, and resume his trek back to Order-held lands.

There was even a chance he could gain some valuable assistance from her in navigating the unfamiliar lands. He would be far less vulnerable if he knew about things such as the creature in the river that she had warned him of earlier that day.

In that moment, Manfred chose to simply enjoy the woman's

company and hospitality, and make the most of his stay. He doubted it would be much longer before more became clear as to her intentions for keeping him around.

***

As night fell, Zora set about bringing a fire to life in the large pit outside. Manfred assisted her with the preparation, and it felt good to engage in some physical activity.

Before much longer had passed, reddish flames licked hungrily at the night air, crackling in the bounty of wood they feasted upon. The clearing was filled with the glow from the pit, and Manfred savored the feeling of the heat against his face.

The wolves remained nearby, their reflective eyes a feral constellation. Manfred remained silent throughout, both amazed and discomfited by the proceedings.

"Come closer, and gaze into the fire with me," Zora invited, the flames dancing in her eyes as she glanced towards Manfred. A smile graced her lips as she gazed back into the fire.

To his eyes, she appeared invigorated by the night, the fire, and the company of the wolves. When he did not step forward immediately, she turned and stared at Manfred for several moments, her brow furrowing slightly and smile fading.

"I have told you that no harm shall come to you, what troubles you now?" she asked, a trace of irritation in her voice.

"You have told me nothing regarding what you would have of me," he replied, highly curious to learn the reason why she was keeping him with her.

"Something any man but one like you would desire greatly, and without hesitation," Zora replied in a lower voice that carried a hint of frustration. The firelight glinted off her eyes, as she peered intently at him.

Her purpose struck him in that moment, and he felt his throat grow dry. There was no denying she was incredibly attractive, and every fiber of his physical being longed with desire for her.

There was a raw hunger dwelling in her eyes that excited him as he gazed upon her face. Manfred felt another heat building inside his own body, one that was not due to the fire blazing in the pit.

"Join with me, monk-warrior, and know the most primal magic, that which is the genesis of all life," she said to him, in a voice thick with eagerness. "Here, under the stars, know what it is to fully be a man."

"There are villages all throughout these woodlands. Are there no men in them?" Manfred asked her in a near whisper, as he wrestled with his natural urges.

It was all he could do to avoid succumbing to the burning temptation. His blood was racing, and he wanted nothing more than to take the beautiful woman right then and there, in the glowing embrace of firelight.

Everything about her was intensely alluring. The way Zora looked, the confidence she radiated, and the fierce independence she exuded called powerfully to him. All he had to do was allow himself the freedom to immerse in the heat of wondrous pleasures.

Yet he knew the words he had spoken as an oath when becoming a full brother in the Order of the Sacred Lady. It was not lost on him that many of his brothers, and many of those men loyal and courageous at that, had tasted the nectar of female delights, and indulged themselves in the fires of passion.

Had it not been for the oath, Manfred knew he would not have hesitated a moment longer. As it was, the words he had spoken upon becoming a brother knight bolstered the shred of willpower keeping him from giving in to the most primal of impulses.

"There are men, but none of the quality I seek," she finally responded. "You are a man who I would have."

"I ... I have taken an oath, or I would do as you ask, without a moment's pause," Manfred replied apologetically. "It is not for a lack of desire that I cannot do this."

A part of him hated himself for resisting. In his younger days he often dreamed of what it would be like to lay with a stunning beauty. Before Manfred was the embodiment of that dream, beckoning powerfully to him.

"Do all of your brothers hold to everything in this oath?" Zora asked.

"No," Manfred replied. "But I must speak for my own actions. I must answer for my own choices. It is my responsibility, and mine alone."

"Right here, in the heat of the fire, under the eternal skies, let us seek ecstasy," she said to him, allowing her long fur cloak to fall to the ground.

Though she remained clothed, the shedding of the cloak revealed enough hints of what lay beneath to stoke the fires within Manfred further. His mind had Zora wrapping her long, shapely legs around him as he gazed spellbound into her dark eyes. His willpower teetered on edge.

"All I ask of you is a few moments, and then I will grant you safe passage out of these lands, so you may return to your brethren," she said. "Is that so difficult?"

"Why do you wish for this?" Manfred asked her, wracked by the urges to satiate his hungers. "Of all things, why this?"

Even with the shadows of night and the limits of the fire, he could see the sadness crossing her face. The reaction was unexpected, and now it was his turn to be surprised.

"My daughter Sveta was taken from me, many years ago," she replied, voice laden with sorrow. "The ones you call heathens captured her in the depths of the forest, before I could do anything about it. All of it was done to serve their sick gods, and the new master they submitted to."

"You said you are not of the same beliefs as the heathens of these lands," Manfred said.

"No, I am not!" she responded sharply, as if spitting the words from her mouth. "They have been born, aged, died, and turned to dust many times over, while my faith has sustained me for centuries."

Her words were hard for Manfred to accept, but he knew the world was filled with all manner of strange and mysterious things. Powers violating all the natural laws were there for the taking, though the cost was never light for anyone choosing such a path.

"Then, you are a witch?" Manfred asked, giving voice to the suspicion he had been harboring since their encounter at the river.

"Yes, as is my daughter," she answered. "... As was my daughter. Sveta is gone, and there is nothing I can do about it now."

"Why?" Manfred asked, incredulous at her admission of futility.

A powerful witch served by a horde of wolves was more than formidable in his eyes. A small group of heathens should not have stood a chance against her.

"She has been given to one who is even greater skilled in the dark magic than I," she answered, and Manfred could sense that she hated openly recognizing that situation. Anger rose in her tone as she continued. "Do you not think I have tried everything I could? I have barely escaped with my life more than once. My only comfort is the knowledge that she yet lives. It is the reason why I was not overwhelmed with despair."

"I ... am deeply sorry," Manfred said, with genuine sympathy.

In that moment the woman before him was no longer a powerful witch. Zora was simply a mother who had lost a daughter.

Her eyes began to glisten, reflecting the firelight. "The pleasures I could show you ... the fires I could summon from within you. Like nothing you have ever known." Zora shook her head ruefully.

"What if I could set your daughter free?" Manfred ventured cautiously, after a long, uncomfortable pause. "What then? Would you allow me to go free?"

She stared at him for several moments. "If you could truly rescue my daughter, I would regard that as full payment for passage out of these woods. I would ask nothing else of you."

Manfred could see the lingering desire in her eyes, but it was evident he had come upon the one thing that superseded the witch's passions and lusts. He had found a way out of the predicament of violating his oaths, but he knew that whatever stymied a centuries-old witch many times was nothing to take lightly.

"Then let me try to free your daughter, and return her to you," Manfred offered.

"And if you fail, and survive?" Zora asked him. Her gaze narrowed. "I will not consider your tribute paid for safe passage."

"Then I shall give you what you ask," Manfred declared, having nothing else to offer her.

"Do not think to deceive me, monk-warrior, or I will make your suffering last long, and there will be nowhere you can hide from me," she warned him. "Not even in your own lands. I may dwell in these woods now, but I have traveled far and wide. The walls of your castles cannot protect you."

As if sensing her agitation, menacing growls swelled from within the trees, as the wolves added their assent to the threat. Manfred felt a chill rising in his bones at the sound, and looked into the host of glowing eyes staring back at him.

"I give you my word, as a Brother in the Order of the Sacred Lady, that I will make the attempt. If I fail, and survive, then you can determine the payment I make to you," he said to her. "Even what you intended this night."

The hint of a smile danced about her full lips. "That is something I already know ... and something you should desire as a man," she replied suggestively. "But let me tell you of the foe you have chosen to go against ... and allow yourself to fill at least one physical need this night.

"As for the foe you will face ... the one who took my daughter ... he is known as the Undying."

***

Before the night aged much further, Manfred had a full belly, and had learned much about the task he volunteered for. The millet gruel, deer meat, and mild drink made from rye bread were a sumptuous feast given how little he had been eating in recent days.

When the fires died down and they finally turned inside for the night, Manfred refused to take the pallet, choosing instead to sleep on hides. It was not long before he fell fast asleep, but the irony of it all was not lost on him.

Here he lay, a monk-warrior sworn to the Order of the Sacred Lady, sheltered by a witch steeped in the darker sorceries. Manfred would be doing her bidding when the sun rose again, but he saw no conflict with his own faith in the matter.

Helping a mother regain her daughter was something that held no evil within it, and in his beliefs the witch and her daughter were still children of the All-Father. It was not for him to judge the state of their spirits, but it was for him to do right by them.

Even so, the circumstances were definitely intriguing to contemplate. Manfred doubted he would ever make full sense of it all, as the ways of the All-Father were indeed mysterious. Eyes heavy, and stomach full, Manfred faded away into a deep, restful slumber.

***

The nascent dawn unveiled bright, clear day. After breaking his fast on an ample portion of millet gruel, Manfred walked with Zora as she prepared a pack of foodstuffs for him, and discussed the perilous task that lay before him. She reiterated many of the things she had spoken to him of the night before.

A considerable hike to the north and west would bring him to the place where the Undying dwelled. Manfred would be going straight back into the territory he had wanted to avoid. Yet ironically he would be seeking out the very entity whose presence had prompted the fateful raid by his Order.

She told him more about the Undying, and the fearsome creatures reputed to serve the powerful being. He hoped dearly that she exaggerated.

Zora warned him of many dangers in the woodlands, especially the creatures of the water. She told him not to trust anything that emerged from a river or stream, no matter how beautiful the appearance.

As she explained, some of the most formidable predators used seduction rather than terror to subdue their quarry. Manfred found a little irony in her words after what had happened the previous night; though he did not deem her a predator in any fashion.

Zora was able to find a woolen cloak that was just big enough for him to use with the garb he was setting out in. He had considerably less girth to cover, as he was shedding a large part of his own equipment. He stared down at the helm, chausses, hauberk, and linen-encased plates, knowing he was giving up effective protection against beasts and heathens alike.

Taking a deep breath, Manfred rested a hand on the circular pommel of his sword, sheathed in its familiar place at his left side. At the very least, he would have the trusted weapon with him. Inscribed on the fuller of the blade were the words he had long ago taken to the core of his heart, 'Defend the defenseless, confront all evil, and seek always the Will of the All-Father.'

The words resonated just as truly with Manfred that morning as they had on the day he had received the sword. He hoped he would always live up to those words, which required conviction, courage, and wisdom to follow. Deep in his heart, he sensed he was going to be put to a most difficult test, and it was good to set his mind and heart on the highest of ideals from the outset.

With the lighter load, there was a noticeable spring in his step as he exited the cabin and returned to join Zora, where she stood alone at the edge of the fire pit. It was approximately the same spot where they had stood together the night before, when Manfred had somehow resisted one of the most powerful of temptations a man could face.

"I am ready," he announced to her.

"Heed my words monk-knight. Do not try to deceive me," Zora warned him, as he prepared to set off. "You cannot go east without those loyal to me seeing you try. I have my own ways of keeping my eyes upon you. I view our pact as you viewed your oath last night."

"It is nothing to be concerned about," Manfred replied. "What kind of brother or knight would I be if my word was so easily broken? You saw last night that I am a man who keeps his word, and in that respect I will not fail you. I do not know what the coming days may bring, or if I shall survive this trial. But though I may die, I will not break my word to you, Zora."

"Everything I have come to know of you causes me to believe you," Zora said, her tone softening. "May you find success where I could not, Manfred of the Order of the Sacred Lady."

Manfred took leave of Zora, and set off through the woods. Almost immediately, he began thinking of every bit of lore that had been shared with him about the heathens and what dwelled within their woods. He smiled to himself as he pondered his ultimate task, attempting to kill a being who could not be killed.

The idea appeared preposterous on the surface, but there was no question the Undying was a figure of great wickedness. By attempting to strike down the Undying, he would be honoring his word to Zora and living up to the goals of the campaign.

A few short flurries of snow broke the monotony of his trek as he hiked onward. He kept alert for any signs of beasts or humans.

His only abiding concern was the tracks he created with each step into the pristine white surface. Should something pick up his trail, it would be very easy to follow.

Walking at a quick pace, he covered a sizable distance over the next few hours. Physically, he felt strong, and the continuous movement kept him comfortable, despite the cold.

The faint sound of laughter froze Manfred in place, but not before his sword was out and he was in a balanced stance. The sound trickled through the trees, stifling his ability to orient upon the direction it came from.

The laughter carried through the air again, this time a little louder, and he looked swiftly from right to left. The woods remained empty;not a thing moved.

Yet whatever made the noise sounded very close. Every instinct cried out that something was both near and very aware of him.

"Come forth, whoever you might be," Manfred called, breaking the tense impasse, though he doubted anything listening to him would understand his Ehrengardian words.

After several moments of deep, uneasy silence, a tall figure moved slowly from behind a tree just ahead of him. At first Manfred thought it to be a man, but many oddities began emerging about its form, as he focused his attention on the being.

The figure's lengthy hair and beard had a green hue, and exhibited the texture of grass. It also had a decidedly pointed contour to its head. It clenched a large wooden club in its right hand.

It said nothing at first, and stood gazing upon Manfred with its bright, penetrating green eyes. He had no idea whether the thing was friend or foe. It was definitely not one of the monstrosities Zora had attributed to serving the Undying.

"Not a foe. The witch shelters you?"

The response and question sounded clearly enough within his mind, though no audible noise had come from the being. The interior 'voice' had a highly unusual quality to it, as if wind through leaves, the song of a bird, and the rush of a stream over rocks had been combined into one unique tone.

"She spared me, to try to do something she was unable to do," Manfred answered slowly, hoping he had interpreted the voice in his head correctly.

There was nothing to confirm that it was the figure before him who had spoken. It was possible there was someone else present.

"You seek to free her daughter. One taken from her long ago."

Manfred nodded. "Yes, I do. Though it would seem I have been sent on an impossible task."

A slight nod from the figure before him indicated to Manfred that it was indeed the speaker of the words within his mind. That revelation came as a small relief, though he was not about to let his guard down.

"Many would say so."

"I will accomplish this task, or I will die," Manfred responded firmly. "I have given her my word."

No voice sounded for several moments, and Manfred wondered what the strange being was thinking. He was careful in his own thoughts, conjecturing that a being who could speak inside his mind could just as easily read his every last contemplation, or deliberation.

"I could help you evade the eyes of the witch, and those loyal to her. Such power is mine to use, for whomever I wish."

Manfred was caught off guard by the statement. The last thing he expected was an offer of help, especially one claiming to conceal him from the powers of the witch. He then recalled that Zora promised to hunt him down in any land he went to.

"I can make it so the witch believes you died in the attempt."

The claim heightened Manfred's wariness, as he strongly suspected the thing had read his very thoughts. Though guarded, he could not help but wonder if the creature had the power to carry out its claims.

"Form and appearance can be changed."

The being moved back behind the tree. Manfred remained in place, but kept his eyes fixed on the spot.

"Something that avoids all notice? That is not hard."

Manfred felt an impulse to look behind him. When he did, his gaze was drawn towards the ground, where a tiny version of the being stood. It was no higher than a blade of grass. His eyes widened in surprise.

"I can command form and appearance. Come with me now and I can see you safely through these woods. You should not heed the desires of a witch."

Perhaps the reason Zora had not mentioned the being was because it opposed her. It if it was an adversary of the witch, and lived in close proximity to her, then it was undoubtedly powerful as well.

Manfred rejected the inner temptation and shook his head. He replied with an adamant tone, "No, I gave my word to Zora. I will see to this task, come whatever may."

The little figure stepped away, and moved out of sight behind the trunk of another tree. Manfred looked around, giving a start when he saw the figure again, returned back to its larger form.

The tall being said nothing to him for several long, pensive moments. At last, the voice sounded once more within Manfred's head.

"Do not look for a green oak. The green oak is the folly of all who have tried. Look instead for the tree watered in blood."

Manfred did not know what to say in reply, as he did not understand what the figure was telling him. He sensed the strange entity was offering important knowledge to him, though, and he took the words to mind.

The woodland entity gave him the slightest of nods, and moved away, disappearing after a few strides behind the trunk of a large oak tree. Manfred stayed in place for a little while longer, unsure if the creature would manifest again.

When it was apparent the thing was indeed gone, Manfred started forward again, and breathed deeply. He had the uneasy suspicion his journey would have come to an end right there, had he answered the being differently. Looking back on the interaction, he suspected the thing had been measuring him in some way.

As things stood, he was alive, and able to continue honoring his promise to Zora. He thought about the words of the forest entity, regarding the avoidance of a green oak and looking for a tree watered by blood. None of it made much sense to him at the present, but perhaps the full meaning would become apparent in due time.

He continued through the woods as the sun traveled across the sky, covering a fair distance over the ensuing hours. There were no more unusual encounters to be had, although more than once he had the distinct impression that something among the trees was watching him.

At last, when it seemed as if the day would stretch on forever, evening arrived. Manfred partook of some of the foodstuffs given to him by Zora, after he had fashioned a small shelter of pine branches. Some dried meat and hard cheese sufficed to stave off the hunger pangs that had manifested late in the day.

Well-concealed, he settled in for the duration of the night. Alone in unfamiliar territory, he prayed for a short while, and then slept lightly, poised for any disturbance.

A little good fortune tilted his way and nothing interrupted his slumber. His body was rested enough when morning's light returned to the forest. After a few prayers, and consuming a little more of his stock of food, Manfred set forth once more.

***

Ringed by stones at its base, the tall wooden pillar exhibited four carved faces of roughly equal size, set side by side. The eyes of the faces stared unblinking and ever watchful, keeping a constant vigil on the north, south, east and west. Manfred knew from his first sight that it was a pillar dedicated to the bizarre, four-headed god of the heathens, Porenutius.

The cult of Berstuk, - a Wizard who allowed himself to be venerated as a god by the forest-dwelling heathens, - would be something much more clandestine. According to Zora, Berstuk had more than a small part to play in the empowerment of the Undying, including the opening of channels to the dark abyss where one such as Porenutius could commune directly with the ambitious sorcerer.

Manfred had little doubt the Undying enjoyed the favor of both the Wizard and a demonic entity. Nothing else served to explain the extraordinary level of power the sorcerer was said to have attained.

Manfred hoped that Berstuk was not in the area at the moment, as he had more than enough on his hands in facing the Undying. A Wizard's presence, especially one that would be hostile to his intentions, was not something the knight could hope to contend with.

The carved pillar indicated Manfred was very close to where he needed to be, and he proceeded forth with the greatest of caution. The heathens were somewhere in the immediate vicinity. He could not afford to have them become aware of him, or the Undying would be well-warned before the monk-warrior had a chance to strike.

With the trees barren, and the underbrush naked, the stark environment proved difficult for concealment. Manfred took each and every step with care, moving at a slow pace and keeping his eyes and ears attuned for the slightest of disturbances. He paused several times to listen for a few moments, and see if he could pick up any sounds of people or beasts.

At last, when the sun's light began casting longer shadows on its approach to dusk, he came across an ancient, massive oak. Several more carved pillars in close proximity testified to the sacred nature of the site, in regard to the heathens.

Taking advantage of a fold in the ground, Manfred kept his profile low as he studied the area. He eyed the tree with great interest, fascinated by the decidedly green hue of the bark.

He had no doubt this was the tree harboring the buried chest spoken of by Zora. She had indicated clearly that Manfred should look for an ancient oak with bark of green.

The last words of the strange forest entity also played about in his mind, casting some doubt on the matter of the green oak. He put the misgivings aside for the moment, believing he should trust more in Zora's words. She was the one he had undertaken the mission for.

Incredibly, the site appeared to be unguarded. Either it was warded by something unseen, or the Undying had left the very means of his destruction completely exposed to anyone with knowledge of his vulnerability.

That was difficult for Manfred to digest, as he pondered whether to approach the tree and begin searching for a spot to dig. As he weighed his options, the sounds of many voices talking carried through the trees to his ears.

Rigid, he oriented on the direction of the voices, which were now growing louder. A large number of people walked into sight, and fortunately they were in front of the rise of ground concealing Manfred.

There were no children among the approaching group, which consisted of men and women ranging from young adults to elders. Their appearances and attire told him at once that they were of a heathen tribe.

Even if Manfred could not understand their words, he could see the excitement and anticipation spread across their faces, and carried in their tones, as they proceeded past the oak tree. He wondered as to their purpose, especially since they were leaving the great oak behind.

His instincts told him to follow them. Groups did not gather at night without something of importance happening, and their bypass of the oak tree had him deeply intrigued. Something of great significance was about to happen, and he chose to find out what it was.

Manfred found that following the large, talkative group of men and women at a distance proved to be easier than he had thought it would be. Using trees to shield him, and keeping to a crouch, Manfred kept pace without taking great risk.

His caution proved excessive, as the men and women appeared fully at ease, unconcerned about potential threats. Only a few times did anyone cast a glance backward, and in the dying light they saw nothing. With his body still, Manfred blended smoothly with trees and shadows.

The group went on a long hike through the forest, until finally the heathen throng headed down a long slope, towards a place situated not far from a riverbank. Just beyond, dark waters flowed steadily within a broad channel, larger than the one where Manfred had met Zora.

More heathens were gathered there already, many of them bearing flaming torches. Other torches were lit and provided to the incoming group as they arrived, swelling the numbers arrayed in the stretch of open ground continuing right up to the river's edge.

From the top of the slope, Manfred gazed in astonishment at an oak tree even larger and more majestic than the green-hued one. In the twilight it carried a surreal appearance, the facing of it illuminated by the firelight from the mass of torches.

Lowering to his belly, he pressed as flat as he could against the ground, allowing only enough of his head to raise to allow for observation. Manfred peered down at the throng, wondering what they were waiting for. There was a palpable sense of expectation running through the crowd, and many individuals spoke in hushed tones to one another.

When the last light of the sun expired, several movements drew Manfred's eyes towards the river. His well-honed discipline prevented him from flinching in surprise at the sight that met his gaze. Silently looking onward, an instinctive feeling of unease began spreading throughout his body.

Emerging from the water and walking up the bank were what looked to be several nubile, young women, with lengthy tresses coursing down from their heads to their slender waists. Despite being unclothed and glistening wet, the females showed no signs of discomfort in the frigid winter air. Water beaded and trickled down their shapely contours, accenting physical attributes that spared nothing to Manfred's imagination.

A haunting music rose and filled the air, created from the voices of the strange women from the river. Manfred had never heard voices more beautiful in his entire life, ebbing and flowing in enchanting harmonies.

He felt the stirring of powerful emotions from deep within, as something called to Manfred's most primal elements. The effect spellbound the crowd, as all talk gave way to the wondrous night music.

A few of the females climbed up into the boughs of trees at the perimeter of the open ground. Others moved towards the humans and began dancing in a broad circle, which was soon joined by some of the men from the crowd. It was a mesmerizing scene, one that threatened to captivate Manfred's focus entirely, until the wary part of him pushed back vigorously against the seductive atmosphere.

As Manfred watched, a couple of the river-women glanced in his direction. He was taken aback, breath halting in his chest for an instant.

Their eyes shone with an ethereal light, as if illuminated from within by a green fire. Any doubts he still harbored about them not being human, even after they came out of frigid waters into wintry air without a single trace of discomfort, their spectral, glowing eyes dispelled all notions that the females were human.

No matter how beautiful their forms, Manfred knew they were not entities to be trifled with. He immediately wondered at the folly of those who were dancing with the river nymphs. Enough lore had been passed to him to warn him of the seductions of such beings, and Zora had firmly cautioned him about the dangers dwelling within the rivers.

Men and women alike continued to join in the dance. Several began taking off the cloaks they wore, spreading them upon the ground until a wide area had been blanketed. It was not much longer before the heathens began shedding their clothes, and started openly engaging in acts of a carnal nature on the area of covered ground.

Manfred had heard accounts of such wanton licentiousness in the heathen lands, but he had deemed the tales to be exaggerations. It was hard for him to believe that such heedless lust could be so enthusiastically embraced; yet he could not deny the evidence captured by his eyes.

As the revelry of flesh continued unabated, he noticed that

the female entities from the water did not take active part. Rather, several of them began leading men away from the orgy, one on one, guiding them back towards the water.

The first pair to depart from the night dance reached the water's edge. In a blur of movement, followed with a large splash, the river nymph displayed exceptional strength as she abruptly grasped the man and bore him downward into the river, taking him beneath the surface in an instant.

As the other pairs reached the water, the same fate met the men. Oddly, despite being in position to witness what was happening to those ahead of them, none of the men resisted. It seemed that they were all within some manner of trance, under the complete control of the river nymphs.

One after another, they were yanked from their feet and disappeared into the dark waters with their alluring captors. None of the men resurfaced.

Manfred did not want to consider what took place in the depths of the river. But surprisingly the crowd did not react to what was happening to their comrades just a short distance away. Bystanders and participants alike kept their full focus on the salacious activity in the firelight.

Finally, only the nymphs in the trees were left of the group that had emerged from the river waters. Without breaking their enrapturing song, they began to descend from the branches.

Slowly, they stepped towards the river, as the indulgences of flesh drew to an end. The men and women began collecting themselves, and their clothing.

A man walked out from somewhere behind the great tree,

and as he did all eyes turned towards him. The song of the nymphs drew to a close as the remaining creatures slipped gracefully back into the river.

The reaction of the crowd told Manfred at once who the figure was. The frivolity permeating the area moments before was replaced with a reverential, subdued hush, as the people bowed their heads towards the Undying.

His appearance was nothing unusual, far less remarkable than Manfred would have imagined for a figure said to be so powerful. The Undying looked to be a rather ordinary man of about middle age, round of face with a dense beard, and thin, straight dark hair that fell to the top of his shoulders.

Clad in a long, dark tunic and cloak, he had a medium-build. A single pendant rested upon his chest from a thin chain about his neck. Manfred was too far away to tell exactly what form the pendant took, but the moonlight glinted brightly off its silvery surface.

Raising his hands, the Undying began speaking to the crowd. His voice was mid-toned and authoritative, and from the first utterance he had them captivated. Though Manfred could not understand a word coming from the Undying's mouth, it was clear that the sorcerer was convening some kind of ceremonial ritual.

Where only men had been taken to their doom by the river nymphs, women were revealed in the next moment to be the substance of the Undying's impending dark rite. At a gesture from the sorcerer, several men dragged forth a pair of frightened-looking young women, for a purpose unmistakable to anyone observing the proceedings.

Clad in long white tunics, the women struggled desperately against their bindings. Extreme terror showed in the firelight reflecting off their faces.

There was no mistaking they were unwilling participants. Worse, the two women were not afforded the hypnotic mercy given the male victims of the nymphs. The women were entirely aware of their peril as they were forced closer to the Undying.

Everything inside Manfred told him to get up and go to their aid. He was on the cusp of rising to his feet when his mind went spinning, as a new figure abruptly joined the ceremony.

Striding out of the darkness from behind the Undying was an utterly terrifying creature. Towering over every man in the clearing, the beast had the lengthy muzzle and face of a dog, though only one large eye was set in the midst of its forehead. Its body was that of a man, brawny and powerful, but its legs were great oddities, very similar to those of a horse.

Its strange form moved with an unusual gait. The beast snarled menacingly at the onlookers, and revealed an arsenal of large jagged teeth and fangs. Several of the men and women quickly stepped back, giving the area before the oak tree a wider berth.

Using a short blade, the Undying stepped behind one of the young women and cut her throat wide open. She was held fast by two of the men who had dragged her before the Undying as her life gurgled out of her gaping wound, the blood flowing into a large bowl held by the sorcerer.

The Undying then turned and walked over to the base of the great oak tree. Chanting rhythmically, he poured the contents of the bowl slowly upon the ground.

The monstrous beast standing before the tree showed no reaction to the Undying, as the sorcerer walked by the creature. The beast's attention was fixed squarely upon the crowd, as if serving as a guardian for that part of the blood ritual.

The next moments were torturous for Manfred to endure. He felt some guilt at not intervening, but he knew restraint was the only choice. He would never strike the Undying down if he recklessly attacked with a horde of heathens and a monstrosity standing between him and the sorcerer.

He clenched his teeth in frustration, a few tears welling as they threatened to break loose. Manfred prayed fervently for the second woman as she was subjected to the same gruesome treatment as her white-garbed companion. A few heartbeats later and her sorrow and terror was all over, as she slumped dead into the grasp of the men holding her.

Below Manfred's face, tears began to fall, striking snow. Alone among those gathered before the massive oak tree, the monk-warrior mourned her passing, and that of her companion.

They were each unique souls, with every bit as much worth as his own. He placed his trust in the boundless mercy of the All-Father, and wished with all his heart that the two women were having all of their fear, sadness and pain washed away; in a place where no evil could ever lay its hand upon them ever again.

The Undying walked away from the woman and back to the tree, with another bowl of fresh blood to pour at its base. Behind the sorcerer, the bodies of the two women were taken away by the men who had been forcibly keeping them in place.

The Undying then held his hands wide, facing the crowd, and chanted loudly for quite some time. The crowed swayed, and at certain times they responded in unison, as if affirming something asked of them by the sorcerer. When he finally concluded, he turned and left the way he had come, followed shortly by the hulking beast.

Not long after, the crowd began to disperse, with different groups splitting off into several directions. They departed in a reverent silence, and Manfred remained in place until well after the last of them had gone.

The dark silence felt surreal, and an icy breeze coursed over Manfred's face, like the breath of sighing ghosts. To be a witness to such wickedness placed added burdens upon his already-strained soul, as such events influenced the way he viewed his fellow humans, and the world the All-Father had made. The only thing he could do in the face of such evil was reach deep inside, muster the inner strength to reach for something higher, and set his sights upon a world far, far better.

Reminding himself that he was on a journey, and not at the destination, he embraced the will to rise and act. Slowly, Manfred got to his feet, stretching his limbs carefully from the rigid posture he had maintained throughout the bizarre ceremony. With a heavier heart, but no less determined than before, Manfred started forward, moving down the slope towards the open ground.

He tried to keep his steps as soft as possible, using the trees to obscure his form. At last, he reached the edge of the clearing. Pausing, he looked around the silent area, careful to make sure there were no people lingering about, or any sign of the Undying's brutish creature.

A feeling of apprehension brought his eyes upward, and his heart jumped within his chest. He had somehow overlooked one of the river nymphs, who had remained in the boughs of a tree to his right. She said nothing, and cast a mesmerizing smile. Staring towards her, he found himself swiftly becoming enchanted; drawn into the fathomless gaze within her bright green eyes.

Lithely, she climbed down from the tree and walked slowly up to Manfred, holding his eyes with her own. She still said nothing, but everything about her beckoned with invitation.

Somehow he knew that everything he desired would be fulfilled, if only he chose to go with her. An overwhelming sense of comfort and reassurance came over him as he gazed into her captivating eyes.

His thoughts became like wisps, as some distant sense of alarm struggled to gain his attention. The nymph nodded slowly to him, and began to back away. He took a step after her, and then another, holding her gaze.

The edge of the riverbank drew closer as they crossed the open ground. He had the powerful, trance-like sensation of being within a wonderful dream. He took no notice when the nymph's lips parted slightly, with the waters just a few steps away, revealing the ends of sharp fangs flanking a span of spiky teeth.

The faint cries of distress at the edge of his consciousness merged into a voice just loud enough to distract him for a moment from his fixation upon the nymph. In that fleeting instance of time, he comprehended his dire circumstance in full.

Though it took an agony of willpower, he acted with alacrity.

Sliding his sword out of its sheath, he brought it around in a sweeping arc.

The steel blade unceremoniously lopped off the head of the river nymph. With her face fixed in a startled-looking expression, the head thudded to the ground in a tangle of long hair. The body followed a moment later, toppling to the side.

Manfred's heart beat faster, a chill falling over him as he found that he stood only a handful of paces from the river's edge. It had taken all the willpower he could summon to break free of the nymph's spell, and he now understood why so many men had been led to their destruction in watery depths.

He looked over at the severed head. In death, the seductive mask had been stolen. The ghostly lights within its eyes had been extinguished, leaving behind two cold, obsidian pools. The thing's lips were spread open, exhibiting the maw of a predator.

Keeping his sword in hand and collecting his focus, he left the riverbank and made his way towards the oak tree. A pang of sorrow stabbed him, as he set his eyes upon the dark stain where the blood of the two women sacrificed in the ritual had been poured.

Two large roots from the oak tree cradled the patch of blood-marked ground. Setting his right knee on the ground, he lay his sword down and pulled out a short dagger. Using it as a pick to break up the solid earth, he began digging.

As he scooped out handfuls of dirt, the words of the strange forest denizen he had encountered played within his mind. 'Look instead for the tree watered in blood.'

With his hands covered in blood and soil, he had little doubt he had interpreted the words correctly. He could only hope the place the sorcerer had chosen to pour the blood held further significance.

After the hole had deepened considerably, Manfred paused and straightened, hearing thumping hoof beats approaching fast. He knew they could only come from one source.

The guardian creature broke out of the darkness and into the moonlit clearing a few moments later. Dropping the dagger and reaching downward, he swiftly grasped the hilt of his sword and got to his feet.

Saliva dripped from the savage thing's jaws as it turned its body to face the lone knight standing before the tree. The beast was armed with a lengthy wooden club, the end of which was studded with iron. The grating, low-pitched growl from the monstrosity's throat chilled the knight's bones, but he managed to keep his balance, as he squared to face it.

The beast roared and bore down upon Manfred, exposing the array of glistening, jagged shards within its widening jaws. Its left set of claws spread in anticipation of tearing into its human quarry, while it raised the timber club grasped in its right.

Manfred eyed the width between the creature's legs, and gauged his timing. Thick hooves pounding the ground, it took only a few more strides before the creature loomed over him.

The odd shape of the beast's legs gave it a wider stance, in order to balance itself. Manfred leapt forward at the last instant, landing within the gap and hitting his knees hard as he slid on the snow. The heavy weapon of the creature swished through air where the knight had been standing an instant before.

Manfred wasted no time and thrust upward with his sword, putting all the strength he could muster into the strike. Steel drove into flesh as the blade found purchase in the creature's groin. Blood gushed over the knight, a howl of terrible agony erupted from the wounded beast.

Manfred shuffled forward, hustling to get his feet under him. He stood and swiveled on the ball of his right foot, taking up a fighting stance.

The creature turned and swiped clumsily at him with its club. The attempted strike missed the knight by a wide margin, though he felt the rush of air across his face.

There was strength behind the swing, enough to shatter Manfred's bones if the blow landed. Yet the beast had not utilized even half the strength that it was capable of. Legs soaked with its own blood, the beast was weakening fast.

Manfred hurried just out of the creature's range. The creature's face had lost much of its rage, as confusion, pain and fear overtook its expression.

Blood continued to stream down its legs to anoint the ground beneath it. Manfred kept his distance, as the beast did not have the strength left to muster another charge. After a few more moments, it began swaying, and then finally crashed to the ground. The beast lay still, and showed no signs of movement.

Manfred was not about to take any chances. Given an opportunity to strike, he ran in and began hacking vigorously at the broad neck of the beast. His sword cleaved through the dense mass of flesh, muscle, and bone on the fifth blow. Without delay, he kicked the dismembered head away from the rest of the creature's body.

Breathing heavily, and blood racing through his veins, he took a few moments to catch his breath before returning to the base of the oak tree. Keeping his sword lying on the ground at his side, and taking up the dagger again, he resumed his excavation with greater urgency.

He cleared out loose dirt, broke up more ground with his dagger, and repeated the process several times until the tip of the dagger abruptly struck hard wood with a resounding clack. The discovery energized Manfred, and spurred him to quicken his pace.

There was no time to celebrate the fact that he had interpreted correctly the sorcerer's choice of spot for the blood during the ritual. There was no telling how much time he had left.

The massive guardian he had slain was not the only servant of the Undying. The river still contained the murderous nymphs, and an abundance of heathens dwelled close to the site.

Finding one edge of the chest, it was not long before he had defined its boundaries, and began clearing the rest of the dirt that the vessel was encased within. Manfred did not pause for rest, but it still took a while before he had freed the wooden chest. Bringing the vessel out of the hole, he ripped it free from a few root tendrils connecting the chest to the oak tree.

Setting the rectangular container down upon flat ground, he took a deep breath, and steeled his nerves as best he could. Setting his hands upon the lid, Manfred found that it was unlocked.

Opening the chest, he grasped quickly in reflex as something tried to leap out of the interior towards him. Catching the strange entity in mid-air, Manfred struggled to hold the thrashing form away from him.

The dark thing within his hands exhibited incredible strength, but he held fast to the entity. After a few moments, it suddenly began shifting into another form, sprouting a set of membranous wings.

Defying all natural laws for something of its size, the entity nearly lifted him from the ground as it tried to flap free. Somehow, the knight managed to keep his feet on the surface, while still holding onto the winged shape.

Manfred realized then that the thing was not trying to get at him, but rather trying to escape. He clutched onto it with everything he had, forcing it slowly down to the ground. Though he could not get a clear look at the entity, it felt vaguely bat-shaped, though that was the closet approximation he could make of the bizarre creature.

Finally, as if succumbing to its captor, the entity's efforts to free itself ebbed. When it finally ceased, the thing's form began shifting again, until the knight founding himself holding an egg-shaped object within his hands.

Manfred's eyes widened, recalling Zora's words to him about what she knew of the Undying. He realized that he was holding the vessel that contained the sorcerer's very soul.

It was the reason why the sorcerer could not be killed. The object safeguarded the Undying's spirit in a way that did not tether the man's soul to the condition of his physical body. The sorcerer could incur wounds that would kill any other man, but they would not sever the bond between his flesh and spirit.

A loud voice broke into his stream of thought, causing

Manfred to look away from the prize he had so assiduously won. Less than ten paces away from the knight stood the Undying.

The sorcerer shouted several words in the heathen tongue. An unmistakable glint of fear showed in his eyes, as his face filled with malice. His attention fixed upon the object held within the knight's palms.

The Undying called out loudly. Out of the darkness behind him stepped a beautiful young woman with lustrous dark hair.

She had a distant look in her eyes, and no emotion reflected in her somber expression. Manfred saw Zora's features within the face of the woman immediately, and knew precisely who she was.

Sveta reached out towards Manfred, and spoke several words in the foreign tongue used by the Undying. Instantly, Manfred felt his body seizing up, as if a paralysis was rapidly coming over him.

Gritting his teeth, he strained to close his hands over the egg-shaped object. Slowly, his hands began converging with the object pressed in between, in the way that many folded their hands in prayer.

Fear danced in his mind as he felt the control leaving his body. He could hear the voice of the Undying speaking in a commanding tone, presumably addressing Sveta once more.

It took every last shred of will he had left to collapse the remaining space between his closing hands. Manfred felt the egg-shaped object break up into fragments, as the flesh of one palm met the other.

With the exception of his eyes, Manfred was a prisoner in his own body. Fixed in place where he stood, he raised his eyes up, to see what the Undying and Sveta were doing.

He could not move, and could not even utter a single word of protest, as the Undying handed the blade he had used during the blood sacrifice over to Sveta. She accepted the blade from the Undying and nodded, and then started towards Manfred.

Helpless, he stared into her eyes as she lingered in front of him. To his surprise, the dull, faraway look he had noted moments before was gone. In its place was a livelier spark, filled with alertness.

He wondered as to the change and her purpose in delaying the inevitable, when he could do nothing to stop her from killing him. The Undying seemed agitated with the delay, as Manfred heard the sorcerer's anger-filled voice speak to the woman again.

Manfred's heart weighed heavy as he awaited the inevitable. He had come so close. The Undying could be killed now, like any other man who drew breath. The mystical vessel was nothing more than fragments in his hands.

Unable to make a sound or move a muscle, there was no way to convey the sorcerer's grave vulnerability to Zora's daughter. The means of freeing her and completing his task was within close grasp, yet it could just as well have been on the other side of the world.

Sveta kept gazing into his eyes, with no change in expression. Manfred thought of the All-Father, and simply hoped that the killing blow would be swift.

He would soon be at the mercy of his Creator, who would weigh his life and determine whether his home would be in Palladium. The knight said an interior prayer of contrition, asking for the healing and cleansing of his spirit before he departed his body.

To his amazement, Sveta abruptly turned back towards the Undying, and said several words to him. A moment later, she walked towards the sorcerer.

The tone of her voice was gentle, even soothing, and she reached out with her left hand to caress the sorcerer's bearded face. He smiled at Sveta, and nodded towards Manfred, as he said a few words to her in response. The Undying still exhibited signs of impatience, but whatever she had said to the sorcerer had pacified him a little.

Moonlight flashed off the silvery blade as Sveta drove the weapon upwards, with determined force, right underneath the Undying's chin. A look of shock was displayed on the sorcerer's face as he trembled, unable to open his mouth. Blood flowed down his neck and began staining the front of his tunic, a few crimson drops sprinkling onto the snow.

Cold laughter emitted from Zora's daughter as the sorcerer fell to his knees. Manfred could not believe his sudden change in fortune as she stood over the dying man, and spoke to him in an icy tone that needed no translation to understand the hatred she was giving vent to. In truth, Manfred underestimated the severity of the animosity she harbored, which was revealed in brutal fashion during the next few moments.

With a hard kick Sveta sent the Undying onto his back. Though little life still remained in the man, she strode forward and began stomping down into his face with the heel of her right boot. Sickening cracks cleaved the night air as she crushed his face down into an unrecognizable, bloody mass.

When she was finished with the frenzy of raw violence, Sveta turned towards the knight. Her face was fixed in a hardened expression, and her eyes glittered with a maniacal edge.

Even though she had killed the Undying, Manfred could glean nothing of her intentions towards him. Yet he could not run or resist, and could only stare helplessly as he awaited her verdict.

Making another gesture with her hand, she spoke a few more words in the unfamiliar tongue. All at once, Manfred felt his control over his body return.

Glancing down at his hands and opening them up, he saw the pieces of the object he had crushed, along with a thin, needle-like element that now lay in two halves within his palms. He had succeeded in breaking the Undying's power, but his mission was not yet complete.

Without further delay, he looked to Sveta and spoke the words Zora had taught him, saying the only heathen words he knew. "Zora, your mother, ward of the forest, and friend of Morana, Vesna, the Morning Star, and the Evening Star, sent me to slay the Undying, and bring you safely back to her."

She stared at him quietly in the aftermath of his words, and he could read the astonishment in her eyes. Manfred discarded the fragments in his hands, letting the pieces fall to the ground.

He took up a small pouch affixed to the belt at his waist. Gingerly, he opened it, and brought forth the small amulet Zora had sent with him.

A luminous smile broke out upon her face as Sveta saw the object, and tears swiftly came to her eyes. Her radiant smile accented the reflection of her mother, and in that moment Manfred marveled at just how beautiful the two women were.

"Come, let us go from here, it is time you are reunited with your mother," Manfred said gently, in the Ehrengardian tongue. "My promise to her is not fulfilled until I bring you back to Zora."

Though he knew Sveta did not understand a word of what he had just said, she clearly perceived the meaning. Nodding, she strode over to him.

He gazed around at the clearing one more time, taking in the excavated hole at the base of the oak tree, the bodies of the Undying and the guardian beast, and the flowing river. There was no sign of the nymphs, or any of the heathens, and he did not want to wait around to see if anyone returned to the site.

Side by side, Manfred and Sveta began the journey back to Zora. It would be a long trek back to her dwelling, but the achievement of his aims, against incredible odds, infused his body with renewed energy.

Looking back upon the events that had transpired, he could not believe that he was still alive, much less had succeeded. Silently, as they continued through the forest, he offered many prayers of thanksgiving to the All-Father.

In the depths of night, nothing disturbed their journey, though Manfred remained vigilant and Sveta exhibited great wariness. By the time morning's light pierced the darkness, they were far from the heathens and well on their way back to Zora's dwelling.

While a language barrier existed between himself and Sveta, he sensed that she knew fully where they were headed. She smiled warmly at Manfred several times when he looked towards her, to see how she was faring.

He knew she had been through a long nightmare, and could not imagine what must be going through her mind now that she was free again. To see her in such relatively good spirits gladdened him. Having Sveta freed from such a vile captivity and able to return to her mother was a reward far better than one of silver or gold.

They stopped a couple of times to rest for a few moments, and he shared all that he had left of the food he had carried with him. On both occasions, Sveta showed an eagerness to resume the journey, and Manfred was more than willing to oblige. The sooner they reached Zora, the sooner he could begin his own trek homeward.

***

A feeling of exquisite joy radiated from within his heart as he strode through the trees, carrying a pack stuffed with food for the journey back to the lands warded by the Order of the Sacred Lady. Manfred had survived a perilous task, and was now on his way home with the knowledge that he had reunited a mother and a daughter. As an added reward, he had overcome a horrific evil; one that would no longer be sacrificing terrified victims as a part of wicked blood rituals.

The monk-knight chuckled to himself, as he could tell that Zora still had hungers of a more libidinous nature towards him. The look in her expressive eyes was unmistakable, as was the underlying intent in her invitation to him, to spend a few more days before departing.

She had kept to her promise amiably enough, though, when Manfred had insisted upon starting back for the Order-held lands. Zora had gone into the sunken storehouse next to her dwelling, and prepared a generous pack of supplies for him to take on the trek.

When she had given him the supplies, Zora made a revelation to him, with more than a little bemusement on her face. The enigmatic forest being Manfred had encountered on his way to face the Undying had thought very highly of him.

"My allies and friends come in many forms," she had remarked, with a laugh, as she looked upon Manfred's surprised countenance. She had cocked her head towards him and grinned broadly. "What? Did you think I would not test you a little, along the way?"

Manfred had shaken his head and smiled in response, thinking of the strange forest entity, who had imparted such crucial wisdom to him. "It does not surprise me."

"I will never forget you," she had replied, her face growing serious. "You returned to me a treasure beyond estimate, one I had thought lost to me forever."

"A mother should not be separated from her daughter," Manfred had replied.

"Even one who wields a pagan magic?" Zora had asked mischievously, raising an eyebrow.

"We all answer for our own choices in this world," Manfred had responded. "You and I choose differently in who we give our loyalties to. But you are still a mother, and Sveta is still your daughter. That was my concern, Zora"

"You are wise beyond your years," she had replied, smiling. "And as one who has lived centuries, I have acquired more than a little of the world's wisdom along the way."

"And may you live a long and healthy life, Zora," Manfred had said.

"I intend on it," she had replied. "You had best be going, so you do not lose any more moments of daylight ... since you refuse to accept my invitation to rest here for a couple of days, with me and my daughter." The seductive look flared once more within her eyes.

Manfred laughed to himself, as he thought of her persistence. He had managed to resist the temptation, though it had been anything but easy.

He hoped that Zora and her daughter found their way to Palladium someday. Many in his Order, and in the Western Church, would think such a thought bordering on the heretical, given that the two women were forest witches engaged in shadowy, darker arts.

For Manfred, there would be no apology, as the hope was consistent with everything he believed and held to heart. To desire that all found their way to the All-Father was nothing to be ashamed of.

Looking forward through the trees, he breathed the crisp wintry air, and listened to his boots crunching on the snow. He was lugging a little added weight, with the rolled up mail, helm, and linen-covered coat of plates he pulled along on a small sled behind him. He was thankful to Zora for the latter, as it made taking the armor back much easier than it would have been otherwise.

Well away from the areas where the heathens had been encountered, Manfred could set his mind on thoughts of seeing his fellow brother-knights once more. Walking onward, he turned his gaze towards the future and more uplifting ruminations.

In a state of friendship, he had left the two women early that morning knowing that he could seek their help if he ever needed it. The thought comforted him after all he had been through in recent days.

Though it was only midday, it already seemed they were a world away. He knew he would never forget them. Manfred had been tested, learning much more about himself and what his faith truly called him to do.

Harsh shouts and cries broke the stillness. Looking about, Manfred quickly realized his predicament. To his great dismay, he saw that he was fully surrounded by heathen warriors.

He also knew it was no random encounter. They were there for him, bent on a mission of vengeance.

Charging across the snow, bearing axe, spear, and mace, the enemy warriors rapidly converged upon him, with murderous intent blazing in their eyes. Dropping his leather pack to the ground, letting his cloak fall free, and loosing his grip on the tethers of the timber sled, he drew his sword and steeled his resolve.

The fury evident in the heathens told Manfred they were men burning to avenge the loss of their sorcery-wielding master. He had probably witnessed several of the figures now attacking him when they had been partaking in the sacrificial ritual. Perhaps one or more had been the men responsible for holding the female victims in place for the Undying's blade.

There were easily a few dozen warriors, and though he was a very capable fighter, Manfred knew deep inside that he could not overcome them all. Gripping his sword hilt firmly, and taking a deep breath, the lone survivor of the woodland battle would now make his final stand.

As the gap between the knight and heathens closed, the woods erupted in howls, bringing many of the enemy warriors skidding to a halt. A few tumbled to the ground, and the shouts that then emerged carried far more fear than anger.

Coming from behind the heathen war band, and surrounding them, were dozens upon dozens of large wolves. Bounding across the snow, the wolves closed the distance rapidly, and were soon tearing into the would-be attackers.

Keeping his grip upon his sword, Manfred stood still, looking on in a state of sheer astonishment as the heathens were overwhelmed in mere moments. What fighting there was came to an end very quickly. Even more incredibly, despite the ferocity of the wolves' attack, not even one of the beasts made a move in the direction of Manfred.

Yet he was still in a tremendous quandary. While not threatened at the moment, Manfred was still encompassed by wolves, who were in even greater numbers than the heathens. Most of the wolves began tearing at the bodies of the dead heathens, and paid the monk-night no heed, except for one.

The great black wolf that Manfred had first met when awakening after the battle between his Order and the heathens padded slowly towards him. The creature drew to a halt several paces away, tongue lolling and triangular ears erect, as it beheld him with its golden, unwavering gaze.

The black wolf trotted past Manfred, and where it headed the others of its kind parted way. To the knight's growing amazement, Manfred realized the wolf was creating a channel for him to depart.

The creature turned and looked at him when there was a safe passage through the sprawling carnage. Manfred gave the beast a slight nod, acknowledging that he understood what the creature had done.

As the wolf stepped aside from the channel and rejoined the other members of the massive pack, Manfred returned his sword back to its scabbard. Taking a couple of moments, he gathered up his leather pack, cloak, and the tethers of the sled.

Manfred then walked down the channel through the bloody ring of fallen heathens and feeding wolves. Deep inside, he knew he was being allowed through unharmed, but nonetheless his nerves stayed on edge until he had passed completely through the lupine ranks.

Turning around, and looking back after a few more paces, he espied two figures standing together on a low ridge in the distance. He knew who they were, and though he left the woods in their friendship Manfred doubted he would see them again in the years left to him in the world.

However, as he had been contemplating before the heathens' thwarted attempt at vengeance, he could not say for certain that he would never see the two women again. Perhaps they would indeed meet again, within the grand, magical worlds to come.

The thought brought a radiant smile to his face and comfort to his weary heart, as he turned and started again towards the east. It was time to rejoin a brotherhood he had been separated from for far too long.

Yet after he had walked a little while longer, something tugged insistently at the back of his mind. He took another glance back, and what he saw brought him to a pause.

Manfred savored a moment of joy that was more pure and buoyant than anything he had felt in a long time. Far above the forest and ridge, two large ravens soared in graceful flight together, ascending towards skies bright and blue.

Lion Heart

Lion Heart

"Courage is resistance to fear, mastery of fear,
not absence of fear."
-Mark Twain

Without a moment to think, Sigananda lunged into the path of the huge Dreganfel, interposing himself between the fearsome predator and Digane. He raised his small oval shield of cowhide, bracing with his spear as the muscular beast thundered towards him.

An ambush predator in the wilderness, Dreganfels were not inclined to chase down their prey. But Digane had been in close proximity, and humans were pitifully slow in comparison to the strides of the monstrous hunting cat.

Signanda had arrived in time to see the Dreganfel's first attack. Exploding out of the high grass, its powerful forelimbs overpowered an Amazu warrior in an instant of violence. Sigananda had come with all the haste he could muster to warn his comrades, knowing they had blundered right into the great cat's hunting territory, but now it was a desperate fight for survival.

Slavering fangs were unveiled to their fullest within the spreading jaws of the creature, as its gaze locked onto Sigananda, reflecting a killing intent. The distance between warrior and Dreganfel was swallowed up in a few bounds. The beast sprang at the last instant with a deep-throated roar, flaring its claws outward as it hurled its bulk towards Sigananda.

A deafening bestial cry encompassed Sigananda as he brought his Ilkwa rushing upward, and fell back in one quick motion, driving the long iron blade deep into the body of the Dreganfel. The creature's momentum carried it overhead, and its body arced downward, landing heavily on the ground behind Sigananda.

With the Ilkwa lodged in the Dreganfel's body, Sigananda hurriedly gripped his timber kerrie, a war club with a heavy, knobbed end. Scrambling up to his feet, he whirled around, and squared his body towards the Dreganfel.

If the creature still held breath, the war club would have to suffice, as there was nothing else for him to wield. The two javelins he had thrown several moments before were too far to reach, both having missed the raging beast that had already slain two others in the small group of Amazu warriors.

The beast struggled laboriously to its paws, its sides heaving as it glared hotly at Sigananda. Blood poured out of the mortal wound it had received, and only a short time remained until the creature's spirit fled its body.

Though a young man, Sigananda was not about to brashly rush in against a wounded predator at bay. The Dreganfel was at its most dangerous, and Signanda maintained his poise as he waited for the end to come.

"Nooooooo!" Signanda shouted urgently, seeing movement out of the periphery of his vision.

Another warrior from his party bounded in, with a hunting spear upraised. The young warrior shouted at the top of his lungs, inexperience preventing him from realizing what he was running into.

The Dreganfel lashed out with blurring speed, mauling the warrior down the length of his right side. The high-pitched feline cry that the beast loosed carried a sharp air of defiance, as it fell upon the warrior savagely. Fangs and claws flashed repeatedly before Signanda could reach the Dreganfel, shredding the doomed warrior with frightening swiftness.

The most gruesome blow was the one that evoked a primal fear in the hearts of veteran Amazu hunters, in every generation. Using the two stout canines jutting into open view from its upper jaws, the predator drove them down with great force into the skull of the hapless warrior, puncturing the bone as if it were little more than an egg shell.

Had the beast been left to itself, it would have dragged the corpse of the dead man into one of the broad-canopied trees dotting the rolling terrain. There, it would feed on the flesh of a human, as its kind had done as long as any could remember.

Looking up as Signananda bore down upon it, the Dreganfel's ears flattened, as its lips peeled back along its short muzzle, baring its fangs. It emitted a piercing, grating cry, which resonated with Sigananda's most elemental instincts, sending a frigid chill through his veins.

The boldness of Signananda caused it to hesitate for a moment. It had never encountered humans who had rushed towards it, as two had just done in a span of moments. The tiny pause was just long enough for Signananda to execute his attack.

With a furious battle cry, Sigananda brought his war club around in an arc that gathered power and speed until it smashed into the beast's skull. The air cracked at the impact, and the Dreganfel crumpled to the ground, stunned, but not quite dead. Its breath came irregularly, and its body swayed as it tried to regain control over itself.

Bringing the club up and down, Sigananda rained several more heavy blows upon the beast, until the primal gleam in its eye had been extinguished. Signananda backed away from the body of the Dreganfel, breathing heavily after the frenzied exertion.

After a few moments, when he was sure the Dreganfel was dead, he looked around for the others of his party with a glowering expression. His eyes settled upon one of the warriors in particular, a sight sparking immediate ire within him.

"What foolishness! Three warriors dead, without need!" Sigananda growled at Digane, who stood a few paces away. "Are you that blind? Did you not see the signs?"

Digane looked downward, making no effort to argue with the man who had just saved his life. The stubby cones of hair formed with the use of clay and tallow masked his sheepish expression. He could not even bring himself to look Sigananda in the eyes.

"Did you not take notice of the trees?" Sigananda berated Digane, pointing emphatically towards one of the large trees dotting the grassland, with its host of strong boughs and expansive shade.

Great herds of prey animals flowed through the open ground on a regular basis, like antelope and gnus. The trees provided a perfect refuge where a Dreganfel could rest in shade, or consume a recent kill.

The mere sight of scattered trees in rolling grassland instilled extreme caution in Signananda. Despite his own great strength and skill with weapons, he knew he stood no chance if he were taken unawares by a Dreganfel.

"You are just lucky I realized your folly, and saw your tracks heading into this area," Sigananda stated firmly, casting a sharp glare at Digane. "Learn from this, or you will die soon, Digane. I will not always be there to put myself before a raging beast trying to kill you."

Lean of build, and long-limbed, Digane was the opposite of Signananda, who brimmed with powerful muscularity and a thick frame. The other warriors with Sigananda kept back, as if they expected the brawny warrior to snap the other man like a twig. The scowl on Signananda's face did not depart, and it was clear he had taken no joy in killing the Dreganfel.

In truth, it was a needless killing of a magnificent creature, a king of the expansive grasslands. Sigananda felt more melancholic than proud, and was sorry that three younger warriors died because of one man's sheer stupidity. Though Signananda and Digane had grown up together, it did not absolve his comrade from accountability.

The more that he dwelled on it, the madder he became. He knew the boundaries of his temper, and realized he had to pull back his ire, before he vented in a manner that boded very ill for Digane.

"Enough of this," Signananda finally snapped, not wanting to scold Digane any more than necessary. "I must take the pelt, and we must see to the fallen warriors. Then let us return to the umuzi, though it is sadness we will be bringing with us."

He looked back towards the bodies of the Dreganfel and the bloodied warrior, and had to choke back another surge of hot anger. None of it had been necessary, as even a modicum of alertness would have easily avoided the deaths. Few things rankled Sigananda's nerves more than senseless killing.

**

The return journey went without incident, though a somber cloud hung over the Amazu party all throughout the march. After a half-day's hike, the band of uFalaza regiment warriors reached the hillside umuzi, the village settlement that both Sigananda and Digane called home.

Moving through high, swaying grasses along the low terrain, they approached a prominent rise. A number of other hills surrounded them, exhibiting nothing but the windswept grasses blanketing their surface.

Arrayed on the slope of the large hill, the umuzi faced in the direction of the rising sun. A wooden palisade encircled the umuzi, the protective boundary constructed of two lines of inward-leaning stakes, crossing near the top, the space formed between the intersecting ends filled with thorns.

Set a short distance away from the umuzi was a pen fashioned of vertical, timber stakes. Containing a number of goats, the enclosure was being tended by a couple of bored-looking youths. Both snapped up straight as they saw Sigananda and the others approaching.

Within the umuzi itself, a series of dome-shaped huts lined the perimeter. Constructed of wood and thatched grass, the largest was positioned near the top, its entrance directly facing the gateway to the umuzi. Small garden plots attended each of the huts, and several wicker containers were held aloft on platforms supported by tall stilts.

A ring of vertical stakes on the inside of the huts marked the border of a cattle corral at the interior. It was empty at the moment, with the main herd out grazing, warded by a number of village men.

When Sigananda arrived in the umuzi, lugging the sizeable pelt of the Dreganfel, an instant commotion was generated. A number of women, children, and some older men gathered around the returning hunting party, staring with fascination at the huge pelt exhibiting the unmistakable spotted pattern of a Dreganfel.

"Did you kill it?" one of the young boys asked Signananda, his voice charged with excitement, as his widened eyes stared at the large hide.

"Yes, to save Digane," Signanda replied evenly, casting a sharp glance towards the one responsible for everything. The other man kept his face fixed forward, still unable to meet Sigananda's accusing gaze.

The youth, probably sensing Sigananda's darkened mood,

refrained from asking other questions. Most of the other villagers kept a wide berth from Sigananda, who carried the aura of a thundercloud as he continued forward. Perhaps a few made comments or asked questions, but Sigananda blocked everything from his mind.

Signananda worked his way to the top of the umuzi, where the most prominent dwelling stood. Without delay, he set the skin of the Dreganfel down before the dome-shaped hut. He straightened back up, relieved to be free of the burden, though he felt nothing but emptiness deeper inside.

It may have been a few moments or a short while, but only the sound of footsteps drawing near roused Sigananda from his brooding stupor. He turned around, to see who was coming.

Mawa, the isangoma of the umuzi, approached Sigananda as he lingered before the chieftain's hut. Her face was covered in white paint, and she carried a gnu's tail in her right hand. Her hair was fashioned into lengthy braids, and a plume of long black feathers sprouted from atop her head, the latter crowned by a headband adorned with small animal bladders.

"A Dreganfel?" Mawa queried, as she neared, eyeing the large hide. "Your hunting foray was eventful."

"Too eventful," Signananda replied morosely. "Three warriors dead, because Digane could not see the obvious signs of a predator's territory, markings that an Amazu child would notice. He led young men in recklessly. He had the experience, and they trusted him."

Mawa frowned, and her voice was soft. "It sorrows my heart to hear this."

"As it does mine," Sigananda concurred, feeling the bitter anger rising up again. "I had gone off to search out signs of possible quarry. From afar I saw where Digane was taking the others. I could not believe what he was doing. I ran as fast as I could to warn them, but I did not get there soon enough."

He looked off down the hill, and saw where Digane and the other warriors were talking with other men and women of the umuzi. From their dour faces, and the tears streaming down the faces of several, Sigananda conjectured the news of the three dead warriors had just been imparted.

A pang of sorrow struck his heart at the thought of the dead warriors' blood-kin, who would be mourning long into the night, until weariness finally overcame them. He did not know the dead men as closely as he did Digane, but Sigananda knew them well enough to know that he would not be spared the ache of lamentation either.

They were young men who had shown much promise as warriors, especially the one who had courageously charged the Dreganfel at the end of the tragic encounter. Named Thimuni, he would likely have grown into a great warrior, a living blessing to his people.

"But I would guess that some of the others still breathe because of you," Mawa said, gently.

Signananda shrugged. "Who can say? I could take no chances. A Dreganfel angered is nothing a warrior with even a splinter of reason can ignore."

"I do not wish to add to your burdens, Sigananda, but there is a matter that cannot wait, not even for grieving," Mawa said, somberly.

Sigananda looked over to her, and knew at once from her countenance that there was something of grave concern weighing her down. A hint of weariness reflected in the lines of her face, and her dark eyes carried a trace of anxiety.

"What concerns you, Mawa?" Sigananda asked, his thoughts turning immediately from the debacle with the Dreganfel.

"There is much talk of Cetshwayo calling up the warriors, to muster in the amakhanda, to prepare for war," Mawa told him, with unblinking eyes.

"War? With who?" Sigananda asked, incredulous.

None of the tribal kingdoms on any border had the strength to wage war with the Amazu people. If anything, all of the rulers who shared borders with the Amazu lived in constant fear of Cetshwayo's ambitions, wondering if he harbored dreams of conquest.

The only plausible scenario for war at the present moment involved aggression on the part of the Amazu. Sigananda gave little credence to the thought, as such a thing would have been highly uncharacteristic for King Cetshwayo.

"The Ewandwe people. And it is said Gibini and Enundu walk among them, and have roused them to war," Mawa said, heavily.

A clammy feeling came over Sigananda at the pair of names. The powers of Gibini and Enundu were far beyond those of the greatest isangoma who ever lived among the Amazu people.

The storied Wizards represented a terrible danger, able to wield arts that could not be resisted with Ilkwa, club, or shield. Sigananda would rather face ten Dreganfels, or a hundred Ewandwe warriors, instead of Gibini and Enundu.

"The Ewandwe could not hope to attack us any other way, unless aided by such powerful sorcery," he said at last, his mood souring fast as he tried to rationalize the unsettling news.

"But they are aided, Sigananda. Make no mistake about it," Mawa replied, evenly. "It emboldens them, and all signs indicate they are preparing for a war of aggression."

"Then Bhambatha must know this already, and the king must know," Sigananda replied. "I know I cannot be the first to learn this. What news do you have of them?"

"They do know, and soon they will gather thousands together for war. The uSuthu … the Ugibabanye …. All the great regiments of the Amazu will be summoned, with their white shields and battle-hardened leaders, and many more. The newer regiments, such as the uFalaza, will be summoned as well.

"A great host will be gathered … and thousands will die, even if the Amazu prevail in open battle against the Ewandwe. Do not underestimate Gibini and Enundu. A harvest of sorrow will be reaped in Amazu lands if they are not stopped soon. The devastation they send upon us will not spare man, woman, or child."

"And you come to me? I am but a new warrior, in a new Ibutho," Sigananda said. "There are warriors among the uSutho of the king who would know better how to confront this peril. Surely your hopes do not rest upon a warrior of the uFalaza."

"Yours will be a life of many triumphs, and many agonies, Sigananda," Mawa said, her gaze piercing into him. Her voice took on a different tonal quality, as if her words were a formal pronouncement. "It will be a life spoken of for ages to come. The account of your life will be the kind of tale that will spark the fires of courage within warriors, long after we have continued our journey into the next realms."

"You have been drinking utshwala," Sigananda scoffed, with a deep chuckle, thinking of the dense, sour liquid that he enjoyed himself. Her words had now ventured into silliness, placing such great hopes upon a young, largely unproven warrior. "Too much of it can harm your judgement."

Mawa's unwavering expression conveyed that she did not share his humor. "I tell you of this, and of what I see in my visions, because the king will choose open battle. I seek to avert the deaths of thousands of the Amazu. You are the only one in this umuzi that will listen to me who has even a slim chance of stopping Gibini and Enundu. The other capable warriors would find me a fool for even seeking to try.

"I will not lie to you, Sigananda. It is most likely that you will die if you accept this task. But if you do not, I fear it is certain death for many, many thousands."

"Stopping both Gibini and Enundu? How? I am no sorcerer. They are not going to meet me with iron in their hands," Sigananda countered. His frown deepened, as he sensed the edge of desperation in Mawa.

"You are the kind of warrior who can find a way," Mawa responded without hesitation, though the words did nothing to bolster his confidence. "My arts strengthen my conviction in this."

"You feel I am the only one foolish enough to undertake something like this," Signananda replied, with a humorless chuckle, shaking his head.

"No, I feel that you are one of only a few who would have a chance, and perhaps the only one of those who would be willing to undertake this desperate task," Mawa said.

Sigananda said nothing in reply, his jaws clenching tight as he realized he had no choice. If what Mawa said was correct, that he was the only one who might have a chance of stopping the two malefic Wizards, then he could not refuse her entreaty.

"Here comes Bhambatha," Mawa said abruptly, looking away, towards the front gate of the umuzi.

A tall, older warrior strode across the open ground, heading straight for Sigananda and Mawa. As with all married males, he wore a fabric head ring, currently hidden beneath a cheetah-skin headband.

He wore a pair of brass armbands, and had bands of cow tail hair under his knees, and above his elbows. A thin loop of hide around his waist served to support a fur groin covering in front, as well as a flap of soft cowhide in back.

Though he was advanced in years, his steps were still limber, and there was no softness to his belly. His eyes held the glint of iron as he looked to Mawa and Sigananda.

Signananda and Mawa both bowed their heads in respect to the umuzi's chieftain.

Bhambatha glanced briefly towards the skin of the Dreganfel. "I have heard of what happened out there. Thank you for intervening on behalf of that fool, Digane," Bhambatha said to Sigananda. "He admitted his stupidity openly, and what you did to save him and the others from being slaughtered."

"It is nothing to be commended, I would confront any danger to one of our people," Sigananda replied, in a low voice.

"Hearing of three warriors slain darkens the matter I must discuss with you," Bhambatha said. "I come to you as the shadow of a terrible danger falls over all our people."

Signananda nodded.

"Mawa has told you of the looming war, and the presence of Gibini and Enundu among our enemies?" Bhambatha asked, his gaze hardening as he spoke the names of the infamous Wizards.

"Yes," Sigananda answered, as Mawa nodded her affirmation at his side.

"Then you know that the uFalaza will be summoned," Bhambatha continued.

Sigananda nodded again. "When my ibutho is called to the ikhanda, I will be ready, as would be any warrior of the Amazu."

"It will not be a war. It will be a massacre, without one javelin thrown," Bhambatha stated, somberly. "This will not be a war decided by thousands clashing under open skies."

"Gibini and Enundu?" Signananda asked, knowing what the other man referred to.

Bhambatha nodded. "They will send a plague amongst us. I am certain of this, as sickness and disease are the weapons those two vile beings wield. No ibutho can stop such a thing. The sorcerers will loose a deadly affliction that will drift into the imizi, all throughout our lands. No umuzi will go untouched as the winds carry disease from one end of Amazu territory to the other."

"Then we must find a way to stop Gibini and Enundu," Sigananda said, though he wondered how such a thing could be accomplished.

"That is why I have come to speak with you. I have already spoken to Mawa, and know her counsel. I release you from your obligations to the uFalaza, so that you can go a different way," Bhambatha said.

Sigananda glanced to Mawa, and recognized at once that the topic had been extensively discussed between the chieftain and the isangoma. He could tell that the two were of the same mind regarding the matter at hand.

"Go to the Lake of Heaven," Bhambatha told Sigananda. "Seek help from the immortals dwelling there. They bear no fondness for the two who seek to destroy us. Then search out the devilry of Gibini and Enundu, and destroy it. You can do what an army cannot. The amabutho will go to confront the Ewandwe that march on our lands. Most eyes will be drawn towards that clash, which is what Gibini and Enundu are counting on. They will not be counting on one such as you, moving to strike at their plans."

Signananda did not know how to respond. He knew that Bhambatha regarded him with high favor, but he had never been singled out in such a way by the chieftain.

Mawa might have had difficulty convincing one of the more veteran warriors in the umuzi regarding the task being discussed, but Bhambatha would not encounter the same resistance. He was the most experienced warrior, and he was the leader of the umuzi. While the few warriors sharing a level of experience close to his might harbor reticence at being told to go on such a daunting journey, they would ultimately cooperate.

There were other concerns as well. The Lake of Heaven, the

enormous lake at the boundaries of Amazu land, spawned many tales speaking of immortal beings. Yet nobody that Sigananda knew had ever encountered one there. He did not have the first idea regarding how to search for the rumored individuals.

"You will not be going alone," Bhambatha stated. "Mawa will go with you."

Sigananda turned towards Mawa, a look of surprise spreading on his face.

"Did you think I would abandon you in this task?" Mawa said, with a grin. "I still have enough strength left in this aging body of mine to make the journey. I may need some time to rest when we return, but I am prepared to go with you."

"Mawa will help you find the immortal ones, and will be there during the journey to give you counsel," Bhambatha said.

The news came as a soothing relief to Sigananda. The things of flesh and blood he could handle, but the chieftain was sending him on a journey that involved realms he did not understand.

An Ilkwa could penetrate the body of a Dreganfel, but the weapon was useless against anything that held no physical form. Whatever was being sent by Gibini and Enundu would almost certainly entail the latter.

"Mawa will help you search out the workings of Gibini and Enundu," Bhambatha said.

A thought struck Sigananda, at that moment. "I should dress for war, as I am going forth like I would for my ibutho."

Bhambatha nodded. "In a way, it is like you are an ibutho of one warrior."

Signananda nodded slowly, taking in the implications of

Bhambatha's words. One warrior was being sent forth to cut down an entire war.

It was a staggering thought, one that Signananda would have to banish from his mind. He would have to keep all of his focus upon the task at hand.

"I will do everything in my ability to carry out this task," Sigananda said.

"I know you will, that is why Mawa and I have asked this of you," Bhambatha replied.

***

The night passed in a state of restlessness. The same concerns tormented him over and over again.

Sigananda understood the things of iron, but not of magic, and he was being asked to seek out individuals whose very nature was intertwined with non-physical arts. Once that had been accomplished, he was to confront the workings of hostile Wizards, and find a way to destroy them. Without question, it was the most difficult task he had ever been assigned, but he was not about to back away from it.

He endured a fitful sleep, waking often, and rolling from one side to the other. Sigananda was relieved when dawn finally broke, and the seemingly interminable night finally came to an end.

He took a few moments to slip on his cowtail arm and leg bands, the former resting just above his elbows, and the latter below his knees. He would not be going forth with the uFalaza, but he was going to war. As Bhambatha had said, he was a regiment consisting of one warrior, and an isangoma.

Pausing for a moment, he assembled his hunting shield. Mostly black, except for a few small spots of white, the cow-hide shield had a sequence of hide lacing running down the back side. A timber shield pole, topped with an ornamental crest of Baka fur, was fitted down the center.

He ran his fingers along the dark, coarse fur, remembering his fierce encounter with the sharp-fanged, long-snouted ape from which the fur had come. Just coming of age, Signananda would have been forgiven for feeling unsettled at the prospects of tangling with a powerful creature only a head shorter than he was, possessed with canines the length of a spear blade, and imbued with strength far exceeding his own. But something emerged within Sigananda that day, as the beast rushed at him, screeching and intent on tearing him apart.

A calm descended on his mind, seeming to slow time itself, and he had seen the opening for his spear that brought down the ape with one strike. Ever since, he had been able to keep his wits collected during the worst of tempests.

Gathering up his weapons, he exited his dwelling, and made his way around the large herd of cattle quartered for the night within the umuzi. Taking in the chilly air with each breath, he felt the grogginess sloughing off, as his body limbered up.

The sky had begun to lighten overhead, the deep black slowly graying with the promise of morning. Gazing east, he saw that the edge of the horizon carried the touch of the sun's glow. Dawn had arrived, with all of its prospects and potential dangers.

Mawa was waiting for him at the gates to the umuzi. Standing with her was a man well familiar to Sigananda. A cumbersome-looking necklace of gourds and horns was slung around his neck. A lengthy walking staff was in one hand, and a large hide pouch was in the other.

Dinizulu, was a prominent inyanga, or healer, regarded as one of the most skilled among all the Amazu. Having an inyanga join him and Mawa for the undertaking was a boon he had not expected.

Sigananda was not entirely surprised to see Dinizulu. The forthcoming journey, involving an active search for Wizards, could well result in the attainment of items useful for healing ailments.

"A good day for a journey," Mawa greeted him, with a welcoming smile.

"A journey whose destination I still do not know," Sigananda replied.

"Those words could describe life itself," Mawa remarked.

"They could, but I still wish I knew what we seek on this journey," Sigananda replied. "When I hunt, I know the animals in the territory I hunt in. When I go to war, I know the kind of warriors I will face in battle. I do not know what I am going to hunt, or what I will have to face on this task."

"I do not know what we will find, but I am ready to gain whatever I can to help our people," Dinizulu interjected.

Signanda smiled. "You are afraid of nothing, Dinizulu. I have long admired your bravery."

Many were the stories telling of the solitary journeys undertaken by Dinizulu, as he sought out rare herbs and remedies to treat a sick member of the umuzi. Dinizulu had courage in abundance, matching that of the great warriors in Sigananda's opinion.

"I do not see it as bravery. It is simply that what must be done, must be done," Dinizulu said evenly.

"Which is why I am here, even if I do not know where this path leads," Sigananda replied, understanding Dinizulu more keenly than ever before.

"Then let us begin with the first step," Mawa said, with a smile.

The trio took their first steps away from the umuzi, and began their trek to the Lake of Heaven. The day proceeded without incident, as they passed under the shadows of hills and along the edges of deep gorges.

It was easy enough to live off the land, with the abundance of game in the area. The inyanga's extensive knowledge of plants and roots also contributed to the available fare. Sigananda took great care to study all signs that he came across, lest they wander into the territory of something dangerous, as Digane had done only a day before.

When night fell across the land, they took up camp in the lee of a great stone, jutting from the side of a hill. Sheltered from the elements, they were able to get a little rest, taking turns at watch, with Sigananda taking the bulk of the time himself.

The shelter was largely unnecessary, as the climate had been consistently dry, and there was no threat of rain that evening. Yet it was still reassuring to have some cover, if only to conceal themselves in the wilderness.

With a bright moon to light their way, they set off before the sun rose. Mawa estimated that they were very close to the Lake of Heaven, a place tied intimately to the world of the Amazu.

It was more familiar to those such as Mawa and Dinizulu, but Sigananda had heard more than a few things about it in the tales he had heard. Wizards of a benevolent disposition were said to live there, working their arts from time to time on behalf of the Amazu people.

While the Wizards did not seem to wish entanglement with the affairs of the Amazu, neither did they shun the people who were their neighbors. Sigananda could only hope that they were receptive to the little delegation sent at the behest of Bhambatha.

After another day's journey, they drew near to the lake, but with night falling, they decided to halt and make camp. After procuring some food for his two companions, he took the first watch, knowing sleep would evade him that night.

He felt both eagerness and anxiety, now that they were close to the first part of their task. Looking upon the sleeping forms of Mawa and Dinizulu, Signananda felt tremendous gratitude that they were there with him.

He had no idea how he was going to summon the immortal beings that dwelled at the lake, and they could not gain aid against Gibini and Enundu if they did not succeed in finding the Wizards. Mawa and Dinizulu had both seemed very calm that evening, and Signanda drew confidence from their demeanors.

***

Sigananda approached the lakeshore at daybreak. Sparkling with crystalline elegance, the lake was vast in size.

Neither the ends of the near shore, nor the opposite one, could be seen from the place where Sigananda came to a halt, at the water's edge. It was the kind of majestic place that seemed appropriate for immortals, the beauty of the scene carrying a timeless essence.

Mawa and Dinizulu came up from behind to join him. For a few moments the three stood in silence, appreciating the grandeur of the lake at sunrise.

"It is time," Mawa said finally, in a calm voice. "I will call to them."

She fell into a deep silence, and closed her eyes. Sigananda watched as her body began to sway, and a low, melodic humming came from within her.

For some time, nothing happened, and Sigananda found himself relaxing, listing to the soothing melodies coming from Mawa. He stood up a little straighter when a figure came into sight, walking at a relaxed pace along the shore towards them. As the individual drew closer, Sigananda saw that it was a woman who approached them, one of most exquisite beauty.

Skin unblemished, like the smoothest ebony, the woman brimmed with the luster of youthful vitality. Her dark eyes were filled with merriment, as her even, snow-white teeth shone brightly in the smile she cast Sigananda and his companions.

Sigananda had seen many beautiful women, both in his umuzi and others he had visited, but none approached the comeliness of the woman standing before him. Mawa had lowered her eyes in reverence, but Sigananda could not stop staring at the woman.

Noticing his unwavering attention, she laughed cheerfully, a harmonious sound that sparked a light feeling of joy within him.

"Mawa. Your visit is unexpected," she addressed them, her voice as elegant as her appearance. She glanced towards Dinuzulu, and nodded her head.

"This is Dinizulu, inyanga of our umuzi," Mawa said, in the way of introduction.

"Welcome Dinizulu, I have heard your name well-spoken of," the woman replied.

Dinizulu, whose eyes were also lowered, gave a slight smile, as he bowed his head towards her.

She then turned her eyes to Sigananda. "I know of you, from visions, and the whispers in my ear. Welcome, Sigananda, warrior of the Amazu."

Signananda's breath caught in his chest as she said his name. The last thing he had anticipated was for her to know his name.

"A danger approaches, great Lomo," Mawa said, in a low, deferential tone. "It is what has brought us to the Lake of Heaven, to seek you and the others who dwell here."

"I desire only peace," Lomo replied, her voice growing more somber, as some of the gaiety left her lively eyes. "But this world assails peace without rest. It is an adversary of peace, in its very nature. Those who wish for peace must be vigilant always, and keep strength. Do you seek peace?"

"Yes, great Lomo. We wish to stop a war, before it begins," Mawa answered. "A war in which many thousands will die."

"To stop a war?" Lomo asked, with a hint of surprise reflected in her tone of voice. "Does war loom over your lands? This I have not heard."

"The Ewandwe gather for war, it is said," Sigananda stated, feeling that he needed to participate in the conversation, if something of importance was going to be asked of him.

"The Ewandwe do not have the strength to wage war against the Amazu," Lomo said, looking at Signanda for a moment. Her eyes shifted back to Mawa. "Who stands with them?"

"Gibini ... and Enundu," Mawa said, a heavy edge to her voice as she spoke the names aloud.

A shadow of alarm passed across Lomo's face, and her eyes flicked between the other three. "Gibini and Enundu are joined in common cause?"

Mawa nodded, with a grave expression.

Lomo stared off across the lake. "Then a great danger is coming to all. Your tidings are a part of something much worse, as a very powerful evil seeks to spread its shadow across your lands and others."

"I do not mean to upset you, great Lomo," Mawa said. "We simply need your help. Whatever Gibini and Enundu have created, we wish to stop it before it reaches the heart of the Amazu people."

"You are wise to have come here, Mawa," Lomo replied, her eyes still fixed towards the lake. "Let me summon Lubangala. He will know better what to do to resist the evil of Gibini and Enundu."

Like Mawa had done earlier, Lomo closed her eyes, and fell silent for several moments. Unlike the isangoma, she did not utter any chant or hum, but her eyes remained oriented towards the lake when she opened them once again.

A mist began forming over the waters, like a cloud

manifesting, spreading outward and down as it grew. As Signanda and the others watched the swelling mass of vapor in the morning sunlight, a rainbow path began to form, arcing along a gentle slope to where it leveled out along the lake surface.

Stretching from the cloud to the shore, the pathway was dazzling in its vibrant appearance. Sigananda was forced to squint, as it was difficult to look upon with its rich, shifting hues.

"This is indeed a sacred place," Mawa said softly, her voice filled with wonder, as they looked upon the iridescent pathway.

As she spoke, another figure approached, first emerging out of the hovering cloud, and then walking along the rainbow path. Sigananda marveled at the spectacle, knowing that powerful arts were at work.

The figure was a man in the middle of his years, tall of height, with broad shoulders. He carried a strong aura about him, something a warrior like Sigananda sensed immediately.

"Lubangala, a guardian of this place, and one who seeks to protect any people from those who would wield the powers of the lower realms," Lomo announced, as the man drew closer.

Lubangala stepped from the kaleidoscopic pathway to the shore. As he did so, the pathway and the cloud dissipated, and faded from view.

Lubangala looked for a moment at Mawa, inclining his head slightly. He then acknowledged Dinizulu with a glance, before he fixed his eyes upon Sigananda. There was a powerful intensity to his gaze, as if he was looking into every shadowy recess within Sigananda's spirit.

After a few moments, he gave another slight incline of his

head, though his expression remained stern. "You will need all your resolve, and all your courage, to stand before Gibini and Enundu," Lubangala told Sigananda. His deep voice had a powerful, authoritative quality, of the kind with a solid foundation of wisdom and experience.

"How do I fight them?" Sigananda asked, wondering how in the world he could combat a pair of the most powerful Wizards ever to walk in their lands.

"They are too strong, even for one such as you," Lubangala replied. "But they will send a vessel into your lands. It will be one in which they will concentrate their power, to deliver the evil they have worked. Empty this vessel, and it will be a long while before they can threaten your people again."

"A vessel?" Sigananda asked, a little perplexed.

"You will know," Lubangala replied. He cast a glance towards Mawa. "And she will help you find the vessel they have chosen."

The response was not what he had hoped for, in terms of clear answers. Another part of him wondered why it would be Mawa that would have to find the vessel, and not one of the immortal Wizards.

"And how can I empty this vessel?" Sigananda asked.

"Jokinam tends a herd of sacred cattle within the lake. We will call him forth, and you are to fill a skin with the milk of one of the cattle," Lubangala instructed.

Lubangala turned towards the water, and spread his hands outward. He called out in a language Sigananda did not understand, his deep tones echoing across the rippling lake surface.

After some time had passed, the surface of the lake began to churn, disturbed by something coming up from beneath it. Shortly, the tips of many pairs of horns broke the surface, water glistening in the sun off the extended outgrowths as they rose upward.

The horns were followed a moment later by the robust bodies of the large cattle they were connected to. The beasts were of a quality far exceeding the best of the Amazu king's own herd. The smallest cow in the emerging group was greater in height and girth than the bull in the herd quartered at Sigananda's umuzi.

The bull of the herd from the lake was a sight to behold when it finally emerged. An enormous, regal creature bulging with muscle, its massive hooves sank deep into the ground as it plodded out of the water.

A man walked out of the water alongside the herd of cattle. He did not have the imposing presence of Lubangala, but he also carried an aura of strength about him. He watched the herd as it sprawled out into the area just beyond the shore, but kept near to Lubangala and the others.

"Hand me a waterskin," Jokinam invited.

Dinuzulu walked forward, and gave him one of the empty skins he had carried along on the journey. Jokinam walked over to one of the nearest cows, and set one knee on the ground.

He proceeded to milk the cow until the skin was full. The cow remained calm throughout, staying completely still and not making any sounds.

Jokinam handed the skin back over to Sigananda when it was full. "The milk has great healing powers, and will negate the arts of Gibini and Enundu in anyone that this is given to."

Signanda accepted the skin, and nodded to the Wizard. "I

thank you."

"Ah, Ketua, you have finally arrived," Lubangala stated.

Sigananda followed Lubangala's gaze. Yet another man had joined them in the interim, standing quietly next to Lomo. The trace of laughter rested in his eyes and face, and the broad smile he gave Signanada was filled with goodwill.

"Ketua will bestow a final gift upon you, before you go forward," Lubangala said. "Stand before him, Sigananda."

About to take the first step, Sigananda hestitated, and looked back to Lubangala. "Can you not send one of your own with us on this journey?"

A grim expression came to the Wizard's face. He shook his head slowly. "No, we cannot. All our strength must be put to another task. As I see it, the One who has mastered the spirits of Gibini and Enundu is also behind this other devilry."

"Is it a threat to the Amazu?" Sigananda asked.

Lubangala shook his head. "Not yet, but no less than Itonde, Esu, and Inkanyamba move to help an upstart warrior in the Akembe lands. It is not a coincidence that they do so as Gibini and Enundu move to strike your lands."

Sigananda looked over to Mawa, who looked aghast at the news. Inkanyamba was said to be able to wield the power of storms, able to summon cyclones from storm-churned skies. Itonde's arts were steeped in the power of death, while Esu was a master at deception.

That all three of them were united in purpose unnerved Sigananda, and he wondered what was underlying all of it. Like Lubangala, he knew in his heart that the actions of the two groups of hostile Wizards were part of something much larger.

"Do not worry yourself over them," Lubangala said, speaking to Sigananda and his companions. "Esu, Itonde, and Inkanyamba are our concern. The vessel sent by Gibini and Enundu are your concern."

"I will do all in my power to stop them," Sigananda said, with resolve.

"Receive a gift from Ketua," Lubangala said.

Signanda nodded, walked up to Ketua, and stood quietly before him. The amiable-looking Wizard gave him a warm smile, and set his hands on the top of Sigananda's head. He uttered some words in the strange language Lubangala had used earlier.

Sigananda did not feel anything in particular, having expected some kind of sensation to pass from the Wizard's hands into him. The magical arts were truly difficult to comprehend, and while Sigananda longed for his world of muscle and iron, he cooperated patiently enough.

Once he was finished with Sigananda, Ketua moved onward and repeated the act with Mawa and Dinizulu.

"You are now ready for your journey, Sigananda of the Amazu people," Lubangala proclaimed.

Sigananda looked to Mawa and Dinizulu. "Then let us begin, with the first step, is that right Mawa?"

Mawa smiled back at him. After thanking the Wizards and taking leave of them, the three resumed their journey.

***

Sigananda and his companions hiked to the south and east, for the better part of two days. Mawa and Dinizulu kept up with him well enough, and Mawa used her arts from time to time to help him adjust his direction.

Towards the end of the second day, Sigananda came across some human tracks. Crouching down, he saw that they were heading north. He also noted the tracks had been made with sandals, and not bare feet. That told him immediately that the impressions had been created by the Ewandwe.

He looked back to Mawa and Dinizulu, who were catching up to him. "Ewandwe. A small number, maybe five."

Mawa closed her eyes, as a steady hum came from inside her. She rotated slightly to the right, and then back to the left, as if honing in on something. At last, her eyes fluttered open, and she looked to Signananda as she pointed in the direction she was facing.

"The vessel is this way. The taint of dark magic is unmistakable, I can feel its corruption in the natural order," she declared, a look of disgust on her face. "They are not far."

When Dinizulu and Mawa started forward, Signanda moved in front of them, stopping the pair in their tracks. He told them firmly. "No, stay back for now. Let me scout this out. Maybe I can see what we are up against."

The other two nodded, as Signanda turned and headed off in the direction Mawa had indicated.

***

Looking over the hill, Sigananda saw several Ewandwe warriors. There were five in all, as he had guessed from the tracks he had come across.

Four of them wore single-feather headdresses, with an adornment worn around their necks that suspended a broad fringe of cow-tails down their backs. The fifth was attired in a distinct fashion from the others, having a kilt of fur strips, as well as another ring of fur strips wrapped around his chest. He had a headdress fitted with long plumes of black feathers.

The first four looked strong enough, but the fifth was a giant of a warrior. He was taller and broader of shoulder than Sigananda, bristling with muscle. He was easily the largest man that Sigananda had ever seen.

After a little observation, it became clear that the group did not feel any imminent threats. They were not careless, but neither were they as disciplined as Sigananda would have been.

Sigananda settled into the grass, finding a more comfortable position as he took up a sustained watch upon the five Ewandwe. He knew that sooner or later a couple of them would leave the others, whether to gather some food, see to a call of nature, or scout out the area.

Like a Dreganfel stalking its quarry, Sigananda would be there when they did.

***

Sigananda reached back and whipped his arm forward, sending the spear tearing through the air. The warrior jerked abruptly, as the spearhead buried deep into his back. The Ewandwe warrior had never seen it coming, nor had he suspected he was being hunted until it was too late.

The man's companion whirled about, bringing spear and shield up, looking around frantically. Sigananda could see the fear splayed across the man's face as he sprang up and lunged towards the Ewandwe warrior with his Ilkwa.

He batted aside the warrior's attempt to strike him, swiftly finding an opening for the Ilkwa. The warrior gasped and crumbled to the ground, as Sigananda pulled the blade free from the other man's side.

After making sure that both Ewandwe warriors were dead, Sigananda set out for their camp. The coming fight would be much more evenly matched with three against one.

The skills displayed by the two he had just cut down told him that he had little to worry about regarding the other two with the single-feathers. The giant warrior he was not as sure of, and he wondered whether he might be the vessel the Wizards at the Lake of Heaven had indicated. He would find out soon enough.

***

Again like a Dreganfel ambushing its prey, Sigananda leaped from the grasses with his Ilkwa. He lanced the Ilkwa into the Ewandwe warrior as he was seeing to a call of nature, hewing him down where he stood.

It was not so far from the camp site that the others failed to hear the grunt of their companion from the Ilkwa blade. There

248

were only two left, and the smaller of the remaining pair rushed at Sigananda, shouting angrily as his footsteps pounded the dry ground.

He reached Sigananda, and a moment later was sprawled out on the ground, his belly opened wide by the Amazu warrior's Ilkwa. His agony did not last long, as Sigananda moved in and finished him off swiftly.

Stomping forward with his war shield and spear in hand, the giant Ewandwe warrior's gaze bored into Sigananda with lethal intent. Sigananda deflected the warrior's first spear thrusts with his own shield, feeling the tremendous power behind them. The Ewandwe giant proved to be skilled and fast for his size, as he blocked some initial counterattacks from Sigananda.

The enemy warrior surged at Sigananda, putting him entirely on the defensive. The giant wielded a combination of power and speed, with a sustained series of rapid spear thrusts and robust strikes using the facing of his shield. One of the latter almost knocked Signanada off balance. That would have been the death of him, as the Ewandwe warrior would have followed with his spear.

As it was, Sigananda incurred several moments of searing pain, as his opponent's spear nicked and slashed his skin in many places. Blood trickled from several light wounds, but none were serious enough to hamper his movements.

Sigananda slashed back desperately with his Ilkwa as he weathered the relentless attack. The giant finally ceased the assault. Signananda could hear the man breathing heavily after the extensive exertion, and recognized his chance to turn the momentum around.

Practiced thousands of times over, a maneuver instilled in him during his warrior training surfaced to the fore. Swinging his shield in an arc from right to left, he brought it sweeping inside the shield of his huge opponent.

He put all of his strength into the move. Entangling the shields and creating an opening, he bared the left side of his huge opponent just enough for a thrust with the Ilkwa. The moment he saw the breach in his enemy's defenses, Sigananda drove the blade deep into flesh.

The huge man grunted as Sigananda shoved forward behind his shield, knocking the Ewandwe warrior backwards and toppling him to the ground. Tearing the Ilkwa free, he stabbed it down into the warrior's chest with full force, killing the man instantly.

Bleeding and exhausted, Sigananda stumbled away from the dead warrior. Collecting his thoughts, as the fires of combat ebbed within his veins, he proceeded to search the area. Looking over the bodies of the slain men, he could find nothing resembling a vessel, nor find any clues as to what it possibly was.

Finally, he realized he had done all he could do. It was time to bring in others who were better suited to determine the identity of the vessel.

He left the site, and returned some time later with Mawa and Dinizulu. Mawa looked around at the fallen warriors, and, accompanied by Dinizulu, she examined each one with scrutiny. After some time had passed, she turned towards Sigananda with a grim expression, shaking her head.

"The taint of the vessel is upon them, but the vessel is not here," Mawa said firmly. "We must continue onward."

***

Trusting his instincts, and Mawa's guidance, Signananda followed the tracks of the five warriors to the north. From time to time, Mawa used her mystic abilities to probe for the vessel, and confirm their direction. Bolstering Siganinda's hopes of finding the vessel, the path she oriented upon paralleled the physical tracks every time.

They eventually came across a place where the tracks of two other individuals separated from the five warriors. Where the warrior's tracks continued south, the other pair went north.

The tracks were much smaller in size, and made with bare feet. The only conclusion Sigananda could make was that they were those of children. The discovery puzzled him, but Mawa's arts indicated that the vessel was indeed somewhere towards the north. With his companions, Sigananda pressed onward, intent on seeking out the ones who had made the smaller set of tracks.

***

Sigananda watched the two small figures heading right towards an umuzi. It took him only a few moments to see that they were children, undoubtedly the ones he had been tracking.

The sight of them triggered an urgent sense of alarm in Sigananda, though they appeared to be carrying nothing. He wished that Mawa was next to him, as he wanted her insights, but she was still coming up from farther behind with Dinizulu.

Sigananda, recognizing fresher tracks, had ranged a short distance ahead of them, eager to see if he could discover the makers of the tracks. Now that he had found them, he regretted his hastiness.

A group of women from the umuzi were well outside the protective palisade, balancing some containers on their head as they went about some menial task. They turned as the children approached, and set the containers down. A couple of women moved towards the children, who kept walking forward.

A feeling of cold dread clutched Sigananda as he watched the children and the Amazu women coming together. Something was very wrong with the situation.

Trusting to his instincts, he began running towards them. His legs churned as fast as he could possibly will them to, but he was slowed down a little by the Ilkwa, shield, and the skin filled with the milk from the lake-dwelling herd.

When he reached the others, the women were all slumping over, sweat beaded all over their bodies. They were shaking as if they were freezing, their teeth clattering within their mouths.

The two children turned towards him, as he slowed down and came to a stop. A boy and a girl, the outer appearances of the children chilled Sigananda's soul.

Their necks looked far too thin to support their large heads, and their limbs were little more than bones wrapped in withered skin. Distended bellies, swollen from advanced starvation, gave them an ungainly appearance.

Dull, lifeless eyes stared at Sigananda, containing no pupils.

Puss oozed from the bottoms of the sockets.

They began shuffling towards him, as he glanced back towards the women on the ground. Most were clearly dead, their sightless eyes staring from faces draped with misery and pain. Looking over them in horror, a hollow death rattle came from the throat of the last woman clinging to a shred of life, as she finally died.

Turning his attention back to the children, he realized the vessel had been found. Before they reached him, he was already feeling lightheaded, as something insidious began to take hold from inside of him.

He knew what was happening. The same supernaturally-empowered plague that killed the women was beginning the process of claiming him.

Above all, he knew he had to empty the two vessels, or the umuzi beyond would be filled with death. It was not a simple matter of killing the children. That was something he would have loathed to do, but would have done if it were the only way of stopping the plague.

The vessels had to be cleaned, including the sorcery involved. Sigananda knew that the bodies of the children would remain vessels, whether they remained alive or not; and they were already well inside the lands of the Amazu.

Casting aside his Ilkwa and shield, both useless for the task at hand, he brought the skin with the milk from Jokinam's herd up. Sigananda lurched towards the first of the children.

Stumbling, and almost tripping, he reached the young boy and grabbed him with one hand. The child made no move to resist, as Sigananda quickly poured the milk past the young one's parched, sore-riddled lips.

Sweat trickled from every pore in his body as he turned towards the second child. He shivered as an icy embrace took firm hold. His teeth chattered, as his vision danced. The plague was advancing within him with every heartbeat.

With every last bit of will he could dredge up, he clutched onto the waterskin. Instead of drinking of the milk himself, he lifted it to the young girl's lips with the last strength left inside him. His muscles began to spasm, right as he got the top to the child's frail lips.

Some of the milk escaped her mouth, but a little dribbled into her. As it coursed down the child's throat, Sigananda sagged to the ground, weakness flooding him.

He did not have any strength left to lift the skin to save himself. His head swimming, and feeling tremendous disorientation, he fell heavily onto his back. Half-conscious, he looked up into the sky, and could only hope that he had done enough.

A couple of heartbeats later, he barely cared. The delirium permeated his slipping consciousness.

With his powerful body, he had lasted longer than the women from the umuzi. Being able to endure a few moments longer was fortuitous in that he was able to reach the children, but the end was going to be the same as that of the hapless women.

"Your tale is not to end here, Sigananda," Mawa's voice sounded faintly, seeming like it came from a far distance.

A faded part of him felt something bump his lips. Something warm trickled down his throat. He slid further, his eyes fluttering, as nothing seemed to matter anymore.

Then, the chill over his body and the tingling deep in his muscles began to recede. The dizziness still pervaded him, but something was resisting the claim of death.

His weakening heartbeats became much more sturdy. It felt as if he was coming out from the depths of a cave, as clarity slowly returned to his mind. Blinking his eyes, he looked upward, and saw Mawa smiling down at him through her painted face.

"My tale ... is not to end here?" Sigananda asked her weakly.

She shook her head. "No, Sigananda, it is not to end here."

He sat up, and looked about, seeing that the two children were standing together, a short distance away. Amazingly, the starved appearance was gone completely. Their bodies were at a normal proportion and weight, and the children's eyes were no longer the pale white orbs they had been.

Dark pupils focused on Sigananda, alert and wary. The children looked very frightened. They huddled close together, dividing their glances between Signananda, Mawa, and Dinizulu.

Signananda had to admit that the sight of a huge warrior, an isangoma with a painted face and strange headdress, and an inyanga with his array of containers made for a strange, intimidating sight to young eyes.

"It is okay, nobody will harm you," Sigananda said gently. They showed no reaction to his words.

"Are you Ewandwe?" Mawa asked gently, using the language of the other tribe. Sigananda knew enough of the Ewandwe tongue to follow the exchange.

The children nodded, but remained silent.

"Then we will see that you are returned home," Mawa said

softly. "We will not keep you from your families."

The fear heightened immediately on the faces of the two children. It was like Mawa had threatened them.

"What frightens you, children?" Mawa asked, a perplexed look on her face.

"The two bad men. They kill all our village," the young boy said, his body trembling.

"The two bad men?" Mawa asked, casting sideways glances to Sigananda and Dinizulu.

"Bad men make us sick," the girl said. "Bad men send us with warriors."

The boy nodded in agreement with his young companion, and added, "Warriors give us drink, and tell us to walk to village. We get sick on way."

"Gibini and Enundu," Mawa said.

The names caused the two children to tense up, and their eyes to widen.

"The bad men?" Mawa asked.

Both nodded emphatically.

"Don't let bad men get us," the young girl begged, panic brimming in her voice.

Mawa shook her head quickly. "No, the bad men will not get you."

"They kill village. Mother and father dead," the boy said, his eyes beginning to tear up.

"Me too," the girl added, also starting to cry.

Mawa moved over, and cradled the two children to her with her arms. To Sigananda, she no longer looked like an isangoma, despite her distinctive garb. She was the image and essence of a mother, working to sooth two frightened children.

Her effect was immediate, as the sobs of the two children lessened, and then stopped. Both of them returned her embrace, hugging onto her tightly.

"It is okay. Bad men will not get you here. We will care for you, and protect you," Mawa said soothingly, continuing to hold the two children close.

She looked to Sigananda and the Dinizulu, and an agreement passed between them.

"You will come with us, to our umuzi, and you will have a wonderful home," Mawa said. "You will have a new family."

The children looked up through their tear-reddened eyes, and a look of hope arose on their faces. The sight brought great joy to Sigananda as he watched.

After taking a few more moments to orient himself, Sigananda got back up to his feet slowly, feeling renewed in both body and soul. The fight had been won, war had been averted, and the malevolent designs of the two enemy Wizards had been overcome.

The joy was dampened a little as his eyes fell upon the bodies of the women from the umuzi. When he spoke, he used the Amazu tongue, so as not to trouble the two children. "And the women who have fallen here?" he asked.

"It is probably best not to touch the bodies now," Dinizulu said. "I will see to it that the bodies are put to flame."

"And I have entreated the Creator-Spirit to welcome their spirits," Mawa said.

"I will pray for them also," Sigananda said, saddened by the suffering they had endured.

"But let us celebrate the two children you have saved this day, Sigananda," Mawa said, drawing his attention back to where she stood with the young ones.

"Yes, that is something wonderful to celebrate. Let us show them to their new homes," Sigananda proclaimed, his mood brightening once again. "We also have some very good tidings to bring to our people."

"I think we should get some rest and food first. The children would not mind that," Dinizulu said.

"No, I do not think they would object," Mawa agreed.

"It is a short journey to that umuzi," Sigananda said, looking off in the direction of the palisade-encircled cluster of huts.

"Then let us begin the journey with the first step," Mawa replied, with a beaming smile, as she took the hands of the two children and started towards the umuzi.

Land of Shadow

Land of Shadow

"Little by little, one travels far."
-J. R. R. Tolkien

Crouched amid a sprawling batch of low brush, and perched atop a lengthy ridgeline, Godfrey peered downward. A group of strange figures gathered out on the flatter stretch of ground occupied his attention in full.

The Avanoran knight observed the entities in a state of fascination and curiosity. Long-limbed, the creatures were lean in build, every striation of muscle visible, and joint pronounced, along their sinewy forms.

Large, hairless craniums held a pair of broad eyes, set well back from their protruding, rounded jaws. Two low-profile nostrils were situated just above their upper lips. Hard to see from a distance, the nasal cavities flowed straight back along the oblong shape of their heads.

With a quality similar to those of a horse, the air passages left the creatures without a projecting nose like most human and humanoid races. Reflective of their nasal structure, the beasts had small ear holes, instead of any external structures.

Their arms were notably lengthy in proportion to their bodies. From what the Avanoran observed, they tended to move about in a hunched posture, bracing themselves often with their upper appendages. He had not seen them run yet, but from their forms he guessed they could use their arms to help propel them forward.

The sandy tones of their skin blended extremely well with the sparse surroundings. He could see a little ornamentation on them in the forms of necklaces, arm bands, and a kind of torque, though the details escaped him at the considerable distance.

Large-footed, they wore no kind of shoe. The only clothing on their bodies was a type of hide kilt, of a hue closely matching the color of their skin, and descending to about the mid-thigh.

Under a sky dotted with puffy, white cloud formations, stretching on seemingly forever, a dry land riddled with scrub and short, misshapen trees radiated in all directions. It was an environment that cast forth a sparse, enduring aura, looking perfectly suited for such rugged-looking creatures.

"Khalan warriors," Godfrey muttered, under his breath.

He had never seen one of the Khalas with his own eyes, but there was no mistaking the features he observed. He had heard more than a few descriptions of the Khala, from those brave or reckless enough to trek through the Shadowlands.

"Not too many of them to be a danger," replied Fulcher, in a low voice. "A small patrol or hunting party, most likely."

"We still need not attract attention," Godfrey responded tersely, casting Fulcher a hard look. His mercenary companion had been prone to underestimate situations before, and the last thing they needed to do in an entirely foreign environment was to presume there was nothing to worry about. "We are yet strangers to these lands."

The large company of Avanorans had pressed eastward for several days, following a harrowing journey by sea. All were hardy mercenary fighters, save for a lone knight of the Order of the High Altar who had catalyzed the expedition.

Bringing ample gold to support the foray, the monk-knight had claimed to be carrying out a request of the Unifier, a storied figure who had recently taken rule over the duchy of Avanor. Whether that was true or not, the monk-knight's gold and the aims of their hiring were more than enough to entice the mercenary band to commit to the highly promising endeavor.

Since they reached its shores, the Shadowlands had already claimed many lives. The deaths had come in a variety of ways that instilled extreme caution in the veteran warriors such as Godfrey.

He was beginning to question his overall judgment in agreeing to go on the journey, the ultimate purpose of which was to locate a propitious site for a fortress. Rumors of jewels, mineral deposits, exotic furs and hides, and much more abounded within the tales filtering back from explorers. Despite the tantalizing claims, the Avanorans were not about to investigate anything, until a well-protected, permanent dwelling site had been established.

The Shadowlands were filled to the brim with dangers. They were like no land Godfrey had ever traveled through before.

To the north, the Wizard Ahriman reigned in his dark mountain fastness, a murky stronghold encompassed by lofty crags and cavernous gorges. No Avanoran of right mind wished to venture there, or even wander close, as many stories told around the campfires spoke of the horrors to be found within the enigmatic being's domain. Things of shadow and flesh, striding the boundaries between the realms of the living and dead, dwelled throughout the northern mountains.

Grey-skinned nightmares with lengthy fangs swooped out of crevice and shadow alike to take unwitting victims. Fiercely loyal to Ahriman, the bloodthirsty, winged creatures warded the main passes leading to the Wizard's massive fortress.

Only a handful of individuals survived an encounter to speak of them, bearing scars for all their remaining years at what had been done to their companions who had not lived to tell the tale. Godfrey had met one such man, who fell into an uncontrollable shaking at the mere mention of the deadly beasts.

Malevolent spirits were said to haunt more than one ancient ruin within the caliginous territory, forsaking hell itself to inhabit decaying corpses and plague the living. Akin to spectral creatures stalking ancient barrows within Midragard, they were not limited to physical means.

Wielding supernatural abilities, and imbued with unnatural strength, they were a pronouncement of death upon anyone unlucky enough to stumble across them. It was said that once they began to pursue a victim, they were relentless, and almost impossible to overcome by natural means.

Beyond those two imposing threats, there were the Khalan tribes dwelling in the harsh lands immediately to the south of the great mountain range. Their territory extended all the way down to the edge of the area where the Avanoran force now traveled. Many of their tribes were said to be under Ahriman's influence, but what was known was that they were not averse to eating the flesh of humans.

As the Avanorans had learned, very painfully, the Khalan tribes were not the only threat to be wary of along the eastward route. Rivers crossing the territory held massive crocodiles, dwarfing those found in the Sun Lands.

The same waters held enormous serpents, scaly brutes longer than some galleys, and capable of swallowing a man whole. Godfrey still recoiled at the remembrance of one Avanoran who had disappeared into one such snake's maw, before it had plunged back into the dark depths of a river they had been fording.

As if that was not enough, they had caught glimpses of other waterborne threats. At a small lake in a gorge, where the water was crystal clear, Godfrey had espied a huge shell in waist-high water just off the shore. He saw it just in time to warn a few Avanorans who were about to cool themselves off in the midday heat. After his comrades had scrambled out of the water, he spotted a number of bones scattered along the lake floor.

As hazardous as any body of water was, the land was no safer. One mounted knight had already been lost to the ambush of a giant spider, whose lair was concealed just under the ground's surface. The terrified scream of the horse, as it was dragged into the lair with the rider, had haunted Godfrey's dreams for several nights afterward.

Fearsome predators abounded, and there was nowhere that Godfrey or any of the others could afford to let their guard down, not even for a heartbeat. Even in a large war band of veteran mercenaries, they were not entirely safe.

Carnivorous baboons, the height of a man, with extended snouts holding dagger-sized canines, roamed in large packs throughout the eastern regions of the Shadowlands. Godfrey hoped that they did not run across one before they had erected a fortress.

The Shadowlands were simply a realm abounding in horrors, as Godfrey had come to find out. He had disciplined himself to constant vigilance, keeping his wits about him at all times.

Not one to be caught unawares, he participated on the probing scouting forays sent out from the main column. He wanted to know about each and every thing they had to be wary of, and there was much to be learned while on scouting duties.

Coming across the group of Khalan warriors, Godfrey had opted to observe them for awhile, a suggestion Fulcher readily agreed to. It was a chance to learn something of one of the main inhabitants of the area, creatures that might become a serious threat to the Avanorans, even after the construction of a fortress.

Making the opportunity even more interesting was the fact that it was a mounted hunting party or patrol. The steeds of the Khalas were exotic, fearsome-looking creatures.

Using one of the short, crooked trees close to the group of Khalan mounts, and the scrub brush around them, Godfrey was able to gauge the size of the steeds. At least twice the length of an average man, and easily over a head taller at their brawny shoulders, the creatures were much larger than the most well-bred of Avanoran war horses.

They had thick, elongated skulls, with pronounced cheek structures that flared out to the sides. A crest of dark bristles ran down their backs. To Godfrey, there were echoes of a boar in the form of the cloven-hoofed creatures. They were nothing he wanted to tangle with at close range.

"Behind you!" Fulcher cried out urgently, his eyes widening, as his warning was joined a heartbeat later by a triumphant, inhuman cry.

As a shadow cloaked him, Godfrey rolled to the side out of instinct. The curved iron blade of a Khalan warrior bit deep into the earth where his body had just been. The deep-set eyes of Godfrey's attacker gleamed, as it swiftly raised the weapon and slashed again at the Avanoran knight.

The blow grazed Godfrey's padded gambeson as he scrambled backwards, seeking to get his feet under him. To his left, the clang of metal broke the air, as Fulcher engaged another attacker blade to blade.

The Khala sprang at Godfrey, the elongated fingers of its oversized hands easily wrapping around the wrist of the knight's sword arm. He felt the great strength in the Khala as his left hand gripped onto the rock-hard muscle and sinew of his enemy's right forearm.

The creature's hot breath was rancid, and its sharp canines were less than a hand's length from Godfrey's face. The Khala's eyes brimmed with wild fury, as it strained vigorously against the Avanoran.

Godfrey sensed the creature would not hesitate to bite him, and resisted with all his might. His attacker pressed in a little closer, a guttural sound coming from its throat.

The Khala loosed a throaty screech as Godfrey snapped his head forward, smashing his iron half-helm into its bestial face. The blow stunned the Khala for a moment, long enough for the Avanoran to free up his left hand.

Without delay, he brought his fist crashing into the round jaw of the Khala, but the impact did little other than to annoy his thick-skulled opponent. The Khala grabbed his arm again, and strained to bite his face, growling savagely. Godfrey exerted with all his might, but the creature was overpowering him.

A look of shock abruptly came to the creature's eyes, as it gagged and hacked up globs of blood. Godfrey felt the strength rapidly draining out of the creature's limbs, and he gave a heave that sent the Khala toppling backwards. A straight blade flashed in an arc, and an inhuman cry of pain lanced the air.

Fulcher stood over the Khala with a bloody sword in hand, and gave Godfrey a grin. "Got the bastard, before he took a chunk out of your pretty little face … but there's more of them coming. Get up quick."

Godfrey got to his feet without delay, and saw that five more of the creatures were hastening towards them, brandishing weapons. They screeched and howled, angered by the deaths of their comrades. As Godfrey had surmised, the Khala used their free arms to help propel themselves across the parched terrain.

Three of the gangly creatures flowed in and surrounded Fulcher. One was armed with a curved blade, and two with spears. The Avanoran's sword flashed in the sunlight, as he parried their first, cautious strikes.

Godfrey did not have time to watch, as the other two Khalas moved in and attacked him, one with a spear, and another with a curved blade. Right at the outset, Godfrey stepped forward and slashed downward, cleaving the shaft of the spear.

Its primary weapon cut in two, the Khalan warrior shrieked in alarm as it was put on the defensive. Godfrey could read the fear flashing within its dark eyes, as he brought his blade upward, in a furious cut. The steel edge bit deeply into the side of the creature, eliciting an agonized howl as blood gushed forth from the lengthy gash in its flank.

Godfrey ripped the blade free, as the Khala slumped down, life draining fast from its mortal wound. He pivoted on his right foot, and saw the Khala with the curved blade loping towards him with lethal intent.

It gave a throaty, grating outcry, waving its weapon overhead as it drew closer to Godfrey. The Khala launched a fierce attack as soon as it was within range.

The strikes of the creature were powerful, but crude and clumsy to a disciplined Avanoran knight. Godfrey's sword quickly found an opening. The blade raced in with power and speed, the steel edge slicing through flesh and bone. Lopping the Khala's head clean off, he watched as the creature's body remained standing for a couple heartbeats longer, before falling over.

Fulcher had already downed two of the Khalas attacking him when Godfrey looked in his direction. He was in the process of going after the remaining Khala, who was backing up under the Avanoran's fierce onslaught.

Staggering it with a backhanded blow using his sword

pommel, sending a spray of blood into the air from the creature's nostrils, Fulcher delivered the killing blow through a thrust to the neck. After the body of the Khala fell to the ground, the air became still once again.

"We took down seven ... with barely a scratch to show for it!" Fulcher boasted, breathing heavily in the wake of the last kill.

"There are likely many more on the way," Godfrey exclaimed solemnly, also working to catch his breath.

He looked down at the inhuman face of one of the attackers. Godfrey knew he could not underestimate the Khalas. They were stronger than a man, and were more than capable of stalking their quarry adeptly. Neither he nor Fulcher had picked up a hint of their approach until they were already upon them.

With knowledge of the terrain and mounts, the Khalas held some daunting advantages. Godfrey did not want to be caught out in the open, and come face to face with one of the Khalas' brutish mounts.

"Keep a look out for others, and let's get away from here, now," Godfrey urged his comrade.

Fulcher nodded his agreement, as his eyes scanned about one more time for other potential attackers. The seven Khalan warriors had come up from behind them, while they were observing the other Khalan party beyond the ridge. There was no telling if more Khalas were concealed within the scattered brush, watching them even now.

Satisfied that no imminent threat loomed, Godfrey and Fulcher raced down the slope. Careful not to get tripped up in the low brush, the knights stayed wary of anything that might emerge suddenly from within it.

Their horses had been tethered within a small group of stunted trees, a few hundred paces from the base of the ridgeline. Godfrey could only hope that the Khalas had not gotten to their steeds first.

The thought spurred him forward as fast as he could move his legs. He kept his sword in hand, listening to the thumping sounds of their footsteps on the dry ground, and the pair's labored breaths, as the mercenaries covered the remaining distance.

The horses neighed and whinnied as the two Avanorans hurried into the cluster of trees, the sounds of the animals coming as a tremendous relief to Godfrey. He and Fulcher wasted no time, and mounted the horses swiftly. Before they had stepped beyond the encircling trees, a dismaying noise filled the air.

Throaty roars announced the approach of several mounted Khalas, the resonant sounds coming from the huge mounts. They were still a good distance away, likely the same band Godfrey and Fulcher had been observing from the ridge-top.

Snapping the reins, and digging his iron prick-spurs into the sides of his mount, Godfrey set his horse into a full gallop. Fulcher kept close as they left the cover of the trees, and set off across the open terrain.

The Khalan warriors screeched when they saw the Avanorans emerge, and maneuvered their brawny mounts to give chase. Thankfully, the massive brutes, while surprisingly fast for their bulk, proved not to be as swift as hale Avanoran horses.

Even so, the Khalas still had a favorable angle on the pair of Avanoran knights. They were able to draw close enough that a couple of them decided to make use of range weapons.

Drawing their mounts to a halt, they quickly set javelins into atlatls. One of the steeds loosed another deep roar, exposing stout tusks within its gaping jaws. Rearing back with their lengthy arms, the Khalas flung the missiles towards Godfrey and Fulcher.

The javelins arced through the air, and the accuracy of the Khalas was proven to be exceptional. One javelin almost struck Fulcher's horse in the rear haunch. Godfrey let out a deep breath, after the other javelin struck his gambeson and fell harmlessly to the ground, failing to penetrate the thick, quilted layer.

It was as close as the Khalas would get to injuring them that day, as the Avanorans pressed their horses onward at haste. The cries of the Khalas faded behind as the Avanorans gained distance, until finally Godfrey could no longer hear them.

The horses had worked up a great lather by the time Godfrey and Fulcher slowed them down to a canter. Turning in his saddle, and eyeing the horizon with rigid scrutiny, he could see no signs of pursuit.

As dry as the ground was, several of the robust Khalan mounts would have kicked up enough dust to be visible from a fair distance. The Khalan band had undoubtedly turned back, as Godfrey thought they would, when they realized that their chase was futile. Nevertheless, Godfrey, like Fulcher, kept up a constant lookout for the Khalas, all the way back to the Avanoran encampment.

When they finally arrived on the outskirts of the ring of low ridge tents and larger, bell-shaped ones, the horses were exhausted. Dismounting, Godfrey and Fulcher walked the beleaguered steeds the remaining distance, the scents of many cook fires stirring Godfrey's mouth into salivation.

His back ached more than a little, and he was weary himself, but it felt good to stroll the remaining distance. The air would soon be cooling precipitously, as night came down. As much as he had been sweating, he looked forward to evening's soothing touch.

"You two look as if you have a tale to tell," greeted an Avanoran named Guillame, who was standing sentry in the area of their approach.

Godfrey nodded, and managed a smile back at the man. "Indeed we do."

Guillame indicated the horses. "Looks like they are in need of some rest too."

"Deserving of a double portion of feed," Godfrey said, patting the neck of his tired mount.

"Anything we should know about from today?" Fulcher inquired.

"Nothing happened on the march," Guillame replied. "I would wager that your tale from today will be the most interesting by far."

"Well, I'm not telling anything about what happened until I get something for my belly," Godrey said, with a grin.

"Plenty of cookfires going now," Guillame told him.

Godrey's grin broadened, the sentry's words like sweet music to his ears.

***

Additional sentries were posted around the boundaries of the camp that night, as Godfrey made certain the Avanorans did not underestimate the Khalas. There was no argument from the other principle leaders of the mercenary contingent, as enough lessons had been learned in blood already.

No attacks occurred that night, though Godfrey did not feel rested when dawn came, having endured a light, restless sleep. After checking on his steed, he passed the early part of the morning tending to his blade. It needed a little work with the whetstone, but overall was not in bad shape. He had little appetite, but ate a small portion of salt pork and hard cheese, washing the meager fare down with a few swigs of wine.

Once the tents had been taken down, and the wagons had been loaded and hitched to horses, the Avanoran contingent set off eastward once again. Eyes watched every horizon for any sign of approaching trouble, as the column got underway.

Like Fulcher, Godfrey opted to stay back with the main body of Avanorans. Both men rode other palfreys to ease the burdens on their primary mounts, and allow them more recovery from the tremendous exertion of the previous day.

The day transpired without incident, as did the one afterwards, as league after league passed by. The monotony was not something to be lamented. If anything, it was a welcome break from what Godfrey and the others had endured, with no deaths suffered, or new horrors uncovered. Even so, Godfrey did not lull into complacency, as everything could change in a heartbeat.

Three days after the encounter with the Khalan warriors, riding near the front of the Avanorans, Godfrey and Fulcher brought their horses to a halt. A couple of Avanoran scouts were approaching from ahead. Scouts returning so early in the day's march indicated that something had been discovered worthy of report.

The other prominent knights in the band gathered with Godfrey and Fulcher, as the scouts neared. The incoming pair did not look particularly rattled, and their horses showed no signs of being hard-pressed, both of which were favorable signs to Godfrey's eyes.

"What news do you bring us?" asked a tall, lean knight named Rogier, as the scouts drew up on the reins of their steeds.

"We are not far from the edge of rolling grasslands, which lead into a broad valley, with forested slopes on its southern edge," the scout to the right, a shorter, stout-looking man named Aimery, announced. "Perhaps a day's march. If that."

"And you returned to tell us this?" Fulcher interjected, with a hint of irritation. "We expected a shift in terrain. This parched scrub land cannot extend forever."

"That is not all," the second scout, a young, broad-shouldered fellow named Conrad responded firmly. "Another reason compelled us to return to you. One that none of us could expect."

"Then what?" Fulcher retorted, impatiently. "Be out with it!"

"I was about to say that we discovered many tracks ... of what, I do not know," Aimery said, casting a sharp, annoyed glance at Fulcher. "We saw nothing, though many tracks we came across looked recently made."

"What kind of tracks?" Fulcher pressed.

"A large, hoofed animal. The tracks are larger than those of a cow or a horse. At least those we are familiar with," Conrad stated. "It may be an animal we do not yet know of."

"And we could find no dung, though these creatures seem to move about in small herds," Aimery said.

"So, it has come to pass that herd animals can evade Avanoran scouts," Fulcher said, chuckling derisively at the two scouts. "No dung? In the vicinity of herd animals? What manner of creature leaves no dung?"

Aimery shook his head. "We found none, I assure you, though my eyes and my skills are both as sharp as ever they have been."

"Maybe it is not a herd animal," suggested another knight, a grizzled fellow with a thinner face. "These lands are filled with strange beasts."

"Do not let wild imagination get the best of you, Robert," Fulcher said. "We must continue forward, and keep our eyes on the look for these herds. A startled herd can be dangerous in itself."

"And perhaps these creatures will be good quarry, whose meat will soon fill our stomachs," Rogier added, with a smile.

From what Godfrey could sense, the two scouts were not as convinced as Fulcher. A strong hint of unease was reflected in their countenances, as the column resumed its forward trek.

After what they had encountered all throughout the Shadowlands, Godfrey was far more inclined to trust the scouts' leanings over Fulcher's. There was something ahead to be wary of, and the Avanoran column was moving right into its territory.

***

As the scouts had indicated, low, rolling grasslands unfurled before the Avanorans by the end of the next day. To the north and south, the hazy outlines of great hills, or perhaps small mountains, came into view.

Godfrey welcomed the change in scenery, having become very tired of the scrub and dusty ground they had been traversing for days on end. The grassland also offered fewer places for concealment, though the Avanoran contingent could be espied from long distances, if anything like the Khalas roamed the region.

The spirits of the other Avanorans were similarly lifted by the change in environment. In the camp that night, there was much more laughter and bawdy jests around the cookfires. After all the tension of previous nights, Godfrey was glad to see the notable shifts in disposition.

After another full day of travel, the mountains to either side became more distinctive, as the contingent funneled into the heart of the broad valley. Scouts coming in from the south confirmed what the earlier reports had said, that forested slopes, abundant with good building timber, rose from the valley's southern edge.

The tidings indicated to Godfrey that they were drawing closer to the destination they were seeking. The thought must have put the depths of his mind more at ease, as that night he enjoyed one of the better slumbers he had attained in quite some time.

On the following day, as the sun neared its zenith in the teal skies, the Avanoran column came to a halt. All eyes were set upon one prominent feature in the landscape.

Within the valley was a singular, lofty rise, surrounded on

all sides by low, flatter terrain. Godfrey and the other Avanoran knights shared knowing glances with each other. He could not believe their good fortune.

The anomalous rise was perfectly suited to be a motte, which would serve as the anchoring element for an expansive bailey. The forests to the south could provide plenty of wood for the outer palisades, timber buildings, and a tower surmounting the great mound.

As if that were not enough, a sparkling stream meandered close to the rise. Flowing with shallow, clear waters, the stream was younger, as it had not cut its track too deeply into the earth. While not a body of water large or deep enough for boats to ply, it was a source of water more than adequate for the needs of a permanent fortification.

"This is it," Fulcher declared, looking to Godfrey with a broad smile breaking out on his face. "We will make camp here. In the next couple of days, we will assess this ground, the available game to be hunted in the vicinity, and determine the manpower needed to build a fortification here."

"You will find no argument here," Godfrey said. "We will not find a more suitable place in all the world."

"No, we will not," Rogier added, before jesting, "And the sooner we can build a fortress, the sooner we will have a place for many beautiful women to dwell."

Rogier's declaration was met with great enthusiasm by the Avanorans within hearing. While Godfrey desired the sensuous touch of a woman again, as the last time had been all the way back in the Theonian Empire, he saw something else regarding the arrival of women in the future.

The presence of women in a new fortress would be an indication of stability. As far as he was concerned, in the midst of the perilous Shadowlands, that was something more precious than gold itself.

"Makes me want to build a fortress today!" another knight, named Orderic, proclaimed spiritedly in response to Rogier, eliciting cheers and laughter from the group.

"Let's build a camp first," Godfrey said, with a chuckle.

"Have you no heart?" laughed Orderic.

"Have you no mind?" Godfrey riposted immediately, laughing himself.

"Never claimed I did!" Orderic countered, without hesitation, as the knights all shared some laughter together.

***

With morale bolstered, tents were erected and the camp was organized much faster than usual. After the encampment site was well-established, Godfrey and the others spent the better part of the next two days probing the region surrounding the rise.

The extended reconnaissance met with great success. To everyone's delight, the area proved to be filled with game.

Fowl and deer populated the woods in abundance, and many streams were discovered that harbored a bounty of fish. Roots and wild berry shrubs of an edible nature were plentiful as well. It was not long until Godfrey was confident a contingent laboring on the fortress could live off the land, if it had to.

There did not seem to be any large-scale threats, such as the huge packs of man-size, flesh eating apes populating the accounts of some explorers. There were some signs of predators to be cautious of, but nothing that would be a danger to a new settlement as a whole.

The only mar on the sequence of favorable discoveries was the continued absence of the creatures responsible for the large tracks Aimery and Conrad had come across. The tracks continued to be uncovered all throughout the grassland and forested slopes. Godfrey studied the tracks himself, again and again, but could not fathom anything beyond the fact that whatever made them was a hoofed animal of considerable weight.

The tracks had some similarities to the imprints made by aurochs, the large, wild cattle found throughout Godfrey's homeland, the Duchy of Avanor. But there were some distinct differences in size and shape. Godfrey wondered if whatever made the tracks was different in temperament as well, thinking of the aggressive aurochs that required a considerable amount of courage to hunt.

Moving through the shadows of the forest, Godfrey occasionally had the tingling sensation of being watched, but never found any source for the unnerving feelings. The other Avanorans probing the wooded slopes talked of experiencing the same sensation, but most agreed it was just the effects of being in a foreign land.

One warrior jested that it was probably other forest spiders, such as the dog-sized one he had cut down one afternoon. The thick-bodied spider's body had been an unsettling sight, but

Godfrey's gut told him it was not the source of the bothersome sensation.

Something was out there, without question, but what, he could not say. He did not doubt that time would tell.

***

Godfrey stared out towards the crimson sun, the huge orb descending amid a tranquil dusk. The temperature was dropping sharply, as it did every night, transitioning towards a deep chill following the bathing warmth of the day.

Though he could not identify the reason, Godfrey felt a deep unease as he pulled his woolen cloak tighter around him. The air felt unusually still, like the holding of a breath.

He saw a small group of Avanorans returning from a foray in the wilderness, hailing them as they drew near. The men looked a little weary, but none appeared to be injured.

"Godfrey, are you in the mood to eat well tonight?" Rogier asked, striding at the head of the small band.

He shook his head. "Not tonight, Rogier. Did you hunt something?"

Rogier grinned, and glanced back towards a couple of Avanorans in the rear of the loose column. The two men were lugging a deer carcass, the legs of which were affixed to a timber pole they were using to carry the body.

"Would a little venison change your mind?" Rogier asked.

"No, though I may be the fool for turning your offer down," Godfrey replied.

"Well, if you care for something a little more unusual, we managed to bring another one of the big spiders down," Rogier said. He waved to another Avanoran, who ambled over, carrying a large hempen sack over his shoulder. Rogier nodded to the man, who set the sack down, and emptied its contents carefully on the ground.

"Bastard was about to get Tancred. They are fast ... very fast," Rogier said, with no trace of his characteristic mirth. "We've found these things live in the hollows of larger trees. Best to keep them in mind when we are in those woods."

The other spider Godfrey had seen was of a beautiful blue coloration, with small orange markings on its legs, and white patches down its back surface. Additional white markings ornamented its eight legs.

Prominent bristles covered that spider's body, just like the one now before him. The spider from the sack was a little smaller, and mainly black in color, with orange chevrons on its back and the same color stripes on its hairy legs.

"Certainly colorful spiders," Godfrey remarked, looking at the bright orange markings set against the deep black.

"Pretty can still kill you," Rogier said.

"Talking about women again?" Godfrey jested, though his heart remained pensive with the brooding atmosphere he sensed.

"Aye, women too, but I'd rather leave this world due to a woman's caress, than the touch of one of those hairy things," Rogier remarked with a chuckle, as his usual levity returned.

"Agreed," Godfrey replied, smiling.

"Well, I'll leave you to your thoughts. After a long day out there, I am hungry, and I mean to have some venison before I get some rest," Rogier said. He looked to the other Avanoran. "Sack it up."

Godfrey saw the grimace on the other man's face, but he obeyed the directive. He was one of the newest members of the mercenary band, far outranked by Rogier. Tentatively, he worked the sack over the spider's body, and got it hoisted back up over his shoulder.

Rogier gave Godfrey a firm pat on the shoulder as he walked by. Godfrey remained in place for a short while, keeping his eyes fixed upon the twilight-illuminated terrain. Cast in a violet hue, one that heralded the coming dark, the twilight always held a timeless element to Godfrey, neither day nor night.

When night settled in full and the two moons had begun their journey, Godrey finally turned away. He made his way back to his tent, and bedded down for the night. As always, he kept his weapons within reach as he lay down. Even in the heart of a mercenary camp, he was not about to take any chances.

He closed his eyes, and listened to the sounds of his breathing, trying to shake the troubling feelings pervading him. Time crept on, and the night steadily deepened, but he still could not fall asleep.

Tossing and turning, Godfrey opened his eyes, letting out a long, deep breath, and surrendering to his restlessness. The discordance still plagued him, and he cursed his inability to gain control over it.

He was the only obstacle to himself, in terms of getting some good rest. He took some extended, cleansing breaths, emptying his mind and trying to relax his body. Godfrey nearly succeeded, until he sensed a vibration in the hard earth underneath his body.

Pulling his woolen coverings off, including his cloak and a coarse blanket, he crept out of the tent, his nerves already set on edge. The cold night air enveloped Godfrey, rousing him swiftly to full alertness.

The vibrations were unmistakably growing stronger, and a sharp feeling of alarm stabbed him. His comrades could castigate him as a fool later if he was wrong, but his every instinct urged him to raise a cry.

Right as he opened his mouth, a warning was sounded by another man. "To arms! Something approaches!" one of the sentries on the camp's perimeter shouted, his voice thick with panic. "To arms! Everyone to arms!"

Godfrey scrambled to get his sword and shield in hand, as shouts of urgency broke out rapidly among the surrounding tents. He cursed in frustration, realizing he did not have time to retrieve his helm.

The ground thundered with the heavy rumbling of hoof beats. Godfrey braced himself, sword and shield at the ready, his hackles rising as the foreboding noise swelled.

Dark, bulky shapes burst into sight, charging through the encampment. At first, he feared they were being attacked by a band of mounted riders, but it quickly became apparent that the situation was far worse.

After a few heartbeats, in which he wondered if his eyes were playing tricks on him in the low ambiance, the reality of what he was seeing began to dawn on him. It settled the question as to what kind of creature made the tracks found all throughout the vicinity of the solitary hillock.

Godfrey's mind spun nonetheless, as he beheld one of the creatures angling directly towards him. His mind struggled to fully comprehend what he was seeing, as it was no wild animal attacking him.

With a gruff bellow, the creature bore down on him with a lance gripped in its massive hands. Its broad, bull-like countenance was made nightmarish by the long, spiky teeth lining its upper and lower jaws, bared in a mask of fury towards Godfrey.

A wide set of horns sprouted from its huge head. Angled forward, the lengthy extensions ended in wickedly sharp points.

The human-like upper torso of the beast was powerful in construct, with more musculature than Godfrey had seen on any human. The brawny torso flowed into the lower, extended portion of its body, reflecting the form of a large bull. A pale strip of furred hide ran down the middle of the bull-like segment, dividing the deep black of the outer coat of fur covering the rest of its body.

Its thick, black hooves loomed as deadly as the horns of its head, and the great lance in its hands. Godfrey knew he was at a terrible disadvantage, but he resolved to defend himself against the beast, with everything he had in him.

Godfrey shifted to the side at the last instant, catching the two-handed slash of the creature's lance on his shield. The leather covering was slashed, and chunks of wood were gouged out as the force of the impact caused him to stagger. The momentum of the creature's charge carried it well past him, giving the knight a slight respite.

Turning, Godfrey kept his body squared towards his assailant. With the sounds of fighting swirling all around him, it was not an easy task to keep his attention locked on the fearsome creature.

Concerns regarding another of the bull-headed creatures emerging abruptly were relentless in his mind, but he kept his discipline intact. The beast slowed to a halt and turned about, its hooves thumping the ground heavily, readying to come at Godfrey again.

At that moment, one of Godfrey's comrades rushed up from behind the beast, with sword raised. Time seemed to slow to a crawl in the next few moments.

The beast swung its head to the side, catching sight of the other Avanoran warrior. It loosed another deep bellow, a sound that chilled Godfrey to the marrow.

With stunning dexterity and speed, the beast lashed out with its rear hooves. A gut-churning crack broke the air as they slammed into the chest of the human. Broken and lifeless from the moment of impact, the Avanoran shot backwards, and tumbled in a contorted heap to the ground.

The fearsome power and speed of the beast instilled great caution in Godfrey. He moved swiftly, putting a ridge-tent between himself and the lance-bearing monster.

The creature roared as it stomped towards him. Its lofty height allowed it to see without difficulty over the low span of the tent. But it was not a reckless beast, willing to risk entanglement by recklessly attempting to charge through the tent.

Godfrey stared into its wide, dark eyes, as it gave a low, menacing snort. The thing looked so surreal in the moonlight, a monster with the traces of man.

He lunged forward and feigned a strike, drawing a lance thrust from the creature, a strike that he was expecting. Twisting, he hacked at the front of the shaft, cleaving the head off, and drawing a bone-rattling roar in response.

The creature stepped forward, grabbing onto the ridge tent and yanking back with astounding force, collapsing the tent as its supports were torn free. With nothing to obstruct it, the bull-creature tromped straight at Godfrey.

Godfrey dropped abruptly to his knees, slashing across a horizontal plane, and keeping his shield angled upward. The steel blade severed one of his attacker's forelegs at the knee joint.

Without hesitation, the knight turned his hand over and brought the blade back through for another strike. Though he did not cleave through its other leg, he sliced deep into the flesh, enough that his steel bit into bone and rendered the appendage useless.

The creature's undulating bellow of pain engulfed Godfrey, as he scrambled to get out of the way of the toppling beast. Roaring, the creature grabbed for him with a frenzied look in its eyes. Catching the top of his shield, the beast ripped it right out of his hands.

Godfrey slashed desperately with his sword, trying to purchase some space to get away. If the beast got a hold on him, he knew he was dead. The creature brought up Godfrey's own shield to block the strikes, allowing the knight just enough time to get beyond the reach of his severely wounded opponent.

His attacker was effectively immobilized, and in a tremendous degree of pain. It was also bleeding profusely, with nothing to stop the thick crimson flow.

The crippled beast roared defiantly, and hurled the shield out of sight, but its vitality was sagging with every moment that passed. Backing away, Godfrey was not willing to take any unnecessary risks by moving in to finish it off. It was going to die, but it could lash out in its final death throes.

He kept a vigil on the dying beast, not wanting any of his comrades to come upon it unwittingly. He looked to each side, hoping he would espy another shield, but there were none to be found.

The beast's head slumped heavily to the ground, and its body became still. While Godfrey could see no signs of breathing and felt it was dead, he still kept a wide berth from the creature as he moved out of the area.

Human shouts and horrific, inhuman roars filled the night, as well as the clash of weapons, the thumps of stomping hooves, and the higher pitched cries of agony; from both human and bestial sources. Avanorans and the massive forms of their inhuman attackers could be seen fighting and moving hurriedly about in the tempestuous battle, but Godfrey was alone in the area he was walking through.

Godfrey trotted forward, as his heart pounded within his chest. Every flicker of a shadow drew his eyes, and he was poised to defend himself in an instant.

He caught sight of a fallen Avanoran, whose head had been separated from his shoulders. A pang of sorrow struck Godfrey as he recognized Orderic, but there was no time to mourn the dead.

Lying in the grass at Orderic's side was a spear, no longer needed by the slain knight.

Sheathing his sword, Godfrey picked up the spear, knowing he needed every finger-length of distance he could get in combat with the bull-headed monsters. Out of the corner of his eye, he caught a flash of movement. He whirled about, just as a javelin thrown with great force sped by his head.

The javelin hurler advanced slowly towards him. The beast passed a war club from its left hand to its right, glowering menacingly at Godfrey and baring its sharp teeth. Coming to a halt, it snorted, and pawed the ground aggressively with its front hooves.

"Come on!" Godfrey yelled at it, summoning as much bravado as he could muster. "Come on, bull man! What are you waiting for?"

To his shock, the creature shouted back at him. If unintelligible to Godfrey, the sounds were unmistakably words. The thing suddenly became less bestial, but it was every bit as dangerous as before.

Godfrey took up a balanced stance, and waited for the beast to make a move towards him. He was not in a position where he could make use of a ridge tent again.

Leveling his spear, he cried out and charged right at the beast. The sudden aggression took the thing by surprise, and it even gave some ground as Godrey jabbed and thrust with the spear.

He ducked as the club whooshed right over his head, gaining an opening to drive the spear tip into the area where the thing's human-like torso melded with the lower, bull-like portion of its body. It was not a killing blow, but it did cause the thing to bellow in furor and agony.

It swatted again at Godfrey with the war club, barely missing him. Feeling the air from the attempt whisk across his face, Godfrey felt a cavernous pit in his stomach.

The creature reared upward, bringing its large hooves into the fight. Godfrey had no shield, and his only chance was to drop to the ground. He braced the end of the spear on the hard ground, and angled its slightly forward, as his attacker came stomping down heavily.

Its weight and momentum impaled it on Godfrey's spear, the shaft burying deep into the same zone where the knight had wounded it before. The creature dropped the war club, and grabbed at the invading spear.

Gaining his feet quickly, Godfrey gripped the end of the spear. He held onto it with all his strength, as the bull creature backed up, and jerked him forward a few paces. Getting his balance and planting his feet solidly, he put his weight behind the shaft and pushed forward, driving the spear even deeper.

A look that Godfrey could only interpret as shock came to the creature's face, as it became still and fell heavily to the ground. A long, wheezing breath exited its nostrils, but the creature's sides heaved no more.

Godfrey felt a wave of relief, but his nerves were sorely rattled at how near he had come to being pounded into the ground under the beast's hooves. He grabbed the hilt of his sword and pulled the blade free.

Dread clutched his stomach as he heard a couple of deep

snorts coming from close proximity; and separate directions. Turning about, he saw that two of the creatures were eyeing him, one to the left, and the other off to his right. One had a lance, and the other a war club.

Tired, and breathing heavy, he knew they would run him down if he were to try and get away. The one with the lance eyed the dead body of its comrade lying just beyond the knight. It looked up to Godfrey, its eyes filling with a burning, murderous hate. With a harsh tone, it loosed several words in its language.

Though Godfrey did not know the words, the creature was a warrior, and he knew that the utterance was some manner of oath. Had the knight seen the killer of one of his own companions, standing by the body, he would have sworn vengeance too.

As he stared at the two creatures, the ground began rumbling again. The knight's final shreds of hope dissipated, as the intensity of the vibrations grew. Feeling the ground shaking through the soles of his leather shoes, he could only hope that the killing blow came swiftly.

Large shapes streamed around him, but the spirited neighs told him at once that they were not another wave of the monstrous assailants. Mounted Avanorans charged by, pressing their attack on the bull-creatures, hacking and slashing with their steel blades. The war horses did their part in the combat, striking out with their hooves.

The Avanorans overwhelmed the bull-creatures, and in moments both of the latter succumbed to a number of wounds. One of the Avanorans was unhorsed with a crushing blow from one of the clubs, and the horse of another knight screamed as it received a vicious spear thrust.

The fighting drew in a few more of the bull-creatures, and a sustained melee developed in front of Godfrey. Blades clashed and blood flowed, as the mounted Avanorans fought with spirited fury.

A few more Avanorans on foot came rushing up in the wake of the riders. Striding towards the edges of the fighting, they sought to help their mounted comrades wherever possible. Godfrey moved to join them, though he paused to take up another discarded spear that he came across.

He stepped forward carefully, eyeing the combatants and looking for an opening. Godfrey was astounded at the sheer power of the bull-creatures, witnessing a few incredible attacks in the span of a few moments.

Off to his left, one of the beasts was disarmed of its spear, but it was not left without weapons. Lowering its head and using its lengthy horns, it charged forward, goring the horse of the rider that had deprived it of its spear. Pulling the blood-coated horns free, the bull-creature shoved the body of the horse to the ground.

Advancing, the bull-creature trampled the knight as he tried to crawl away. Godfrey's blood ran cold as he watched the knight being brutally pulverized, knowing how close he had come to the same terrible fate.

Another display of extraordinary strength took place just a short distance in front of Godfrey. Another one of the bull-creatures rushed forward, lowering itself and clutching onto the breast of a war horse with its huge hands.

Anchored by the grip, hands digging into the horse's flesh,

the bull-creature drove upwards and executed an astounding thrust, upending the steed in spectacular fashion. The horse toppled backwards, collapsing heavily and casting its rider out of the saddle.

The bull-creature surged in without hesitation. It landed several heavy blows with its extended war club on both rider and steed, before either had a chance of getting their legs back under them.

It did not have long to savor its triumph, as Godfrey utilized its distraction, recognizing a chance for his own attack. Running in, he put everything that he could into a lance thrust that caught the monster flush in the ribs. The spear blade drove deep into its body, eliciting a breathy grunt from the beast. After a brief hesitation, the creature collapsed to the ground.

Hearing a bellow, Godfrey saw another attacker coming in fast from the side. Without time to dislodge the spear, he took up his sword, right as the creature reached him. With no time to assess, he could only react.

His opponent's muscular arm began the downward swing with the war club. Thrusting his sword up under the broad jaw of the creature, Godfrey felt the impact of his enemy's weapon with a blinding flash of pain. Fortune was with him again, as his strike caused a slight shift in the club's trajectory, rendering it into a glancing blow; rather than a mortal one landing flush on his skull.

The sword was yanked out of his hands, as his legs went out from under him and he landed on his knees. He barely registered his massive opponent falling before him, not knowing whether the beast was still alive or not.

He blinked his eyes rapidly, spots dancing all across his vision. Godfrey knew he was teetering on the edge of unconsciousness, and did everything he could to avoid sliding into blackness.

A murky grogginess began to cloud his mind, slowly overpowering the primal part of him clinging desperately to survival. If one of the beasts came across him now, he was defenseless.

A flurry of cries went up among the Avanorans. "The hill! The hill!"

At the lingering edges of his consciousness, Godfrey heard the footsteps of several men running by him. The sounds of fighting were quickly moving away from where the dazed knight struggled to gain his feet. He got one foot set flat against the ground, and tried to lurch upward. Woozy and swaying, he fell to the side, his head throbbing and swimming.

"You have more than done your part. I am keeping you out of the end of this one," Fulcher's voice interjected firmly, as Godfrey felt strong hands holding him down. "Just stay right here, Godfrey."

Unable to resist or argue, Godfrey remained in place. His vision then misted over fully, and his consciousness slipped into total darkness.

***

Picks and shovels broke the ground apart, and scooped it away, as a deepening moat gradually took shape. Encompassing the base of the hill, and the perimeter of the palisade that would soon be erected, the moat would be fed by the stream running through the valley. A channel to suit that purpose was already underway.

The site had already served as a beacon for other humans. A lone traveler, a foreigner who claimed to be from far to the east, with yellow-toned skin and slanted eyes, had arrived during the construction.

Oddly, he spoke the Gallean tongue quite fluently, and even said that he knew the Unifier. The monk-knight from the Order of the High Altar traveling with them warmed very quickly to the stranger, who was regarded by all as the first guest of the fortress.

The mystery of what the bull-creatures were was solved, as the man called them Burujin. It seemed as good of a name as any that the Avanorans could come up with, and they adopted it.

While the man was interesting company, and filled with captivating tales, the men of the large mercenary band looked forward to the time when the first women arrived at the fortress. They knew others could not be summoned until the fortress was in place. The knowledge motivated them greatly, and all the Avanorans did their part to plant the seeds of order into the midst of a dangerous wilderness.

In time, a bridge would span the water, leading into a capacious bailey filled with workshops, storehouses, pens, byres, dwellings, and even a church. The motte within the palisade would support a stout, square tower, which would serve a dual purpose; as part of the fortress' defenses, and also as a residence for the commander.

It would be a fortification that could easily resist the kind of assault the encampment had suffered. The Burujin would be hard pressed to breach the moat and palisade, especially when the wall-walk would be providing protection for archers loosing a stream of missiles at any attacker.

**

Godfrey rested, taking a bite of dried, salted meat. His eyes were fixed on the landscape, wondering why the Burujin had been so desperate to drive the Avanorans from the area. From what his comrades had told him, the Burujin had taken up positions all around the motte, facing outward, and fighting to the very last.

There was more to their attack than merely driving out foreigners. Something had compelled them to desperation, though Godfrey had no inkling regarding its nature.

A grim, bloody toll had been paid on both sides. Timber grave markers would soon be replaced with stone ones, to honor the first Avanorans to spill their blood on the site of the fortress. The cemetery plot was located outside the moat, in a stretch of open ground well-within sight of the walls.

The bodies of the slain Burujin had been committed to flame. There had been no sign of others since the battle, though the stranger from the east insisted that there were other Burujin tribes.

It all would have to remain a mystery, at least for the time being, as Godfrey slowly got to his feet. He felt the stiffness in his knees, and was glad a permanent residence was not too far in the offing.

He paused as a wave of lightheadedness came over him. His

head still ached from the heavy blow he had suffered in the battle, the area of the club's impact tender to the touch.

His body had endured enough campaigns and wars for four men, and it was long past time to settle. Things would not be dull in the great valley, and times of hardship would certainly come to pass in the future, but years of incessant journeying would finally come to an end. That alone would make the struggle of forging a new life out of the wilderness well worth it.

Godfrey smiled, as he realized he had the best of both realms. He could set down roots, and still look forward to adventures.

A Few Words About the Stories from Stephen Zimmer

Into Glory Ride

The Trogens are one of my favorite races in the world of Ave, if not my favorite of them all. I wanted to have a story centered on the Trogens among the first releases in the Chronicles of Ave as I wanted readers to get a better acquainted with them on their home ground.

In the Fires in Eden series, the reader meets the Trogens in the service of the Unifier, fighting in return for the promise of assistance in liberating their lands from the Elves. Clearly, the Trogens are very tough warriors, so it may be difficult for the reader to imagine the kind of adversity they have been going through with the Elves.

This story gives the reader those kinds of insights, while also documenting a very historic moment the Trogen lands; when they take the Harraks for the first time into battle. Much more is explained as to why the Trogens are having such a difficult time with the Elves, who have chosen to suppress and destabliize them.

You also get some nice insights into the Sea Wolf Clan, and what Sea Wolves are, as well as other creatures in the Trogen world. The reader also gets to be front and center during an Elven raid and the battle that follows. This includes an introduction to a type of Skiantha, the Lavions, that have not been described in the first three novels of the series..

I think readers of the series will find a lot in this short story, especially those who have been expressing a growing infinity for the Trogens. The Trogens play a huge part in the series, so I sincerely hope that this short story sheds some more light on their world. I love immersing in the Trogen world and hope that the reader does too!

Touch of Serenity

I have been long-fascinated with the mythologies, heroic figures, and deities of the Far East, such as the storied legacies of China and Japan. Ave has its own regions inspired heavily by these places, and "A Touch of Serenity" gives the reader a chance for a wonderful sneak peek ahead of the time that they will be revealed more in the Fires in Eden series.

The story itself is loaded with powerful figures of Chinese mythology, and also shows a little about the kinds of dragons, demonic entities, and supernatural elements that can be found in this region of Ave. The reader also gets to meet a nice array of Wizards inhabiting the region. The Divine Emperor and the Empire of Heaven are big parts of the history of Ave too, and let's just say tha this part of Ave factors into the Fires in Eden Series in a significant way.

Yet amid all the lofty and powerful figures, this story centers upon a commoner, conscripted to labor in the construction of an extensive wall. It is a story about seizing the moment, and not being afraid to follow a calling. It also establishes a wonderful character that I hope to bring more of to readers in the future.

This is the kind of character that I enjoy working with the most. It shows what any of us are capable of, if we open our hearts to respond to cries for help.

Moonlight's Grace

"Moonlight's Grace" is a very special story to me for several reasons, but there are a few prime ones in particular. For one thing, I get to play in the realm of the Irish part of my heritage, which gives it a very personal aspect. Secondly, this story allowed me to explore genuine romance, and what love really means.

Having been to Ireland, England, Wales, and Scotland, and visited medieval period monasteries, and studying the Viking raids of the eighth, ninth, and tenth centuries especially, I had a strong vision in mind for where I wanted to take this story.

The Midragardan raid and the conflict with the Druids form the backdrop to the Finnian and Brigit story. Moonlight's Grace is about the couple, first and foremost, introducing Brigit for possible future tales as she is a major figure in Gael history.

The reader is given a nice look into the land of Gael, which as of the time that this story is being published has not yet been visited in the Fires in Eden series. It gives some deeper understanding of Midragard's history, and also reveals more concerning the mystical side of Ave.

It is a story of the power of love, the influence of culture, and it points toward something transcendant. I hope readers enjoy their first direct meeting with the Gael.

Winter's Embrace

The stories of the Teutonic Knights and the Eastern Crusades I've always found very interesting. When people talk about the Crusades it is mainly in reference to the events that took place in the Middle East, from the first campaign called by Urban II, to the clash of Richard the Lionheart and Saladin, to the Fall of Acre late in the 13th century. Yet there remains a whole period of history centering around Eastern Europe that is rarely explored, filled with all kinds of fascinating individuals, campaigns, and events that had a profound effect on European history.

"Winter's Embrace" let me immerse into a story of a warrior-monk in the Order of the Sacred Lady, who is the sole survivor of a heathen ambush deep in winter. By himself, he ends up carrying out the Order's mission, but in a way he definitely did not foresee when he agrees to assist in a forest witch in the rescue of her daughter from a wicked sorcerer called the Undying.

The story allowed me to explore a deeper level of what it means to be true to one's faith. Manfred, in my view, does not betray what he stands for in helping the witch. If anything, he grows stronger in the path he has embraced through the experience. It is definitely a tale depicting growth in a figure who already is possessed of strength and wisdom. That wisdom grows, as does his strength, when he is brought to a deeper understanding.

The reader of the Fires in Eden series gets to explore some regions near Ehrengard that they haven't been introduced to yet. They will also get to learn a whole lot more about the Order of the Sacred Lady, who have been encountered in the Fires in Eden Series as of the time this story is being published.

Those familiar with Slavic mythical figures and creatures will have a feast in this tale, as there are many elements derived from that tradition. The challenges set before Manfred are considerable, but not insurmountable.

I'm looking forward to telling more of Manfred's exploits in the future too!

Lion Heart

"Lion Heart" was a really fun one for me to write, as it gave me a chance to go into an area of Ave that is not even mentioned in the early Fires in Eden books. The lands of the Amazu are far to the north and west of the Sun Lands, across a great desert wasteland. The culture of the Amazu is heavily influenced by the Zulu people of our world.

I think this story is important because it gives the reader another peek into the kind of range that will be found in the Fires in Eden series. It centers upon a legendary warrior in the Amazu culture, Sigananda, in a time long before the coming of the otherworlders as described in *Crown of Vengeance*.

Sigananda is shown in his youth, not long after being accepted to full warrior status. The journey that he is sent on is when his legacy really begins to take flight. I intend to share more tales of Sigananda in the future. I think readers will find him interesting in that while he is a force of nature as a fighter, he also exhibits other dimensions that do not detract from his lethal skill.

The reader gets a great look into Amazu culture, and is introduced to many of the more prominent Wizards that dwell in that region of Ave. There is a lot to glean in the text, and I hope readers really have fun exploring this corner of Ave!

On Land of Shadow

The Shadowlands are mentioned early in the Fires in Eden series, primarily as the lands where Gunther found the Jaghuns that he eventually brought back to Saxany and started a small pack with. The Shadowlands are one of the more dangerous places in all of Ave. There are many unique cultures that inhabit these lands, as well as a wide array of dangerous creatures in the wilderness.

This story focuses in on a band of Avanoran mercenaries, who have been contracted to seek out and establish a fortress.

Story Notes

Through the eyes of Godfrey, the reader gets to learn more about the Shadowlands and why it is such a perilous place. The Shadowlands are going to factor significantly in the Fires in Eden series, so this gives the reader a little bit of a preview of what they can look forward to. I haven't given everything away, not by a long shot, but this does have some elements that factor into the novels.

I have really been looking forward to unveiling the Khalas and Burujin. I think readers that have enjoyed the Trogens and the Unguhur will find the cultures and races of the Shadowlands to be equally compelling. While this story takes place not long after the Unifier has risen to power in Avanor, it is clear that the Khalan tribes are well under the influence of Ahriman.

The reason why the Burujin fought so hard against the Avanorans when they encamped around the mound they discovered is not revealed here. I intend to answer some of those questions in another story for the Chronicles of Ave, taking place much earlier than the time of this one. Other answers will be found in the Fires in Eden series, but that is all I am going to say for now. Can 't give away any big spoilers!

About the Author

Stephen Zimmer is an award-winning author of speculative fiction, whose works include the Fires in Eden Series (Epic Fantasy), the Rising Dawn Saga (epic-scale Urban Fantasy), the Harvey and Solomon tales (Steampunk), the Hellscapes tales (Horror), and the Rayden Valkyrie tales (Sword and Sorcery).

He is also a writer-director in moviemaking, with feature and short film credits such as Shadows Light, The Sirens, and Swordbearer.

Further information on Stephen can be found at:
www.stephenzimmer.com

Transcend reality with Seventh Star Press!

On the following pages we would like to introduce you to some of our titles featuring Sword and Sorcery, Post-Apocalyptic Fantasy, Epic Fantasy, YA Fantasy, and more!

To get more information on Seventh Star Press and our titles, please visit:

www.seventhstarpress.com

or connect with us at:
www.twitter.com/7thstarpress
www.facebook.com/seventhstarpress

More from Stephen Zimmer:

The Rising Dawn Saga, an epic-scale urband fantasy series that explores the dystopian and apocalyptic!

Book One: The Exodus Gate
Softcover ISBN: 9780615267470
eBook ISBN: 9780982565674

Book Two: The Storm Guardians
Softcover ISBN: 9780982565636
eBook ISBN: 9780982565681

Book Three: The Seventh Throne
Softcover ISBN: 9780983740247
eBook ISBN: 9780983740223

The Rising Dawn Saga titles feature cover art and illustrations from the award-winning Matthew Perry

Grand Epic Fantasy from Stephen Zimmer!
Explore the world of Ave in the Fires in Eden Series!
Epic Fantasy for those who enjoy authors like George R.R.
Martin and Steven Erikson!

Explore post-apocalyptic fantasy worlds
in the Seventh Star Press anthology
The End Was Not the End
from editor Joshua H. Leet!

softcover ISBN: 978-1-937929-07-7
eBook ISBN: 978-1-937929-15-2

Action-driven Fantasy from D.A. Adams!
Begin your journey into The Brotherhood of Dwarves, the
popular YA Fantasy series and action-filled saga where the
dwarves are not just sidekicks!

Softcover ISBN: 9781937929916   Softcover ISBN: 9781937929923

eBook ISBN: 9781937929930   eBook ISBN: 9781937929-947

Softcover ISBN: 9780983740254   Softcover ISBN: 9781937929787

eBook ISBN: 9781937929909   eBook ISBN: 9781937929770

YA Fantasy From Jackie Gamber!
The highly-acclaimed Leland Dragon Series from Jackie
Gamber! Strong character-driven YA Fantasy for those
who enjoy authors such as Christopher Paolini.

Softcover ISBN: 9780983108672

eBook ISBN: 9780983108696

Softcover ISBN: 9781937929893

eBook ISBN: 9781937929817

Gorias La Gaul adventures from Steven Shrewsbury!
Enter an ancient world of heroes, blood, and steel in the
tales of Gorias La Gaul! Hard-hitting Sword & Sorcery in
the vein of Robert E. Howard!.

Softcover ISBN: 9781937929800   Softcover ISBN: 9780983108634

eBook ISBN: 9781937929831   eBook ISBN: 9780983108641

Softcover: 978-1-937929-28-2

eBook: 978-1-937929-29-9

Want more Sword and Sorcery?
Pick up the anthologies *Thunder on the Battlefield:*
Sword, and *Thunder on the Battlefield: Sorcery,*
from editor James R. Tuck!
(author of the Deacon Chalk novels)
Available in print and eBook!

Thunder on the Battlefield: Sword
Softcover: 978-1-937929-24-4
eBook: 978-1-937929-25-1

Thunder on the Battlefield: Sorcery
Softcover: 978-1-937929-26-8
eBook: 978-1-937929-27-5